CONTRARY MARY

TEMPLE BAILEY

1st WORLD
LIBRARY
Literary Society

Contrary Mary

Temple Bailey

© 1st World Library, 2006
PO Box 2211
Fairfield, IA 52556
www.1stworldlibrary.com
First Edition

LCCN: 2006938110

Softcover ISBN: 978-1-4218-3412-2
Hardcover ISBN: 978-1-4218-3312-5
eBook ISBN: 978-1-4218-3512-9

Purchase *"Contrary Mary"*
as a traditional bound book at:
www.1stWorldLibrary.com/purchase.asp?ISBN=978-1-4218-3412-2

1st World Library is a literary, educational organization
dedicated to:

- Creating a free internet library of downloadable ebooks

- Hosting writing competitions and offering book
publishing scholarships.

1ˢᵗ World Library Literary Society

Giving Back to the World

"If you want to work on the core problem, it's early school literacy."

- James Barksdale, former CEO of Netscape

"No skill is more crucial to the future of a child, or to a democratic and prosperous society, than literacy."

- Los Angeles Times

Literacy... means far more than learning how to read and write... The aim is to transmit... knowledge and promote social participation."

- UNESCO

"Literacy is not a luxury, it is a right and a responsibility. If our world is to meet the challenges of the twenty-first century we must harness the energy and creativity of all our citizens."

- President Bill Clinton

"Parents should be encouraged to read to their children, and teachers should be equipped with all available techniques for teaching literacy, so the varying needs and capacities of individual kids can be taken into account."

- Hugh Mackay

To My Sister

CONTENTS

CHAPTER I

In Which Silken Ladies Ascend One Stairway, and a Lonely Wayfarer Ascends Another and Comes Face to Face With Old Friends.

The big house, standing on a high hill which overlooked the city, showed in the moonlight the grotesque outlines of a composite architecture. Originally it had been a square substantial edifice of Colonial simplicity. A later and less restrained taste had aimed at a castellated effect, and certain peaks and turrets had been added. Three of these turrets were excrescences stuck on, evidently, with an idea of adornment. The fourth tower, however, rounded out and enlarged a room on the third floor. This room was one of a suite, and the rooms were known as the Tower Rooms, and were held by those who had occupied them to be the most desirable in the barn-like building.

To-night the house had taken on an unwonted aspect of festivity. Its spaciousness was checkered by golden-lighted windows. Delivery wagons and automobiles came and went, some discharging loads of deliciousness at the back door, others discharging loads of loveliness at the front.

Following in the wake of one of the front door loads of fluttering femininity came a somewhat somber pedestrian. His steps lagged a little, so that when the big door opened, he was still at the foot of the terrace which led up to it. He waited until the door was shut before he again advanced. In the glimpse that he thus had of the interior, he was aware of a sort of pink effulgence, and in that shining light, lapped by it, and borne up, as it were, by it toward the wide stairway, he saw slender girls in faint-hued frocks—a shimmering celestial company.

As he reached the top of the terrace the door again flew open, and he gave a somewhat hesitating reason for his intrusion.

"I was told to ask for Miss Ballard—Miss Mary Ballard."

It seemed that he was expected, and that the guardian of the doorway understood the difference between his business and that of the celestial beings who had preceded him.

He was shown into a small room at the left of the entrance. It was somewhat bare, with a few law books and a big old-fashioned desk. He judged that the room might have been put to office uses, but to-night the desk was heaped with open boxes, and odd pieces of furniture were crowded together, so that there was left only a small oasis of cleared space. On the one chair in this oasis, the somber gentleman seated himself.

He had a fancy, as he sat there waiting, that neither he nor this room were in accord with the things that were going on in the big house. Outside of the closed door the radiant guests were still ascending the stairway on shining wings of light. He could hear the music of their laughter, and the deeper note of men's voices, rising and growing fainter in a sort of transcendent harmony.

When the door was finally opened, it was done quickly and was shut quickly, and the girl who had entered laughed breathlessly as she turned to him.

"Oh, you must forgive me—I've kept you waiting?"

If their meeting had been in Sherwood forest, he would have known her at once for a good comrade; if he had met her in the Garden of Biaucaire, he would have known her at once for more than that. But, being neither a hero of ballad nor of old romance, he knew only that here was a girl different from the silken ladies who had ascended the stairs. Here was an air almost of frank boyishness, a smile of pleasant friendliness, with just enough of flushing cheek to show womanliness and warm blood.

Even her dress was different. It was simple almost to the point of plainness. Its charm lay in its glimmering glistening sheen, like the inside of a shell. Its draperies were caught up to show slender feet in low-heeled slippers. A quaint cap of silver tissue held closely the waves of thick fair hair. Her eyes were like the sea in a storm—deep gray with a glint of green.

These things did not come to him at once. He was to observe them as she made her explanation, and as he followed her to the Tower Rooms. But first he had to set himself straight with her, so he said: "I was sorry to interrupt you. But you said— seven?"

"Yes. It was the only time that the rooms could be seen. My sister and I occupy them—and Constance is to be married— to-night."

This, then, was the reason for the effulgence and the silken ladies. It was the reason, too, for the loveliness of her dress.

"I am going to take you this way." She preceded him through a narrow passage to a flight of steps leading up into the darkness. "These stairs are not often used, but we shall escape the crowds in the other hall."

Her voice was lost as she made an abrupt turn, but, feeling his way, he followed her.

Up and up until they came to a third-floor landing, where she stopped him to say, "I must be sure no one is here. Will you wait until I see?"

She came back, presently, to announce that the coast was clear, and thus they entered the room which had been enlarged and rounded out by the fourth tower.

It was a big room, ceiled and finished in dark oak, The furniture was roomy and comfortable and of worn red leather. A strong square table held a copper lamp with a low spreading shade. There was a fireplace, and on the mantel above it a bust or two.

But it was not these things which at once caught the attention of Roger Poole.

Lining the walls were old books in stout binding, new books in cloth and fine leather—the poets, the philosophers, the seers of all ages. As his eyes swept the shelves, he knew that here was the living, breathing collection of a true book-lover—not a musty, fusty aggregation brought together through mere pride of intellect. The owner of this library had counted the heart-beats of the world.

"This is the sitting-room," his guide was telling him, "and the bedroom and bath open out from it." She had opened a connecting door. "This room is awfully torn up. But we have just finished dressing Constance. She is down-stairs now in the Sanctum. We'll pack her trunks to-morrow and send them, and then if you should care to take the rooms, we can put back the bedroom furniture that father had. He used this suite, and brought his books up after mother died."

He halted on the threshold of that inner room. If the old house below had seemed filled with rosy effulgence, this was the heart of the rose. Two small white beds were side by side in an alcove. Their covers were of pink overlaid with lace, and the chintz of the big couch and chairs reflected the same enchanting hue. With all the color, however, there was the freshness of simplicity. Two tall glass candlesticks on the dressing table, a few photographs in silver and ivory frames— these were the only ornaments.

Yet everywhere was lovely confusion—delicate things were thrown half-way into open trunks, filmy fabrics floated from unexpected places, small slippers were held by receptacles never designed for shoes, radiant hats bloomed in boxes.

On a chair lay a bridesmaid's bunch of roses. This bunch Mary Ballard picked up as she passed, and it was over the top of it that she asked, with some diffidence, "Do you think you'd care to take the rooms?"

Did he? Did the Peri outside the gates yearn to enter? Here within his reach was that from which he had been cut off for five years. Five years in boarding-houses and cheap hotels, and now the chance to live again—as he had once lived!

"I do want them—awfully—but the price named in your letter seems ridiculously small—"

"But you see it is all I shall need," she was as blissfully unbusinesslike as he. "I want to add a certain amount to my income, so I ask you to pay that," she smiled, and with increasing diffidence demanded, "Could you make up your mind—now? It is important that I should know—to-night."

She saw the question in his eyes and answered it, "You see— my family have no idea that I am doing this. If they knew, they wouldn't want me to rent the rooms—but the house is mine— I shall do as I please."

She seemed to fling it at him, defiantly.

"And you want me to be accessory to your—crime."

She gave him a startled glance. "Oh, do you look at it—that way? Please don't. Not if you like them."

For a moment, only, he wavered. There was something distinctly unusual in acquiring a vine and fig tree in this fashion. But then her advertisement had been unusual—it was that which had attracted him, and had piqued his interest so that he had answered it.

And the books! As he looked back into the big room, the rows of volumes seemed to smile at him with the faces of old friends.

Lonely, longing for a haven after the storms which had beaten him, what better could he find than this?

As for the family of Mary Ballard, what had he to do with it? His business was with Mary Ballard herself, with her frank laugh and her friendliness—and her arms full of roses!

"I like them so much that I shall consider myself most fortunate to get them."

"Oh, really?" She hesitated and held out her hand to him. "You don't know how you have helped me out—you don't know how you have helped me—"

Again she saw a question in his eyes, but this time she did not answer it. She turned and went into the other room, drawing back the curtains of the deep windows of the round tower.

"I haven't shown you the best of all," she said. Beneath them lay the lovely city, starred with its golden lights. From east to west the shadowy dimness of the Mall, beyond the shadows, a line of river, silver under the moonlight. A clock tower or two showed yellow faces; the great public buildings were clear-cut like cardboard.

Roger drew a deep breath. "If there were nothing else," he said, "I should take the rooms for this."

And now from the lower hall came the clamor of voices.

"*Mary! Mary!*"

"I must not keep you," he said at once.

"*Mary!*"

Poised for flight, she asked, "Can you find your way down alone? I'll go by the front stairs and head them off."

"*Mary—!*"

With a last flashing glance she was gone, and as he groped his way down through the darkness, it came to him as an amazing revelation that she had taken his coming as a thing to be thankful for, and it had been so many years since a door had been flung wide to welcome him.

CHAPTER II

In Which Rose-Leaves and Old Slippers Speed a Happy Pair;
and in Which Sweet and Twenty Speaks a New and Modern
Language, and Gives a Reason for Renting a Gentleman's
Library.

In spite of the fact that Mary Ballard had seemed to Roger Poole like a white-winged angel, she was not looked upon by the family as a beauty. It was Constance who was the "pretty one," and tonight as she stood in her bridal robes, gazing up at her sister who was descending the stairs, she was more than pretty. Her tender face was illumined by an inner radiance. She was two years older than Mary, but more slender, and her coloring was more strongly emphasized. Her eyes were blue and her hair was gold, as against the gray-green and dull fairness of Mary's hair. She seemed surrounded, too, by a sort of feminine *aura*, so that one knew at a glance that here was a woman who would love her home, her husband, her children; who would lean upon masculine protection, and suffer from masculine neglect.

Of Mary Ballard these things could not be said at once. In spite of her simplicity and frankness, there was about her a baffling atmosphere. She was like a still pool with the depths as yet unsounded, an uncharted sea—with its mystery of undiscovered countries.

The contrast between the sisters had never been more marked than when Mary, leaning over the stair-rail, answered the breathless, "Dearest, where have you been?" with her calm:

"There's plenty of time, Constance."

And Constance, soothed as always by her sister's tranquillity, repeated Mary's words for the benefit of a ponderously anxious Personage in amber satin.

"There's plenty of time, Aunt Frances."

That Aunt Frances *was* a Personage was made apparent by certain exterior evidences. One knew it by the set of her fine shoulders, the carriage of her head, by the diamond-studded lorgnette, by the string of pearls about her neck, by the osprey in her white hair, by the golden buckles on her shoes.

"It is five minutes to eight," said Aunt Frances, "and Gordon is waiting down-stairs with his best man, the chorus is freezing on the side porch, and *everybody* has arrived. I don't see *why* you are waiting—"

"We are waiting for it to be eight o'clock, Aunt Frances," said Mary. "At just eight, I start down in front of Constance, and if you don't hurry you and Aunt Isabelle won't be there ahead of me."

The amber train slipped and glimmered down the polished steps, and the golden buckles gleamed as Mrs. Clendenning, panting a little and with a sense of outrage that her nervous anxiety of the preceding moment had been for naught, made her way to the drawing-room, where the guests were assembled.

Aunt Isabelle followed, gently smiling. Aunt Isabelle was to Aunt Frances as moonlight unto sunlight. Aunt Frances was married, Aunt Isabelle was single; Aunt Frances wore amber, Aunt Isabelle silver gray; Aunt Frances held up her head like a queen, Aunt Isabelle dropped hers deprecatingly; Aunt Frances' quick ears caught the whispers of admiration that followed her, Aunt Isabelle's ears were closed forever to all the music of the universe.

No sooner had the two aunts taken their places to the left of a floral bower than there was heard without the chanted wedding chorus, from a side door stepped the clergyman and the bridegroom and his best man; then from the hall came the little procession with Mary in the lead and Constance leaning on the arm of her brother Barry.

They were much alike, this brother and sister. More alike than Mary and Constance. Barry had the same gold in his hair, and blue in his eyes, and, while one dared not hint it, in the face of his broad-shouldered strength, there was an almost feminine charm in the grace of his manner and the languor of his movements.

There were no bridesmaids, except Mary, but four pretty girls held the broad white ribbons which marked an aisle down the length of the rooms. These girls wore pink with close caps of old lace. Only one of them had dark hair, and it was the dark-haired one, who, standing very still throughout the ceremony, with the ribbon caught up to her in lustrous festoons, never took her eyes from Barry Ballard's face.

And when, after the ceremony, the bride turned to greet her friends, the dark-haired girl moved forward to where Barry stood, a little apart from the wedding group.

"Doesn't it seem strange?" she said to him with quick-drawn breath.

He smiled down at her. "What?"

"That a few words should make such a difference?"

"Yes. A minute ago she belonged to us. Now she's Gordon's."

"And he's taking her to England?"

"Yes. But not for long. When he gets the branch office started over there, they'll come back, and he'll take his father's place in the business here, and let the old man retire."

She was not listening. "Barry," she interrupted, "what will Mary do? She can't live here alone—and she'll miss Constance."

"Oh, Aunt Frances has fixed that," easily; "she wants Mary to shut up the house and spend the winter in Nice with herself and Grace—it's a great chance for Mary."

"But what about you, Barry?"

"Me?" He shrugged his shoulders and again smiled down at her. "I'll find quarters somewhere, and when I get too lonesome, I'll come over and talk to you, Leila."

The rich color flooded her cheeks. "Do come," she said, again with quick-drawn breath, then like a child who has secured its coveted sugar-plum, she slipped through the crowd, and down into the dining-room, where she found Mary taking a last survey.

"Hasn't Aunt Frances done things beautifully?" Mary asked; "she insisted on it, Leila. We could never have afforded the orchids and the roses; and the ices are charming—pink hearts with cupids shooting at them with silver arrows—"

"Oh, Mary," the dark-haired girl laid her flushed cheek against the arm of her taller friend. "I think weddings are wonderful."

Mary shook her head. "I don't," she said after a moment's silence. "I think they're horrid. I like Gordon Richardson well enough, except when I think that he is stealing Constance, and then I hate him."

But the bride was coming down, with all the murmuring voices behind her, and now the silken ladies were descending the stairs to the dining-room, which took up the whole lower west wing of the house and opened out upon an old-fashioned garden, which to-night, under a chill October moon, showed its rows of box and of formal cedars like sharp shadows against the whiteness.

Into this garden came, later, Mary. And behind her Susan Jenks.

Susan Jenks was a little woman with gray hair and a coffee-colored skin. Being neither black nor white, she partook somewhat of the nature of both races. Back of her African gentleness was an almost Yankee shrewdness, and the firm will which now and then degenerated into obstinacy.

"There ain't no luck in a wedding without rice, Miss Mary. These paper rose-leaf things that you've got in the bags are mighty pretty, but how are you going to know that they bring good luck?"

"Aunt Frances thought they would be charming and foreign, Susan, and they look very real, floating off in the air. You must stand there on the upper porch, and give the little bags to the guests."

Susan ascended the terrace steps complainingly. "You go right in out of the night, Miss Mary," she called back, "an' you with nothin' on your bare neck!"

Mary, turning, came face to face with Gordon's best man, Porter Bigelow.

"Mary," he said, impetuously, "I've been looking for you everywhere. I couldn't keep my eyes off you during the service —you were—heavenly."

"I'm not a bit angelic, Porter," she told him, "and I'm simply freezing out here. I had to show Susan about the confetti."

He drew her in and shut the door. "They sent me to hunt for you," he said. "Constance wants you. She's going up-stairs to change. But I heard just now that you are going to Nice. Leila told me. Mary—you can't go—not so far away—from me."

His hand was on her arm.

She shook it off with a little laugh.

"You haven't a thing to do with it, Porter. And I'm not going—to Nice."

"But Leila said—"

Her head went up. It was a characteristic gesture. "It doesn't make any difference what *any one* says. I'm not going to Nice."

Once more in the Tower Rooms, the two sisters were together for the last time. Leila was sent down on a hastily contrived errand. Aunt Frances, arriving, was urged to go back and look after the guests. Only Aunt Isabelle was allowed to remain. She could be of use, and the things which were to be said she could not hear.

"Dearest," Constance's voice had a break in it, "dearest, I feel so selfish—leaving you—"

Mary was kneeling on the floor, unfastening hooks. "Don't worry, Con. I'll get along."

"But you'll have to bear—things—all alone. It isn't as if any one knew, and you could talk it out."

"I'd rather die than speak of it," fiercely, "and I sha'n't write anything to you about it, for Gordon will read your letters."

"Oh, Mary, he won't."

"Oh, yes, he will, and you'll want him to—you'll want to turn your heart inside out for him to read, to say nothing of your letters."

She stood up and put both of her hands on her sister's shoulders. "But you mustn't tell him, Con. No matter how much you want to, it's my secret and Barry's—promise me, Con—"

"But, Mary, a wife can't."

"Yes, she *can* have secrets from her husband. And this belongs to us, not to him. You've married him, Con, but we haven't."

Aunt Isabelle, gentle Aunt Isabelle, shut off from the world of sound, could not hear Con's little cry of protest, but she looked up just in time to see the shimmering dress drop to the floor, and to see the bride, sheathed like a lily in whiteness, bury her head on Mary's shoulder.

Aunt Isabelle stumbled forward. "My dear," she asked, in her thin troubled voice, "what makes you cry?"

"It's nothing, Aunt Isabelle." Mary's tone was not loud, but Aunt Isabelle heard and nodded.

"She's dead tired, poor dear, and wrought up. I'll run and get the aromatic spirits."

With Aunt Isabella out of the way, Mary set herself to repair the damage she had done. "I've made you cry on your wedding day, Con, and I wanted you to be so happy. Oh, tell Gordon, if you must. But you'll find that he won't look at it as you and I have looked at it. He won't make the excuses."

"Oh, yes he will." Constance's happiness seemed to come back to her suddenly in a flood of assurance. "He's the best man in the world, Mary, and so kind. It's because you don't know him that you think as you do."

Mary could not quench the trust in the blue eyes. "Of course he's good," she said, "and you are going to be the happiest ever, Constance."

Then Aunt Isabelle came back and found that the need for the aromatic spirits was over, and together the loving hands hurried Constance into her going away gown of dull blue and silver, with its sable trimmed wrap and hat.

"If it hadn't been for Aunt Frances, how could I have faced Gordon's friends in London?" said Constance. "Am I all right now, Mary?"

"Lovely, Con, dear."

But it was Aunt Isabelle's hushed voice which gave the appropriate phrase. "She looks like a bluebird—for happiness."

At the foot of the stairway Gordon was waiting for his bride— handsome and prosperous as a bridegroom should be, with a dark sleek head and eager eyes, and beside him Porter Bigelow, topping him by a head, and a red head at that.

As Mary followed Constance, Porter tucked her hand under his arm.

"Oh, Mary, Mary, quite contrary,
Your eyes they are so bright,
That the stars grow pale, as they tell the tale
To the other stars at night,"

he improvised under his breath. "Oh, Mary Ballard, do you know that I am holding on to myself with all my might to keep from shouting to the crowd, 'Mary isn't going away. Mary isn't going away.'"

"Silly—"

"You say that, but you don't mean it. Mary, you can't be

hard-hearted on such a night as this. Say that I may stay for five minutes—ten—after the others have gone—"

They were out on the porch now, and he had folded about her the wrap which she had brought down with her. "Of course you may stay," she said, "but much good may it do you. Aunt Frances is staying and General Dick—there's to be a family conclave in the Sanctum—but if you want to listen you may."

And how the rose-leaves began to flutter! Susan Jenks had handed out the bags, and secretly, and with much elation had leaned over the rail as Constance passed down the steps, and had emptied her own little offering of rice in the middle of the bride's blue hat!

It was Barry, aided and abetted by Leila, who brought out the old slippers. There were Constance's dancing slippers, high-heeled and of delicate hues, Mary's more individual low-heeled ones, Barry's outworn pumps, decorated hurriedly by Leila for the occasion with lovers' knots of tissue paper.

And it was just as the bride waved "Good-bye" from Gordon's limousine that a new slipper followed the old ones, for Leila, carried away by the excitement, and having at the moment no other missile at hand, reached down, and plucking off one of her own pink sandals, hurled it with all her might at the moving car. It landed on top, and Leila, with a gasp, realized that it was gone forever.

"It serves you right." Looking up, she met Barry's laughing eyes.

She sank down on the step. "And they were a new pair!"

"Lucky that it's your birthday next week," he said. "Do you want pink ones?'"

"*Barry!*"

Her delight was overwhelming. "Heavens, child," he condoned her, "don't look as if I were the grand Mogul. Do you know I sometimes think you are eight instead of eighteen? And now, if you'll take my arm, you can hippity-hop into the house. And I hope that you'll remember this, that if I give you pink slippers you are not to throw them away."

In the hall they met Leila's father—General Wilfred Dick. The General had married, in late bachelorhood, a young wife. Leila was like her mother in her dark sparkling beauty and demure sweetness. But she showed at times the spirit of her father—the spirit which had carried the General gallantly through the Civil War, and had led him after the war to make a success of the practice of law. He had been for years the intimate friend and adviser of the Ballards, and it was at Mary's request that he was to stay to share in the coming conclave.

He told Leila this. "You'll have to wait, too," he said. "And now, why are you hopping on one foot in that absurd fashion?"

"Dad, dear, I lost my shoe—"

"Her very best pink one," Barry explained; "she threw it after the bride, and now I've got to give her another pair for her birthday."

The General's old eyes brightened as he surveyed the young pair. This was as it should be, the son of his old friend and the daughter of his heart.

He tried to look stern, however. "Haven't I always kept you supplied with pink shoes and blue shoes and all the colors of the rainbow shoes!" he demanded. "And why should you tax Barry?"

"But, Dad, he wants to." She looked eagerly at Barry for confirmation. "He wants to give them to me—for my birthday—"

"Of course I do," said Barry, lightly. "If I didn't give her slippers, I should have to give her something else—and far be it from me to know what—little—lovely—Leila—wants—"

And to the tune of his chant, they hippity-hopped together up the stairs in a hunt for some stray shoe that should fit little-lovely-Leila's foot!

A little later, the silken ladies having descended the stairway for the last time, Aunt Frances took her amber satin stateliness to the Sanctum.

Behind her, a silver shadow, came Aunt Isabelle, and bringing up the rear, General Dick, and the four young people; Leila in a pair of mismated slippers, hippity-hopping behind with Barry, and Porter assuring Mary that he knew he "hadn't any business to butt in to a family party," but that he was coming anyhow.

The Sanctum was the front room on the second floor. It had been the Little Mother's room in the days when she was still with them, and now it had been turned into a retreat where the young people drifted when they wanted quiet, or where they met for consultation and advice. Except that the walnut bed and bureau had been taken out nothing had been changed, and their mother's books were still in the low bookcases; religious books, many of them, reflecting the gentle faith of the owner. On mantel and table and walls were photographs of her children in long clothes and short, and then once more in long ones; there was Barry in wide collars and knickerbockers, and Constance and Mary in ermine caps and capes; there was Barry again in the military uniform of his preparatory school; Constance in her graduation frock, and Mary with her hair up for the first time. There was a picture of their father on porcelain in a blue velvet case, and another picture of him above the mantel in an oval frame, with one of the Little Mother's, also in an oval frame, to flank it. In the fairness of the Little Mother one traced the fairness of Barry and Constance. But the fairness and features of the father were Mary's.

Mary had never looked more like her father than now when, sitting under his picture, she stated her case. What she had to say she said simply. But when she had finished there was the silence of astonishment.

In a day, almost in an hour, little Mary had grown up! With Constance as the nominal head of the household, none of them had realized that it was Mary's mind which had worked out the problems of making ends meet, and that it was Mary's strength and industry which had supplemented Susan's waning efforts in the care of the big house.

"I want to keep the house," Mary repeated. "I had to talk it over to-night, Aunt Frances, because you go back to New York in the morning, and I couldn't speak of it before to-night because I was afraid that some hint of my plan would get to Constance and she would be troubled. She'll learn it later, but I didn't want her to have it on her mind now. I want to stay here. I've always lived here, and so has Barry—and while I appreciate your plans for me to go to Nice, I don't think it would be fair or right for me to leave Barry."

Barry, a little embarrassed to be brought into it, said, "Oh, you needn't mind about me—"

"But I do mind." Mary had risen and was speaking earnestly. "I am sure you must see it, Aunt Frances. If I went with you, Barry would be left to—drift—and I shouldn't like to think of that. Mother wouldn't have liked it, or father." Her voice touched an almost shrill note of protest.

Porter Bigelow, sitting unobtrusively in the background, was moved by her earnestness. "There's something back of it," his quick mind told him; "she knows about—Barry—"

But Barry, too, was on his feet. "Oh, look here, Mary," he was expostulating, "I'm not going to have you stay at home and miss a winter of good times, just because I'll have to eat a few meals in a boarding-house. And I sha'n't have to eat many.

When I get starved for home cooking, I'll hunt up my friends. You'll take me in now and then, for Sunday dinner, won't you, General?—Leila says you will; and it isn't as if you were never coming back—Mary."

"If we close the house now," Mary said, "it will mean that it won't be opened again. You all know that." Her accusing glance rested on Aunt Frances and the General. "You all think it ought to be sold, but if we sell what will become of Susan Jenks, who nursed us and who nursed mother, and what shall we do with all the dear old things that were mother's and father's, and who will live in the dear old rooms?" She was struggling for composure. "Oh, don't you see that I—I can't go?"

It was Aunt Frances' crisp voice which brought her back to calmness. "But, my dear, you can't afford to keep it open. Your income with what Barry earns isn't any more than enough to pay your running expenses; there's nothing left for taxes or improvements. I'm perfectly willing to finance you to the best of my ability, but I think it very foolish to sink any more money—here—"

"I don't want you to sink it, Aunt Frances. Constance begged me to use her little part of our income, but I wouldn't. We sha'n't need it. I've fixed things so that we shall have money for the taxes. I—I have rented the Tower Rooms, Aunt Frances!"

They stared at her stunned. Even Leila tore her adoring eyes from Barry's face, and fixed them on the girl who made this astounding statement.

"Mary," Aunt Frances gasped, "do you meant that you are going to take—lodgers—?"

"Only one, Aunt Frances. And he's perfectly respectable. I advertised and he answered, and he gave me a bank reference."

"*He*. Mary, is it a man?"

Mary nodded. "Of course. I should hate to have a woman fussing around. And I set the rent for the suite at exactly the amount I shall need to take me through this year, and he was satisfied."

She turned and picked up a printed slip from the table.

"This is the way I wrote my ad," she said, "and I had twenty-seven answers. And this seemed the best—"

"Twenty-seven!" Aunt Frances held out her hand. "Will you let me see what you wrote to get such remarkable results?"

Mary handed it to her, and through the diamond-studded lorgnette Aunt Frances read:

"To let: Suite of two rooms and bath; with Gentleman's Library. House on top of a high hill which overlooks the city. Exceptional advantages for a student or scholar."

"I consider," said Mary, as Aunt Frances paused, "that the Gentleman's Library part was an inspiration. It was the bait at which they all nibbled."

The General chuckled, "She'll do. Let her have her own way, Frances. She's got a head on her like a man's."

Aunt Frances turned on him. "Mary speaks what is to me a rather new language of independence. And she can't stay here alone. She *can't*. It isn't proper—without an older woman in the house."

"But I want an older woman. Oh, Aunt Frances, please, may I have Aunt Isabelle?"

She had raised her voice so that Aunt Isabelle caught the name. "What does she want, Frances?" asked the deaf woman; "what does she want?"

"She wants you to live with her—here." Aunt Frances was thinking rapidly; it wasn't such a bad plan. It was always a problem to take Isabelle when she and her daughter traveled. And if they left her in New York there was always the haunting fear that she might be ill, or that they might be criticized for leaving her.

"Mary wants you to live with her," she said, "While we are abroad, would you like it—a winter in Washington?"

Aunt Isabelle's gentle face was illumined. "Do you really *want* me, my dear?" she asked in her hushed voice. It had been a long time since Aunt Isabelle had felt that she was wanted anywhere. It seemed to her that since the illness which had sent her into a world of silence, that her presence had been endured, not coveted.

Mary came over and put her arms about her. "Will you, Aunt Isabelle?" she asked. "I shall miss Constance so, and it would almost be like having mother to have—you—"

No one knew how madly the hungry heart was beating under the silver-gray gown. Aunt Isabella was only forty-eight, twelve years younger than her sister Frances, but she had faded and drooped, while Frances had stood up like a strong flower on its stem. And the little faded drooping lady yearned for tenderness, was starved for it, and here was Mary in her youth and beauty, promising it.

"I want you so much, and Barry wants you—and Susan Jenks—"

She was laughing tremulously, and Aunt Isabelle laughed too, holding on to herself, so that she might not show in face or gesture the wildness of her joy.

"You won't mind, will you, Frances?" she asked.

Aunt Frances rose and shook out her amber skirts "I shall of course be much disappointed," she pitched her voice high and spoke with chill stateliness, "I shall be very much disappointed that neither you nor Mary will be with us for the winter. And I shall have to cross alone. But Grace can meet me in London. She's going there to see Constance, and I shall stay for a while and start the young people socially. I should think you'd want to see Constance, Mary."

Mary drew a quick breath. "I do want to see her—but I have to think about Barry—and for this winter, at least, my place—is here."

Then from the back of the room spoke Porter Bigelow.

"What's the name of your lodger?"

"Roger Poole."

"There are Pooles in Gramercy Park," said Aunt Frances. "I wonder if he's one of them."

Mary shook her head. "He's from the South."

"I should think," said Porter, slowly, "that you'd want to know something of him besides his bank reference before you took him into your house."

"Why?" Mary demanded.

"Because he might be—a thief, or a rascal," Porter spoke hotly.

Over the heads of the others their eyes met. "He is neither," said Mary. "I know a gentleman when I see one, Porter."

Then the temper of the redhead flamed. "Oh, do you? Well, for my part I wish that you were going to Nice, Mary."

CHAPTER III

In Which a Lonely Wayfarer Becomes Monarch of All He Surveys; and in Which One Who Might Have Been Presented as the Hero of This Tale is Forced, Through No Fault of His Own, to Take His Chances With the Rest.

When Roger Poole came a week later to the big house on the hill, it was on a rainy day. He carried his own bag, and was let in at the lower door by Susan Jenks.

Her smiling brown face gave him at once a sense of homeyness. She led the way through the wide hall and up the front stairs, crisp and competent in her big white apron and black gown.

As he followed her, Roger was aware that the house had lost its effulgence. The flowers were gone, and the radiance, and the stairs that the silken ladies had once ascended showed, at closer range, certain signs of shabbiness. The carpet was old and mended. There was a chilliness about the atmosphere, as if the fire, too, needed mending.

But when Susan Jenks opened the door of the Tower Room, he was met by warmth and brightness. Here was the light of leaping flames and of a low-shaded lamp. On the table beside the lamp was a pot of pink hyacinths, and their fragrance made the air sweet. The inner room was no longer a rosy bower, but a man's retreat, with its substantial furniture, its simplicity, its absence of non-essentials. In this room Roger set down his bag, and Susan Jenks, hanging big towels and little ones in the bathroom, drawing the curtains, and coaxing the fire, flitted cozily back and forth for a few minutes and then withdrew.

It was then that Roger surveyed his domain. He was monarch of all of it. The big chair was his to rest in, the fire was his, the low lamp, all the old friends in the bookcases!

He went again into the inner room. The glass candlesticks were gone and the photographs in their silver and ivory frames, but over the mantel there was a Corot print with forest vistas, and another above his little bedside table. On the table was a small electric lamp with a green shade, a new magazine, and a little old bulging Bible with a limp leather binding.

As he stood looking down at the little table, he was thrilled by the sense of safety after a storm. Outside was the world with its harsh judgments. Outside was the rain and the beating wind. Within were these signs of a heart-warming hospitality. Here was no bleak cleanliness, no perfunctory arrangement, but a place prepared as for an honored guest.

Down-stairs Mary was explaining to Aunt Isabelle. "I'll have Susan Jenks take some coffee to him. He's to get his dinners in town, and Susan will serve his breakfast in his room. But I thought the coffee to-night after the rain—might be comfortable."

The two women were in the dining-room. The table had been set for three, but Barry had not come.

The dinner had been a simple affair—an unfashionably nourishing soup, a broiled fish, a salad and now the coffee. Thus did Mary and Susan Jenks make income and expenses meet. Susan's good cooking, supplementing Mary's gastronomic discrimination, made a feast of the simple fare.

"What's his business, my dear?"

"Mr. Poole's? He's in the Treasury. But I think he's studying something. He seemed to be so eager for the books—"

"Your father's books?"

"Yes. I left them all up there. I even left father's old Bible. Somehow I felt that if any one was tired or lonely that the old Bible would open at the right page."

"Your father was often lonely?"

"Yes. After mother's death. And he worked too hard, and things went wrong with his business. I used to slip up to his bedroom sometimes in the last days, and there he'd be with the old Bible on his knee, and mother's picture in his hand." Mary's eyes were wet.

"He loved your mother and missed her."

"It was more than that. He was afraid of the future for Constance and me. He was afraid of the future for—Barry—"

Susan Jenks, carrying a mahogany tray on which was a slender silver coffee-pot flanked by a dish of cheese and toasted biscuit, asked as she went through the room: "Shall I save any dinner for Mr. Barry?"

"He'll be here," Mary said. "Porter Bigelow is taking us to the theater, and Barry's to make the fourth."

Barry was often late, but to-night it was half-past seven when he came rushing in.

"I don't want anything to eat," he said, stopping at the door of the dining-room where Mary and Aunt Isabelle still waited. "I had tea down-town with General Dick and Leila's crowd. And we danced. There was a girl from New York, and she was a little queen."

Mary smiled at him. To Aunt Isabella's quick eyes it seemed to be a smile of relief. "Oh, then you were with the General and Leila," she said.

"Yes. Where did you think I was?"

"Nowhere," flushing.

He started up-stairs and then came back. "I wish you'd give me credit for being able to keep a promise, Mary. You know what I told Con—"

"It wasn't that I didn't believe—" Mary crossed the dining-room and stood in the door.

"Yes, it was. You thought I was with the old crowd. I might as well go with them as to have you always thinking it."

"I'm not always thinking it."

"Yes, you are, too," hotly.

"Barry—please—"

He stood uneasily at the foot of the stairs. "You can't understand how I feel. If you were a boy—"

She caught him up. "If I were a boy? Barry, if I were a boy I'd make the world move. Oh, you | men, you have things all your own way, and you let it stand still—"

She had raised her voice, and her words floating up and up reached the ears of Roger Poole, who appeared at the top of the stairway.

There was a moment's startled silence, then Mary spoke.

"Barry, it is Mr. Poole. You don't know each other, do you?"

The two men, one going up the stairway, the other coming down, met and shook hands. Then Barry muttered something about having to run away and dress, and Roger and Mary were left alone.

It was the first time that they had seen each other, since the night of the wedding. They had arranged everything by telephone, and on the second short visit that Roger had made to his rooms, Susan Jenks had looked after him.

It seemed to Roger now that, like the house, Mary had taken on a new and less radiant aspect. She looked pale and tired. Her dress of white with its narrow edge of dark fur made her taller and older. Her fair waved hair was parted at the side and dressed compactly without ornament or ribbon. He was again, however, impressed by the almost frank boyishness of her manner as she said:

"I want you to meet Aunt Isabella. She can't hear very well, so you'll have to raise your voice."

As they went in together, Mary was forced to readjust certain opinions which she had formed of her lodger. The other night he had been divorced from the dapper youths of her own set by his lack of up-to-dateness, his melancholy, his air of mystery.

But to-night he wore a loose coat which she recognized at once as good style. His dark hair which had hung in an untidy lock was brushed back as smoothly and as sleekly as Gordon Richardson's. His dark eyes had a waked-up look. And there was a hint of color in his clean-shaven olive cheeks.

"I came down," he told her as he walked beside her, "to thank you for the coffee, for the hyacinths; for the fire, for the—welcome that my room gave me."

"Oh, did you like it? We were very busy up there all the morning, Aunt Isabelle and I and Susan Jenks."

"I felt like thanking Susan Jenks for the big bath towels; they seemed to add the final perfect touch."

She laughed and repeated his remark to Aunt Isabelle.

"Think of his being grateful for bath towels, Aunt Isabelle."

After his presentation to Aunt Isabelle, he said, smiling:

"And there was another touch—the big gray pussy cat. She was in the window-seat, and when I sat down to look at the lights, she tucked her head under my hand and sang to me."

"*Pittiwitz*? Oh, Aunt Isabelle, we left Pittiwitz up there. She claims your room as hers," she explained to Roger. "We've had her for years. And she was always there with father, and then with Constance and me. If she's a bother, just put her on the back stairs and she will come down."

"But she isn't a bother. It is very pleasant to have something alive to bear me company."

The moment that his remark was made he was afraid that she might interpret it as a plea for companionship. And he had no right—What earthly right had he to expect to enter this charmed circle?

Susan Jenks came in with her arms full of wraps. "Mr. Porter's coming," she said, "and it's eight o'clock now."

"We are going out—" Mary was interested to note that her lodger had taken Aunt Isabelle's wrap, and was putting her into it without self-consciousness.

Her own wrap was of a shimmering gray-green velvet which matched her eyes, and there was a collar of dark fur.

"It's a pretty thing," Roger said, as he held it for her. "It's like the sea in a mist."

She flashed a quick glance at him. "I like that," she said in her straightforward way. "It is lovely. Aunt Frances brought it to me last year from Paris. Whenever you see me wear anything that is particularly nice, you'll know that it came from Aunt Frances—Aunt Isabelle's sister. She's the rich member of the family. And all the rest of us are as poor as poverty."

Outside a motor horn brayed. Then Porter Bigelow came in— a perfectly put together young man, groomed, tailored, outfitted according to the mode.

"Are you ready, Contrary Mary?" he said, then saw Roger and stopped.

Porter was a gentleman, so his manner to Roger Poole showed no hint of what he thought of lodgers in general, and this one in particular. He shook hands and said a few pleasant and perfunctory things. Personally he thought the man looked down and out. But no one could tell what Mary might think. Mary's standards were those of the dreamer and the star gazer. What she was seeking she would never find in a Mere Man. The danger lay however, in the fact that she might mistakenly hang her affections about the neck of some earth-bound Object and call it an Ideal.

As for himself, in spite of his Buff-Orpington crest, and his cock-o'-the-walk manner, Porter was, as far Mary was concerned, saturated with humility. He knew that his money, his family's social eminence were as nothing in her eyes. If underneath the weight of these things Mary could find enough of a man in him to love that could be his only hope. And that hope had held him for years to certain rather sedate ambitions, and had given him moral standards which had delighted his mother and had puzzled his father.

"Whatever I am as a man, you've made me," he said to Mary two hours later, in the intermission between the second and third acts of the musical comedy, which, for a time, had claimed their attention. Aunt Isabelle, in front of the box, was smiling gently, happy in the golden light and the nearness of the music. Barry was visiting Leila and the General who were just below, in orchestra chairs.

"Whatever I am as a man, you've made me," Porter repeated, "and now, if you'll only let me take care of you—"

Hitherto, Mary had treated his love-making lightly, but tonight she turned upon him her troubled eyes. "Porter, you know I can't. But there are times when I wish—I could—"

"Then why not?"

She stopped him with a gesture. "It wouldn't be right. I'm simply feeling lonely and lost because Constance is so far away. But that isn't any reason for marrying you. You deserve a woman who cares, who really cares, heart and soul. And I can't, dear boy."

"I was a fool to think you might," savagely, "a man with a red head is always a joke."

"As if that had anything to do with it."

"But it has, Mary. You know as well as I do that when I was a youngster I was always Reddy Bigelow to our crowd—Reddy Bigelow with a carrot-head and freckles. If I had been poor and common, life wouldn't have been worth living. But mother's family and Dad's money fixed that for me. And I had an allowance big enough to supply the neighborhood with sweets. You were a little thing, but you were sorry for me, and I didn't have to buy you. But I'd buy you now—with a house in town and a country house, and motor cars and lovely clothes—if I thought it would do any good, Mary."

"You wouldn't want me that way, Porter."

"I want you—any way."

He stopped as the curtain went up, and darkness descended. But presently out of the darkness came his whisper, "I want you—any way."

They had supper after the play, Leila and the General joining them at Porter's compelling invitation.

Pending the serving of the supper, Barry detained Leila for a moment in a palm-screened corner of the sumptuous corridor.

"That girl from New York, Leila—Miss Jeliffe? What is her first name?"

"Delilah."

"It isn't."

Leila's light laughter mocked him. "Yes, it is, Barry. She calls herself Lilah and pronounces it as I do mine. But she signs her cheques De-lilah."

Barry recovered. "Where did you meet her?"

"At school. Her father's in Congress. They are coming to us to-morrow. Dad has asked me to invite them as house guests until they find an apartment."

"Well, she's dazzling."

Leila flamed. "I don't see how you can like—her kind—"

"Little lady," he admonished, "you're jealous. I danced four dances with her, and only one with your new pink slippers."

She stuck out a small foot. "They're lovely, Barry," she said, repentantly, "and I haven't thanked you."

"Why should you? Just look pleasant, please. I've had enough scolding for one day."

"Who scolded?"

"Mary."

Leila glanced into the dining-room, where, in her slim fairness, Mary was like a pale lily, among all the tulip women, and poppy women, and orchid women, and night-shade women of the social garden.

"If Mary scolded you, you deserved it," she said, loyally.

"You too? Leila, if you don't stick to me, I might as well give up."

His face was moody, brooding. She forgot the Delilah-dancer of the afternoon, forgot everything except that this wonderful man-creature was in trouble.

"Barry," she said, simply, like a child, "I'll stick to you until I—die."

He looked down into the adoring eyes. "I believe you would, Leila," he said, with a boyish catch in his voice; "you're the dearest thing on God's great earth!"

The chilled fruit was already on the table when they went in, and it was followed by a chafing dish over which the General presided. Red-faced and rapturous, he seasoned and stirred, and as the result of his wizardry there was placed before them presently such plates of Creole crab as could not be equaled north of New Orleans.

"To cook," said the General, settling himself back in his chair and beaming at Mary who was beside him, "one must be a poet—to me there is more in that dish than merely something to eat. There's color—the red of tomatoes, the green of the peppers, the pale ivory of mushrooms, the snow white of the crab—there's atmosphere—aroma."

"The difference," Mary told him, smiling, "between your cooking and Susan Jenks' is the difference between an epic— and a nursery rhyme. They're both good, but Susan's is unpremeditated art."

"I take off my hat to Susan Jenks," said the General—"when her poetry expresses itself in waffles and fried chicken."

Mary was devoting herself to the General. Porter Bigelow who was on the other side of her, was devoting himself to Aunt Isabelle.

Aunt Isabelle was serenely content in her new office of chaperone.

"I can hear so much better in a crowd." she said, "and then there's so much to see."

"And this is the time for the celebrities," said Porter, and wrote on the corner of the supper card the name of a famous Russian countess at the table next to them. Beyond was the Speaker of the House; the British Ambassador with his fair company of ladies; the Spanish Ambassador at a table of darker beauties.

Mary, listening to Porter's pleasant voice, was constrained to admit that he could be charming. As for the freckles and "carrot-head," they had been succeeded by a fine if somewhat florid complexion, and the curled thickness of his brilliant crown gave to his head an almost classic beauty.

As she studied him, his eyes met hers, and he surprised her by a quick smile of understanding.

"Oh, Contrary Mary," he murmured, so that the rest could not hear, "what do you think of me?"

She found herself blushing, "*Porter.*"

"You were weighing me in the balance? Red head against my

lovely disposition?"

Before she could answer, he had turned back to Aunt Isabelle, leaving Mary with her cheeks hot.

After supper, the young host insisted that Leila and the General should go home in his limousine with Barry and Aunt Isabelle.

"Mary and I will follow in a taxi," he said in the face of their protests.

"Young man," demanded the twinkling General, "if I accept, will you look upon me in the light of an incumbrance or a benefactor?"

"A benefactor, sir," said Porter, promptly, and that settled it.

"And now," said Porter, as, having seen the rest of the party off, he took his seat beside the slim figure in the green velvet wrap, "now I am going to have it out with you."

"But—Porter!"

"I've a lot to say. And we are going to ride around the Speedway while I say it."

"But—it's raining."

"All the better. It will be we two and the world away, Mary."

"And there isn't anything to say."

"Oh, yes, there is—*oodles*."

"And Aunt Isabelle will be worried."

He drew the rug up around her and settled back as placidly as if the hands on the moon face of the clock on the post-office tower were not pointing to midnight. "Aunt Isabelle has been told," he informed her, "that you may be a bit late. I wrote it on the supper card, and she read it—and smiled."

He waited in silence until they had left the avenue, and were on the driveway back of the Treasury which leads toward the river.

"Porter, this is a wild thing to do."

"I'm in a wild mood—a mood that fits in with the rain and wind, Mary. I'm in such a mood that if the times were different and the age more romantic, I would pick you up and put you on my champing steed and carry you off to my castle."

He laughed, and for the moment she was thrilled by his masterfulness. "But, alas, my steed is a taxi—the age is prosaic —and you—I'm afraid of you, Contrary Mary."

They were on the Speedway now, faintly illumined, showing a row of waving willow trees, spectrally outlined against a background of gray water.

"I'm afraid of you. I have always been. Even when you were only ten and I was fifteen. I would shake in my shoes when you looked at me, Mary; you were the only one then—you are the only one—now."

Her hand lay on the outside of the rug. He put his own over it.

"Ever since you said to-night that you didn't care—there's been something singing—in my brain, and it has said, 'make her care, make her care.' And I'm going to do it. I'm not going to trouble you or worry you with it—and I'm going to take my chances with the rest. But in the end I'm going to—win."

"There aren't any others."

"If there aren't there will be. You've kept yourself protected so far by that little independent manner of yours, which scares men off. But some day a man will come who won't be scared—and then it will be a fight to the finish between him—and me."

"Oh, Porter, I don't want to think of marrying—not for ten million years."

"And yet," he said prophetically, "if to-morrow you should meet some man who could make you think he was the Only One, you'd marry him in the face of all the world."

"No man of that kind will ever come."

"What kind?"

"That will make me willing to lose the world."

The rain was beating against the windows of the cab.

"Porter, please. We must go home."

"Not unless you'll promise to let me prove it—to let me show that I'm a man—not a—boy."

"You're the best friend I've ever had. I wish you wouldn't insist on being something else."

"But I do insist—"

"And I insist upon going home. Be good and take me."

It was said with decision, and he gave the order to the driver. And so they whirled at last up the avenue of the Presidents and along the edges of the Park, and arrived at the foot of the terrace of the big house.

There was a light in the tower window.

"That fellow is up yet," Porter said. He had an umbrella over her, and was shielding her as best he could from the rain. "I don't like to think of him in the house."

"Why not?"

"Oh, he sees you every day. Talks to you every day. And what do you know of him? And I who've known you all my life must be content with scrappy minutes with other people around. And anyhow—I believe I'd be jealous of Satan himself, Mary."

They were under the porch now, and she drew away from him a bit, surveying him with disapproving eyes.

"You aren't like yourself to-night, Porter."

He put one hand on her shoulder and stood looking down at her. "How can I be? What am I going to do when I leave you, Mary, and face the fact that you don't care—that I'm no more to you—than that fellow up there in the—tower?"

He straightened himself, then with the madness of his earlier mood upon him, he said one thing more before he left her:

"Contrary Mary, if I weren't such a coward, and you weren't so—wonderful—I'd kiss you now—and *make* you—care—"

CHAPTER IV

In Which a Little Bronze Boy Grins in the Dark;
and in Which Mary Forgets That There is Any One
Else in the House.

Up-stairs among his books Roger Poole heard Mary come in. With the curtains drawn behind him to shut out the light, he looked down into the streaming night, and saw Porter drive away alone.

Then Mary's footstep on the stairs; her raised voice as she greeted Aunt Isabelle, who had waited up for her. A door was shut, and again the house sank into silence.

Roger turned to his books, but not to read. The old depression was upon him. In the glow of his arrival, he had been warmed by the hope that things could be different; here in this hospitable house he had, perchance, found a home. So he had gone down to find that he was an outsider—an alien—old where they were young, separated from Barry and Porter and Mary by years of dark experience.

To him, at this moment, Mary Ballard stood for a symbol of the things which he had lost. Her youth and light-heartedness, her high courage, and now, perhaps, her romance. He knew the look that was in Porter Bigelow's eyes when they had rested upon her. The look of a man who claims—his own. And behind Bigelow's pleasant and perfunctory greeting Roger had felt a subtle antagonism. He smiled bitterly. No man need fear him. He was out of the running. He was done with love, with romance, with women, forever. A woman had spoiled his life.

Yet, if before the other, he had met Mary Ballard? The possibilities swept over him. His life to-day would have been different. He would be facing the world, not turning his back to it.

Brooding over the dying fire, his eyes were stern. If it had been his fault, he would have taken his punishment without flinching. But to be overthrown by an act of chivalry—to be denied the expression of that which surged within him. Daily he bent over a desk, doing the work that any man might do, he who had been carried on the shoulders of his fellow students, he whose voice had rung with a clarion call!

In the lower hall, a door was again opened, and now there were footsteps ascending. Then he heard a little laugh. "I've found her—Aunt Isabelle, she insists upon going up."

He clicked off his light and very carefully opened his door. Mary was in the lower hall, the heavy gray cat hugged up in her arms. She wore a lace boudoir cap, and a pale blue dressing-gown trailed after her. Seen thus, she was exquisitely feminine. Faintly through his consciousness flitted Porter Bigelow's name for her—Contrary Mary. Why Contrary? Was there another side which he had not seen? He had heard her flaming words to Barry, "If I were a man—I'd make the world move—" and he had been for the moment repelled. He had no sympathy with modern feminine rebellions. Women were women. Men were men. The things which they had in common were love, and that which followed, the home, the family. Beyond these things their lives were divided, necessarily, properly.

He groped his way back through the darkness to the tower window, opened it and leaned out. The rain beat upon his face, the wind blew his hair back, and fluttered the ends of his loose tie. Below him lay the storm-swept city, its lights faint and flickering. He remembered a test which he had chosen on a night like this.

"O Lord, Thou art my God. I will exalt Thee, I will praise Thy name, for Thou hast done wonderful things; Thou hast been a strength to the poor, a strength to the needy in distress . . . a refuge from the storm—"

How the words came back to him, out of that vivid past. But to-night—why, there was no—God! Was he the fool who had once seen God—in a storm?

He shut the window, and finding a heavy coat and an old cap put them on. Then he made his way, softly, down the tower steps to the side door. Mary had pointed out to him that this entrance would make it possible for him to go and come as he pleased. To-night it pleased him to walk in the beating rain.

At the far end of the garden there was an old fountain, in which a bronze boy rode on a bronze dolphin. The basin of the fountain was filled with sodden leaves. A street lamp at the foot of the terrace illumined the bronze boy's face so that it seemed to wear a twisted grin. It was as if he laughed at the storm and at life, defying the elements with his sardonic mirth.

Back and forth, restlessly, went the lonely man, hating to enter again the rooms which only a few hours before had seemed a refuge. It would have been better to have stayed in his last cheap boarding-house, better to have kept away from this place which brought memories—better never to have seen this group of young folk who were gay as he had once been gay—better never to have seen—Mary Ballard!

He glanced up at the room beneath his own where her light still burned. He wondered if she had stayed awake to think of the young Apollo of the auburn head. Perhaps he was already her accepted lover. And why not?

Why should he care who loved Mary Ballard?

He had never believed in love at first sight. He didn't believe in it now. He only knew that he had been thrilled by a look, warmed by a friendliness, touched by a frankness and sincerity such as he had found in no other woman. And because he had been thrilled and warmed and touched by these things, he was feeling to-night the deadly mockery of a fate which had brought her too late into his life.

* * * * * *

Coming in, shivering and excited after her ride with Porter, Mary had found evidence of Aunt Isabelle's solicitous care for her. Her fire was burning brightly, the covers of her bed were turned down, her blue dressing-gown and the little blue slippers were warming in front of the blaze.

"No one ever did such things for me before," Mary said with appreciation, as the gentle lady came in to kiss her niece good-night. "Mother wasn't that kind. We all waited on her. And Susan Jenks is too busy; it isn't right to keep her up. And anyway I've always been more like a boy, taking care of myself. Constance was the one we petted, Con and mother."

"I love to do it," Aunt Isabelle said, eagerly. "When I am at Frances' there are so many servants, and I feel pushed out. There's nothing that I can do for any one. Grace and Frances each have a maid. So I live my own life, and sometimes it has been—lonely."

"You darling." Mary laid her cool young lips against the soft cheek. "I'm dead lonely, too. That's why I wanted you."

Aunt Isabelle stood for a moment looking into the fire. "It has been years since anybody wanted me," she said, finally.

There was no bitterness in her tone; she simply stated a fact. Yet in her youth she had been the beauty of the family, and the toast of a county.

"Aunt Isabelle," Mary said, suddenly, "is marriage the only way out for a woman?"

"The only way?"

"To freedom. It seems to me that a single woman always seems to belong to her family. Why shouldn't you do as you please? Why shouldn't I? And yet you've never lived your own life. And I sha'n't be able to live mine except by fighting every inch of the way."

A flush stained Aunt Isabelle's cheeks. "I have always been poor, Mary—"

"But that isn't it," fiercely. "There are poor girls who aren't tied—I mean by conventions and family traditions. Why, Aunt Isabelle, I rented the Tower Rooms not only in defiance of the living—but of the dead. I can see mother's face if we had thought of such a thing while she lived. Yet we needed the money then. We needed it to help Dad—to save him—" The last words were spoken under her breath, and Aunt Isabelle did not catch them.

"And now everybody wants me to get married. Oh, Aunt Isabelle, sit down and let's talk it out. I'm not sleepy, are you?" She drew the little lady beside her on the high-backed couch which faced the fire. "Everybody wants me to get married, Aunt Isabelle. And to-night I had it out with—Porter."

"You don't love him?"

"Not—that way. But sometimes—he makes me feel as if I couldn't escape him—as if he would persist and persist, until he won. But I don't want love to come to me that way. It seems to me that if one loves, one knows. One doesn't have to be shown."

"My dear, sometimes it is a tragedy when a woman knows."

"But why?"

"Because men like to conquer. When they see love in a woman's eyes, their own love—dies."

"I should hate a man like that," said Mary, frankly. "If a man only loves you because of the conquest, what's going to happen when you are married and the chase is over? No, Aunt Isabelle, when I fall in love, it will be with a man who will know that I am the One Woman. He must love me because I am Me— Myself. Not because some one else admires me, or because I can keep him guessing. He will know me as I know him—as his Predestined Mate!"

Thus spoke Sweet and Twenty, glowing. And Sweet and Forty, meeting that flame with her banked fires, faltered. "But, my dear, how can you know?"

"How did you know?"

The abrupt question drove every drop of blood from Aunt Isabelle's face. "Who told you?"

"Mother. One night when I asked her why you had never married. You don't mind, do you?"

Aunt Isabelle shook her head. "No. And, Mary, dear, I've faced all the loneliness, all the dependence, rather than be untrue to that which he gave me and I gave him. There was one night, in this old garden. I was visiting your mother, and he was in Congress at the time, and the garden was full of roses—and it was—moonlight. And we sat by the fountain, and there was the soft splash of the water, and he said: 'Isabelle, the little bronze boy is throwing kisses at you—do you see him— smiling?' And I said, 'I want no kisses but yours'—and that was the last time. The next day he was killed—thrown from his horse while he was riding out here to see—me.

"It was after that I was so ill. And something teemed to snap in my head, and one day when I sat beside the fountain I found that I couldn't hear the splash of the water, and things began to go; the voices I loved seemed far away, and I could tell that the wind was blowing only by the movement of the leaves, and the birds rounded out their little throats—but I heard—no music—"

Her voice trailed away into silence.

"But before the stillness, there were others who—wanted me—for I hadn't lost my prettiness, and Frances did her best for me. And she didn't like it when I said I couldn't marry, Mary. But now I am glad. For in the silence, my love and I live, in a world of our own."

"Aunt Isabelle—darling. How lovely and sweet, and sad—" Mary was kneeling beside her aunt, her arm thrown around her, and Aunt Isabelle, reading her lips, did not need to hear the words.

"If I had been strong, like you, Mary, I could have held my own against Frances and have made something of myself. But I'm not strong, and twenty-five years ago women did not ask for freedom. They asked for—love."

"But I want to find freedom in my love. Not be bound as Porter wants to bind me. He'd put me on a pedestal and worship me, and I'd rather stand shoulder to shoulder with my husband and be his comrade. I don't want him to look up too far, or to look down as Gordon looks down on Constance."

"Looks down? Why, he adores her, Mary."

"Oh, he loves her. And he'll do everything for her, but he will do it as if she were a child. He won't ask her opinion in any vital matter. He won't share his big interests with her, and so he'll never discover the big fine womanliness. And she'll shrivel to his measure of her."

Aunt Isabelle shook her head, smiling. "Don't analyze too much, Mary. Men and women are human—and you may lose yourself in a search for the Ideal."

"Do you know what Porter calls me, Aunt Isabelle? Contrary Mary. He says I never do things the way the people expect. Yet I do them the way that I must. It is as if some force were inside of me—driving me—on."

She stood up as she said it, stretching out her arms in an eager gesture. "Aunt Isabelle, if I were a man, there'd be something in the world for me to do. Yet here I am, making ends meet, holding up my part of the housekeeping with Susan Jenks, and taking from the hands of my rich friends such pleasures as I dare accept without return."

Aunt Isabelle pulled her down beside her. "Rebellious Mary," she said, "who is going to tame you?"

They laughed a little, clinging to each other, and than Mary said, "You must go to bed, Aunt Isabelle. I'm keeping you up shamefully."

They kissed again and separated, and Mary made ready for bed. She took off her cap, and all her lovely hair fell about her. That was another of her contrary ways. She and Constance had been taught to braid it neatly, but from little girlhood Mary had protested, and on going to bed with two prim pigtails had been known to wake up in the middle of the night and take them down, only to be discovered in the morning with all her fair curls in a tangle. Scolding had not availed. Once, as dire punishment, the curls had been cut off. But Mary had rejoiced. "It makes me look like a boy," she had told her mother, calmly, "and I like it."

Another of her little girl fancies had been to say her prayers aloud. She said them that way to-night, kneeling by her bed with her fair head on her folded hands.

Then she turned out the light, and drew her curtains back. As she looked out at the driving rain, the flare of the street lamp showed a motionless figure on the terrace. For a moment she peered, palpitating, then flew into Aunt Isabelle's room.

"There's some one in the garden."

"Perhaps it's Barry."

"Didn't he come with you?"

"No. He went on with Leila and the General."

"But it is two o'clock, Aunt Isabelle."

"I didn't know; I thought perhaps he had come."

Going back into her room, Mary threw on her blue dressing-gown and slippers and opened her door. The light was still burning in the hall. Barry always turned it out when he came. She stood undecided, then started down the back stairs, but halted as the door opened and a dark figure appeared.

"Barry—"

Roger Poole looked up at her. "It isn't your brother," he said. "I—I must beg your pardon for disturbing you. I could not sleep, and I went out—" He stopped and stammered. Poised there above him with all the wonder of her unbound hair about her, she was like some celestial vision.

She smiled at him. "It doesn't matter," she said; "please don't apologize. It was foolish of me to be—frightened. But I had forgotten that there was any one else in the house."

She was unconscious of the effect of her words. But his soul shrank within him. To her he was the lodger who paid the rent. To him she was, well, just now she was, to him, the Blessed Damosel!

Faintly in the distance they heard the closing of a door. "It's Barry," Mary said, and suddenly a wave of self-consciousness swept over her. What would Barry think to find her at this hour talking to Roger Poole? And what would he think of Roger Poole, who walked in the garden on a rainy night?

Roger saw her confusion. "I'll turn out this light," he said, "and wait—"

And she waited, too, in the darkness until Barry was safe in his own room, then she spoke softly. "Thank you so much," she said, and was gone.

CHAPTER V

In Which Roger Remembers a Face and Delilah Remembers a Voice—and in Which a Poem and a Pussy Cat Play an Important Part.

Since the night of his arrival, Roger had not intruded upon the family circle. He had read hostility in Barry's eyes as the boy had looked up at him; and Mary, in spite of her friendliness, had forgotten that he was in the house! Well, they had set the pace, and he would keep to it. Here in the tower he could live alone—yet not be lonely, for the books were there—and they brought forgetfulness.

He took long walks through the city, now awakening to social and political activities. Back to town came the folk who had fled from the summer heat; back came the members of House and of Senate, streaming in from North, South, East and West for the coming Congress. Back came the office-seekers and the pathetic patient group whose claims were waiting for the passage of some impossible bill.

There came, too, the sightseers and trippers, sweeping from one end of the town to the other, climbing the dome of the Capitol, walking down the steps of the Monument, venturing into the White House, piloted through the Bureau where the money is made, riding on "rubber-neck wagons," sailing about in taxis, stampeding Mt. Vernon, bombarding Fort Myer, and doing it all gloriously under golden November skies.

And because of the sightseers and statesmen, and the folk who had been away for the summer, the shops began to take on beauty. Up F Street and around Fourteenth into H swept the eager procession, and all the windows were abloom for them.

Roger walked, too, in the country. In other lands, or at least so their poets have it, November is the month of chill and dreariness. But to the city on the Potomac it comes with soft pink morning mists and toward sunset, with amethystine vistas. And if, beyond the city, the fields are frosted, it is frost of a feathery whiteness which melts in the glory of a warmer noon. And if the trees are bare, there is yet pale yellow under foot and pale rose, where the leaves wait for the winter winds which shall whirl them later in a mad dance like brown butterflies. And there's the green of the pines, and the flaming red of five-fingered creepers.

It was on a sunny November day, therefore, as he followed Rock Creek through the Park that Roger came to the old Mill where a little tea room supplied afternoon refreshment.

As it was far away from car lines, its patronage came largely from those who arrived in motors or on horseback, and a few courageous pedestrians.

Here Roger sat down to rest, ordering a rather substantial repast, for the long walk had made him hungry.

It was while he waited that a big car arrived with five passengers. He recognized Porter Bigelow at once, and there were besides two older men and two young women.

The taller of the two young women had eyes that roved. She had blue black hair, and she wore black—a small black hat with a thin curved plume, and a tailored suit cut on lines which accentuated her height and slenderness. Her furs were of leopard skins. Her cheeks were touched with high color under her veil.

The other girl had also dark hair. But she was small and bird-like. From head to foot she was in a deep dark pink that, in the wool of her coat and the chiffon of her veil, gave back the hue of the rose which was pinned to her muff.

But it was on the girl in black that Roger fixed his eyes. Where had he seen her?

They chose a table near him, and passed within the touch of his hand. Porter did not recognize him. The tall man in the old overcoat and soft hat was not linked in his memory with that moment of meeting in Mary's dining-room.

"Everybody mixes up our names, Porter," the girl with the rose was saying as they sat down; "the girls did at school, didn't they, Lilah?"

"Yes," the girl in black did not need many words with her eyes to talk for her.

"Was it big Lilah and little Leila?" Porter asked.

"No," the dark eyes above the leopard muff widened and held his gaze. "It was dear Leila, and dreadful Lilah. I used to shock them, you know."

The three men laughed. "What did you do?" demanded Porter, leaning forward a little.

Men always leaned toward Delilah Jeliffe. She drew them even while she repelled.

"I smoked cigarettes, for one thing," she said; "everybody does it now. But then—I came near being expelled for it."

The little rose girl broke in hotly. "I think it is horrid still, Lilah," she said.

Lilah smiled and shrugged. "But that wasn't the worst. One

day—I eloped."

She was making them all listen. The old men and the young one, and the man at the other table.

"I eloped with a boy from Prep. He was nineteen, and I was two years younger. We started by moonlight in Romeo's motor car—it was great fun. But the clergyman wouldn't marry us. I think he guessed that we were a pair of kiddies from school—and he scolded us and sent me back in a taxi—"

The tall, thin old gentleman was protesting. "My dear—"

"Oh, you didn't know, Daddy darling," she said. "I got back before I was discovered, and let myself in by the door I had unlocked. But I couldn't keep it from the girls—it was such fun to make them—shiver."

"And what became of Romeo?" Porter asked.

"He found another Juliet—a lovely little blonde and they are living happy ever after."

Leila's eyes were round. "But I don't see," she began.

"Of course you don't, duckie. To me, the whole thing was an adventure along the road—to you, it would have been a heart-break."

Her words came clearly to Roger. That, then, was what love meant to some women—an adventure along the road. One man served for pleasuring, until at some curve in the highway she met another.

Lilah was challenging her audience. "And now you see why I was dreadful Lilah. I fit the name they had for me, don't I?"

Her question was put at Porter, and he answered it. "It is women who set the pace for us," he said; "if they adventure, we venture. If they lead, we follow."

General Dick broke in. With his halo of white hair and his pink face, he looked like an indignant cherub. "The way you young people treat serious subjects is appalling;" then he felt his little daughter's hand upon his arm.

"Lilah is always saying things that she doesn't mean, Dad. Please don't take her seriously."

"Nobody takes me seriously," said Lilah, "and that's why nobody knows me as I really am."

"I know you," said her father, "and you're like a little mare that I used to drive out on the ranch. As long as I'd let her have her head, she was lovely. But let me try to curb her, and she'd kick over the traces."

They all laughed at that; then their tea came, and a great plate of toast, and the conversation grew intermittent and less interesting.

Yet the man at the other table had his attention again arrested when Lilah said to Porter, as she drew on her gloves:

"We are invited to Mary Ballard's for Thanksgiving, and you're to be there."

"Yes—mother and father are going South, so I can escape the family feast."

"Mary Ballard is—charming—" It was said tentatively, with an upward sweep of her lashes.

But Porter did not answer; and as he stood behind her chair, there was a deeper flush on his florid cheeks. Mary's name he held in his heart. It was rarely on his lips.

Mary had not wanted Delilah and her father for Thanksgiving.

"But we can't have Leila and the General without them," she said to Barry, after a conversation with Leila over the telephone, "and it wouldn't seem like Thanksgiving without the Dicks."

"Delilah," said Barry, comfortably, "is good fun. I'm glad she is coming."

"She may be good fun," said Mary, slowly, "but she isn't—our kind."

"Leila said that to me," Barry told her. "I don't quite see what you girls mean."

"Well, you wouldn't," Mary agreed; "men don't see. But I should think when you look at Leila you'd know the difference. Leila is like a little wild rose, and Delilah Jeliffe is a—tulip."

"I like tulips," murmured Barry, audaciously.

Mary laughed. What was the use? Barry was Barry. And Delilah Jeliffe would flit in and out of his life as other girls had flitted; but always there would be for him—Leila.

"If you were a woman," she said, "you'd know by her clothes, and the pink of her cheeks, and by the way she does her hair—she's just a little too much of—everything—Barry."

"There's just enough of Delilah Jeliffe," said Barry, "to keep a man guessing."

"Guessing what?" Mary demanded with a spark in her eyes.

"Oh, just guessing," easily.

"Whether she likes you?"

Barry nodded.

"But why should you want to know, Barry? You're not in love with her."

His blue eyes danced. "Love hasn't anything to do with it, little solemn sister; it's just in the—game."

Later they had a tilt over inviting Mary's lodger.

"It seems so inhospitable to let him spend the day up there alone."

"I don't see how he could possibly expect to dine with us," Barry said, hotly. "You don't know anything about him, Mary. And I agree with Porter—a man's bank reference isn't sufficient for social recognition. And anyhow he may not have the right kind of clothes."

"We are to have dinner at three o'clock," she said, "just as mother always had it on Thanksgiving Day. If you don't want me to ask Roger Poole, I won't. But I think you are an awful snob, Barry."

Her eyes were blazing.

"Now what have I done to deserve that?" her brother demanded.

"You haven't treated him civilly," Mary said. "In a sense he's a guest in our house, and you haven't been up to his rooms since he came—and he's a gentleman."

"How do you know?"

"Because I do."

"Yet the other day you hinted that Delilah Jeliffe wasn't a lady, not in your sense of the word—and that I couldn't see the difference because was a man. I'll let you have your opinion of Delilah Jeliffe if you'll let me have mine of Roger Poole."

So Mary compromised by having Roger down for the evening. "We shall be just a family party for dinner," she said. "But later, we are asking some others for candle-lighting time. We want everybody to come prepared to tell a story or recite, or to sing, or play—in the dark at first, and then with the candles."

His pride urged him to refuse—to spurn this offer of hospitality from the girl who had once forgotten that he was in the house!

But as he stood there on the threshold of the Tower Rooms, her smile seemed to draw him, her voice called him, and he was young—and desperately lonely.

So as he dressed carefully on Thanksgiving afternoon, he had a sense of exhilaration. For one night he would let himself go. He would be himself. No one should snub him. Snubs came from self-consciousness—he who was above them need not see them.

When at last he entered the drawing-room, it was unillumined except for the flickering flame of a fire of oak logs. The guests, assembling wraith-like among the shadows, were given, each, an unlighted candle.

Roger found a place in a big chair beside the piano, and sat there alone, interested and curious. And presently Pittiwitz, stealing toward the hearth, arched her back under his hand, and he reached down and lifted her to his knee, where she stretched herself, sphinx-like, her amber eyes shining in the dusk.

With the last guest seated, Barry stood before them, and gave the key to the situation.

"Everybody is to light a candle with some stunt," he explained. "You know the idea. All of you have some parlor tricks, and you're to show them off."

There were no immediate volunteers, so Barry pounced on Leila.

"You begin," he said, and drew her into the circle of the firelight.

She looked very childish and sweet as she stood there with her unlighted candle, and sang a lullaby. Mary Ballard played her accompaniment softly, sitting so near to Roger in his dim corner that the folds of her velvet gown swept his foot.

And when the song was finished, Leila touched a match to her candle and stood on tiptoe to set it on the corner of the mantel, where it glimmered bravely.

General Dick and Mr. Jeliffe came next. Solemnly they placed two cushions on the hearth-rug, solemnly they knelt thereon, facing each other. Then intently and conscientiously they played the old game of "Pease porridge hot, pease porridge cold." The General's fat hands met Mr. Jeliffe's thin ones alternately and in unison. Not a mistake did they make, and, ending out of breath, the General found it hard to rise, and had to be picked by Porter, like a plump feather pillow.

And now the candles were three!

Then Barry and Delilah danced, a dance which they had practiced together. It had in it just a hint of wildness, and just a hint of sophistication, and Delilah in her dress of sapphire chiffon, with its flaring tunic of silver net, seemed in the nebulous light like some strange bird of the night.

And now the candles were five!

Following, Leila went to the piano, and Porter and Mary gave a minuet. They had learned it at dancing-school, and it had been years since they had danced it. But they did it very well; Porter's somewhat stiff bearing accorded with its stateliness, and Mary, having added to her green velvet gown a little Juliet cap of lace and a lace fan, showed the radiant, almost boyish beauty which had charmed Roger on the night of the wedding.

His pulses throbbed as he watched her. They were a well-matched pair, this young millionaire and the pretty maid. And as their orderly steps went through the dance, so would their orderly lives, if they married, continue to the end. But what could Porter Bigelow teach Mary Ballard of the things which touch the stars?

And now the candles were seven! And the spirit of the carnival was upon the company. Song was followed by story, and story by song—until at last the room seemed to swim in a golden mist.

And through that mist Mary saw Roger Poole! He was leaning forward a little, and there was about him the air of a man who waited.

She spoke impetuously.

"Mr. Poole," she said, "please—"

There was not a trace of awkwardness, not a hint of self-consciousness in his manner as he answered her.

"May I sit here?" he asked. "You see, my pussy cat holds me, and as I shall tell you about a cat, she gives the touch of local color."

And then he began, his right hand resting on the gray cat's head, his left upon his knee.

He used no gestures, yet as he went on, the room became still with the stillness of a captured audience. Here was no stumbling elocution, but a controlled and perfect method, backed by a voice which soared and sang and throbbed and thrilled—the voice either of a great orator, or of a great actor.

The story that he told was of Whittington and his cat. But it was not the old nursery rhyme. He gave it as it is written by one of England's younger poets. Since he lacked the time for it all, he sketched the theme, rounding it out here and there with a verse—and it seemed to Mary that, as he spoke, all the bells of London boomed!

> "'*Flos Mercatorum*,' moaned the bell of All Hallowes,
> 'There was he an orphan, O, a little lad, alone!'
> 'Then we all sang,' echoed happy St. Saviour's,
> 'Called him and lured him, and made him our own.'"

And now they saw the little lad stealing toward the big city, saw all the color and glow as he entered upon its enchantment, saw his meeting with the green-gowned Alice, saw him cold and hungry, faint and footsore, saw him aswoon on a doorstep.

> "'Alice,' roared a voice, and then, O like a lilied angel,
> Leaning from the lighted door, a fair face unafraid,
> Leaning over Red Rose Lane, O, leaning out of Paradise
> Drooped the sudden glory of his green-gowned maid!"

Touching now a lighter note, his voice laughed through the lovely lines; of the ship which was to sail beyond the world; of how each man staked such small wealth as he possessed; "for in those days Marchaunt adventurers shared with their prentices the happy chance of each new venture."

But Whittington had nothing to give. "Not a groat," he tells sweet Alice. "I staked my last groat in a cat!"

> "'Ay, but we need a cat,'
> The Captain said. So when the painted ship
> Sailed through a golden sunrise down the Thames,
> A gray tail waved upon the misty poop,
> And Whittington had his venture on the seas!"

The ringing words brought tumultuous applause. Pittiwitz,

startled, sat up and blinked. People bent to each other, asking: "Who is this Roger Poole?" Under his breath Barry was saying, boyishly, "Gee!" He might still wonder about Mary's lodger, he would never again look down on him. And Delilah Jeliffe sitting next to Barry murmured, "I've heard that voice before—but where?"

Again the bells boomed as the story swept on to the fortune which came to the prentice lad—the price paid for his cat in Barbary by a king whose house was rich in gems but sorely plagued with rats and mice.

Then Whittington's offer of his wealth to Alice, her refusal, and so—to the end.

> "'I know a way,' said the Bell of St. Martin's.
> 'Tell it and be quick,' laughed the prentices below!
> 'Whittington shall marry her, marry her, marry her!
> Peal for a wedding,' said the Big Bell of Bow."

Roger stopped there, and with Pittiwitz in his arms, rose to light his candle. All about him people were saying things, but their words seemed to come to him through a beating darkness. There was only one face—Mary's, and she was leaning toward him, or was it above him? "It was wonderful," she said.

"It is a great poem."

"I don't mean that—it was the way you—gave it."

Outwardly calm, he carried his candle and set it in its place.

Then he came back to Mary—Mary with the shining eyes. This was his night! "You liked it, then?"

For a moment she did not speak, then she said again, "It was wonderful."

There were other people about them now, and Roger met

them with the ease of a man of the world. Even Barry had to admit that his manners were irreproachable, and his clothes. As for his looks, he was not to be matched with Mary's auburn Apollo—one cannot compare a royal stag and a tawny-maned lion!

During the rest of the program, Roger sat enthroned at Mary's side, and listened. He watched the candles, an increasing row of little pointed lights. He went down to supper, and again sat beside Mary—and knew not what he ate. He saw Porter's hot eyes upon him. He knew that to-morrow he must doff his honors and be as he had been before. However, "who knows but the world may end to-night," he told himself, desperately.

Thus he played with Fate, and Fate, turning the tables, brought him at last to Delilah Jeliffe as the guests were saying "good-bye."

"Somewhere I've heard your voice," she said with the upsweep of her lashes. "It isn't the kind that one is likely to forget."

"Yet you have forgotten," he parried.

"I shall remember," she said. "I want to remember—and I shall want to hear it again."

He shook his head. "It was my—swan song—"

"Why?"

He shrugged. "One isn't always in the mood—"

And now it was she who shook her head. "It isn't a mood with you, it's your life."

She had him there, so he carried the conversation lightly to another topic. "I had not thought to give Whittington until I saw Pittiwitz."

"And Mary's green gown?"

Again he parried. "It was dark. I could not see the color of her gown."

"But 'love has eyes.'" The words were light and she meant them lightly. And she went away laughing.

But Roger did not laugh.

And when Mary came to look for him he was gone.

And up-stairs, his evening stripped of its glamour, he told himself that he had been a fool! The world would *not* end to-night. He had to live the appointed length of his days, through all the dreary years.

CHAPTER VI

In Which Mary Brings Christmas to the Tower Rooms; and in Which Roger Declines a Privilege for Which Porter Pleads.

On Christmas Eve, Mary and Susan Jenks brought up to Roger a little tree. It was just a fir plume, but it was gay with tinsel and spicy with the fragrance of the woods, and it was topped by a wee wax angel.

In vain Mary and Barry and even Aunt Isabelle had urged Roger to join their merrymaking downstairs. Aunt Frances, having delayed her trip abroad until January, was coming; and except for Leila and General Dick and Porter Bigelow, it was to be strictly a family affair.

But Roger had refused. "I'm not one of you," he had told Mary. "I'm a bee, not a butterfly, and I shouldn't have joined you on Thanksgiving night. When you're alone, if I may, I'll come down—but please—not with your guests."

He had not joined them often, however, and he had never again shown the mood which had possessed him when his voice had charmed them. Hence they grew, as the days went on, to know him as quiet, self-contained man, whose eyes burned now and then, when some subject was broached which moved him, but who, for the most part, showed at least an outward serenity.

They grew to like him, too, and to depend upon him. Even Aunt Isabelle went to him for advice. He had such an attentive manner, and when he spoke, he gave his opinion with an air of comforting authority.

But always he avoided Porter Bigelow, he avoided Leila, and most of all, he avoided Delilah Jeliffe, although that persistent young person would have invaded the Tower Rooms, if Mary had not warned her away.

"He is very busy, Lilah," she said, "and when he isn't, he comes down here."

"Don't you ever go up?" Delilah's tone was curious.

"No," said Mary, "Why should I?"

Delilah shrugged. "If a man," she said, "had looked at me as he looked at you on Thanksgiving night, I should be, to say the least—interested—"

Mary's head was held high. "I like Roger Poole," she said, "and he's a gentleman. But I'm not thinking about the look in his eyes."

Yet she did think of it, after all, for such seed does the Delilah-type of woman sow. She thought of him, but only with a little wonder—for Mary was as yet unawakened—Porter's passionate pleading, the magic of Roger Poole's voice—these had not touched the heart which still waited.

"Since Mahomet wouldn't come to the mountain," Mary remarked to her lodger as Susan deposited her burden, "the mountain had to come to Mahomet. And here's a bit of mistletoe for your door, and of holly for your window."

He took the wreaths from her. "You are like the spirit of Christmas in your green gown."

"This?" She was wearing the green velvet—with a low collar of lace. "Oh, I've had this for ages, but I like it—" She broke off to say, wistfully, "It seems as if you ought to come down—as if up here you'd be lonely."

Susan Jenks, hanging the mistletoe over the door, was out of range of their voices.

"I am lonely," Roger said, "but now with my little tree, I shall forget everything but your kindness."

"Don't you love Christmas?" Mary asked him. "It's such a friendly time, with everybody thinking of everybody else. I had to hunt a lot before I found the wax angel. It needed such a little one—but I always want one on my tree. When I was a child, mother used to tell me that the angel was bringing a message of peace and good will to our house."

"If the little angel brings me your good will, I shall feel that he has performed his mission."

"Oh, but you have it," brightly. "We are all so glad you are here. Even Barry, and Barry hated the idea at first of our having a lodger. But he likes you."

"And I like Barry," he said. "He is youth—incarnate."

"He's a dear," she agreed. Then a shadow came into her eyes. "But he's such a boy, and—and he's spoiled. Everybody's too good to him. Mother was—and father, though father tried not to be. And Leila is, and Constance—and Aunt Isabelle excuses him, and even Susan Jenks."

Susan Jenks, having hung all the wreaths, had departed, and was not there to hear this mention of her shortcomings.

"I see—and you?" smiling.

She drew a long breath. "I'm trying to play Big Sister—and

sometimes I'm afraid I'm more like a big brother—I haven't the—patience."

His attentive face invited further confidence. It was the face of a man who had listened to many confidences, and instinctively she felt that others had been helped by him.

"You see I want Barry to pass the Bar examination. All of the men of our family have been lawyers, But Barry won't study, and he has taken a position in the Patent Office. He's wasting these best years as a clerk."

Then she remembered, and begged, "Forgive me—"

"There's nothing to forgive," he said. "I suppose I am wasting my years as a clerk in the Treasury Department—but there's this difference, your brother's life is before him—mine is behind me. His ambitions are yet to be fulfilled. I have no—ambitions."

"You don't mean that—you can't mean it?"

"Why not?"

"Because you're a man! Oh, I should have been the man of our family—and Barry and Constance should have been the girls." Her eyes blazed.

"You think then, as I heard you say the other night on the stairs, that the world is ours; yet we men let it stand still."

Her head went up. "Yes. Perhaps you do have to fight for what you get. But I'd rather die fighting than smothered."

He laughed a good boyish laugh. "Does Barry know that you feel that way?"

"I'm afraid," penitently, "that I make him feel it, sometimes. And he doesn't know that it is because I care so much. That it is because I want him to be like—father."

He smiled into her misty eyes. "Perhaps if you weren't so militant—in your methods—"

"Oh, that's the trouble with Barry. Everybody's too good to him. And when I try to counteract it, Barry says that I nag. But he doesn't understand."

Her voice broke, and by some subtle intuition he was aware that her burden was heavier than she was willing to admit.

She stood up and held out her hand. "Thank you so much—for letting me talk to you."

He took her hand and stood looking down at her.

"Will you remember that always—when you need to talk things out—that the Tower Room—is waiting?"

And now there were steps dancing up the stairs, and Barry whirled in with Little-Lovely Leila.

"Mary," he said, "we are ready to light the tree, and Aunt Frances is having fits because you aren't down. You know she always has fits when things are delayed. Poole, you are a selfish hermit to stay off up here with a tree of your own."

Roger, who had stepped forward to speak to Leila, shook his head. "I don't deserve to be invited. And you're all too good to me."

"Oh, but we're not," Leila spoke in her pretty childish way; "we'd love to have you down. Everybody's just crazy about you, Mr. Poole."

They shouted at that.

"Leila," Barry demanded, "are you crazy about him? Tell me

now and get the agony over."

Leila, tilting herself on her pink slipper toes almost crowed with delight at his teasing: "I said, *everybody*—"

Barry advanced to where she stood in the doorway.

"Leila Dick," he announced, "you're under the mistletoe, and you can't escape, and I'm going to kiss you. It's my ancient and hereditary privilege—isn't it, Poole? It's my ancient and hereditary privilege," he repeated, and now he was bending over her.

"Barry," Mary expostulated, "behave yourself."

But it was Leila who stopped him. Her little hands held him off, her face was white. "Barry," she whispered, "Barry— *please*—"

He dropped her hands.

"You blessed baby," he said, with all his laughter gone. "You're like a little sweet saint in an altar shrine!"

Then, with another sudden change of mood, he whirled her away as quickly as he had come, and Mary, following, stopped on the threshold to say to Roger:

"We shall all be away to-morrow. We are to dine at General Dick's. But I am going to church in the morning—the six o'clock service. It's lovely with the snow and the stars. There'll be just Barry and me. Won't you come?"

He hesitated. Then, "No," he said, "no," and lest she should think him unappreciative, he added, "I never go to church."

She came back to him and stood by the fire. "Don't you believe in it?" She was plainly troubled for him. "Don't you believe in the angels and the shepherds, and the wise men, and the Babe in the Manger?"

"No," he said dully, "I don't believe."

"Oh," it was almost a cry, "then what does Christmas mean to you? What can it mean to anybody who doesn't believe in the Babe and the Star in the East?"

"It means this, Mary Ballard," he said, impetuously, "that out of all my unbelief—I believe in you—in your friendliness. And that is my star shining just now in the darkness."

She would have been less than a woman if she had not been thrilled by such a tribute. So she blushed shyly. "I'm glad," she said and smiled up at him.

But as she went down-stairs, the smile faded. It was as if the shadow of the Tower Rooms were upon her. As if the loneliness and sadness of Roger Poole had become hers. As if his burden was added to her other burdens.

Aunt Frances, more regal than ever in gold and amethyst brocade, was presiding over a mountainous pile of white boxes, behind which the unlighted tree spread its branches.

"My child," she said reprovingly, as Mary entered, "I wonder if you were ever in time for anything."

And Porter whispered in Mary's ear as he led her to the piano: "Is this a merry Christmas or a Contrary-Mary Christmas? You look as if you had the weight of the world on your shoulders."

She shook her head. Tears were very near the surface. He saw it and was jealously unhappy. What had brought her in this mood from the Tower Rooms?

And now Barry turned off the lights, and in the darkness Mary struck the first chords and began to sing, "Holy Night—"

As her voice throbbed through the stillness, little stars shone out upon the tree until it was all in shining glory.

Up-stairs, Roger heard Mary singing. He went to his window and drew back the curtains. Outside the world was wrapped in snow. The lights from the lower windows shone on the fountain, and showed the little bronze boy in a winding sheet of white.

But it was not the little bronze boy that Roger Poole saw. It was another boy—himself—singing in a dim church in a big city, and his soul was in the words. And when he knelt to pray, it seemed to him that the whole world prayed. He was bathed in reverence. In his boyish soul there was no hint of unbelief— no doubt of the divine mystery.

He saw himself again in a church. And now it was he who spoke to the people of the Shepherds and the Star. And he knew that he was making them believe. That he was bringing to them the assurance which possessed his own soul—and again there were candles on the altar, and again he sang, and the choir boys sang, and the song was the one that Mary Ballard was singing—

He saw himself once more in a church. But this time there was no singing. There were no candles, no light except such as came faintly through the leaded panes. He was alone in the dimness, and he stood in the pulpit and looked around at the empty pews. Then the light went out behind the windows, and he knelt in the darkness; but not to pray. His head was hidden in his arms. Since then he had never shed a tear, and he had never gone to church.

* * * * * *

Mary's song was followed by carols in which the other voices joined—Porter's and Barry's and Leila's; General Dick's breathy tenor, Aunt Isabelle's quaver, Aunt Frances' dominant note—with Susan Jenks and the colored maid who helped her on such occasions, piping up like two melodious blackbirds in the hall.

Then General Dick played Santa Claus, handing out the parcels with felicitous little speeches.

Constance had sent a big box from London. There were fads and fripperies from Grace Clendenning in Paris, while Aunt Frances had evidently raided Fifth Avenue and had brought away its treasures.

"It looks like a French shop," said Leila, happy in her own gifts of gloves and silk stockings and slipper buckles and beads, and the crowning bliss of a little pearl heart from Barry.

Porter's offering to Mary was a quaint ring set with rose-cut diamonds and emeralds.

Aunt Frances, hovering over it, exclaimed at its beauty. "It's a genuine antique?"

He admitted that it was, but gave no further explanation.

Later, however, he told Mary, "It was my grandmother's. She belonged to an old French family. My grandfather met her when he was in the diplomatic service. He was an Irishman, and it is from him I get my hair."

"It's a lovely thing. But—Porter—it mustn't bind me to anything. I want to be free."

"You are free. Do you remember when you were a kiddie that I gave you a penny ring out of my popcorn bag? You didn't think that ring tied you to anything, did you? Well, this is just another penny prize package."

So she wore it on her right hand and when he said "Good-night," he lifted the hand and kissed it.

"Girl, dear, may this be the merriest Christmas ever!"

And now the tears overflowed. They were alone in the lower hall and there was no one to see. "Oh, Porter," she wailed, "I'm missing Constance dreadfully—it isn't Christmas—without her. It came over me all at once—when I was trying to think that I was happy."

"Poor little Contrary Mary—if you'd only let me take care of you."

She shook her head. "I didn't mean to be—silly, Porter."

"You're not silly." Then after a silence, "Shall you go to early service in the morning?"

"Yes."

"May I go?"

"Of course. Barry's going, too."

"You mean that you won't let me go with you alone."

"I mean nothing of the kind. Barry always goes. He used to do it to please mother, and now he does it—for remembrance."

"I'm so jealous of my moments alone with you. Why can't Leila stay with you to-night, then there will be four of us, and I can have you to myself. I can bring the car, if you'd rather."

"No, I like to walk. It's so lovely and solemn."

"Be sure to ask Leila."

She promised, and he went away, having to look in at a dance given by one of his mother's friends; and Mary, returning to join the others, pondered, a little wistfully, on the fact that

Porter Bigelow should be so eager for a privilege which Roger Poole had just declined.

CHAPTER VII

In Which Aunt Frances Speaks of Matrimony as a Fixed
Institution and is Met by Flaming Arguments; and in
Which a Strange Voice Sings Upon the Stairs.

Aunt Frances stayed until after the New Year. But before she
went she sounded Aunt Isabelle.

"Has Mary said anything to you about Porter Bigelow?"

"About Porter?"

"Yes," impatiently, "about marrying him. Anybody can see
that he's dead in love with her, Isabelle."

"I don't think Mary wants to marry anybody. She's an
independent little creature. She should have been the boy,
Frances."

"I wish to heaven she had," Aunt Frances' tone was fervent. "I
can't see any future for Barry, unless he marries Leila. If he
were not so irresponsible, I might do something for him. But
Barry is such a will-o'-the-wisp."

Aunt Isabelle went on with her mending, and Aunt Frances
again pounced upon her.

"And it isn't just that he is irresponsible. He's—Did you
notice on Christmas Day, Isabelle—that after dinner he

wasn't himself?"

Aunt Isabelle had noticed. And it was not the first time. Her quick eyes had seen things which Mary had thought were hidden. She had not needed ears to tell the secret which was being kept from her in that house.

Yet her sense of loyalty sealed her lips. She would not tell Frances anything. They were dear children.

"He's just a boy, Frances," she said, deprecatingly, "and I am sorry that General Dick put temptation in his way."

"Don't blame the General. If Barry's weak, no one can make him strong but himself. I wish he had some of Porter Bigelow's steadiness. Mary won't look at Porter, and he's dead in love with her."

"Perhaps in time she may."

"Mary's like her father," Aunt Frances said shortly. "John Ballard might have been rich when he died, if he hadn't been such a dreamer. Mary calls herself practical—but her head is full of moonshine."

Aunt Frances made this arraignment with an uncomfortable memory of a conversation with Mary the day before. They had been shopping, and had lunched together at a popular tea room. It was while they sat in their secluded corner that Aunt Frances had introduced in a roundabout way the topic which obsessed her.

"I am glad that Constance is so happy, Mary."

"She ought to be," Mary responded; "it's her honeymoon."

"If you would follow her example and marry Porter Bigelow, my mind would be at rest."

"But I don't want to marry Porter, Aunt Frances. I don't want to marry anybody."

Aunt Frances raised her gold lorgnette, "If you don't marry," she demanded, "how do you expect to live?"

"I don't understand."

"I mean who is going to pay your bills for the rest of your life? Barry isn't making enough to support you, and I can't imagine that you'd care to be dependent on Gordon Richardson. And the house is rapidly losing its value. The neighborhood isn't what it was when your father bought it, and you can't rent rooms when nobody wants to come out here to live. And then what? It's a woman's place to marry when she meets a man who can take care of her—and you'll find that you can't pick Porter Bigelows off every bush—not in Washington."

Thus spoke Worldly-Wisdom, not mincing words, and back came Youth and Romance, passionately. "Aunt Frances, a woman hasn't any right to marry just because she thinks it is her best chance. She hasn't any right to make a man feel that he's won her when she's just little and mean and mercenary."

"That sounds all right," said the indignant dame opposite her, "but as I said before, if you don't marry,—what are you going to do?"

Faced by that cold question, Mary met it defiantly. "If the worst comes, I can work. Other women work."

"You haven't the training or the experience." Aunt Frances told her coldly; "don't be silly, Mary. You couldn't earn your shoe-strings."

And thus having said all there was to be said, the two ate their salad with diminished appetite, and rode home in a taxi in stiff silence.

Aunt Frances' mind roamed back to Aunt Isabelle, and fixed on her as a scapegoat. "She's like you, Isabelle," she said, "with just the difference between the ideals of twenty years ago and to-day. You haven't either of you an idea of the world as a real place—you make romance the rule of your lives—and I'd like to know what you've gotten out of it, or what she will."

"I'm not afraid for Mary." There was a defiant ring in Aunt Isabelle's voice which amazed Aunt Frances. "She'll make things come right. She has what I never had, Frances. She has strength and courage."

It was this conversation with Aunt Frances which caused Mary, in the weeks that followed, to bend for hours over a yellow pad on which she made queer hieroglyphics. And it was through these hieroglyphics that she entered upon a new phase of her friendship with Roger Poole.

He had gone to work one morning, haggard after a sleepless night.

As he approached the Treasury, the big building seemed to loom up before him like a prison. What, after all, were those thousands who wended their way every morning to the great beehives of Uncle Sam but slaves chained to an occupation which was deadening?

He flung the question later at the little stenographer who sat next to him. "Miss Terry," he asked, "how long have you been here?"

She looked up at him, brightly. She was short and thin, with a sprinkle of gray in her hair. But she was well-groomed and nicely dressed in her mannish silk shirt and gray tailored skirt.

"Twenty years," she said, snapping a rubber band about her note-book.

"And always at this desk?"

"Oh, dear, no. I came in at nine hundred, and now I am getting twelve hundred."

"But always in this room?"

She nodded. "Yes. And it is very nice. Most of the people have been here as long as I, and some of them much longer. There's Major Orr, for example, he has been here since just after the War."

"Do you ever feel as if you were serving sentence?"

She laughed. She was not troubled by a vivid imagination. "It really isn't bad for a woman. There aren't many places with as short hours and as good pay."

For a woman? But for a man? He turned back to his desk. What would he be after twenty years of this? He waked every morning with the day's routine facing him—knowing that not once in the eight hours would there be a demand upon his mentality, not once would there be the thrill of real accomplishment.

At noon when he saw Miss Terry strew bird seed on the broad window sill for the sparrows, he likened it to the diversions of a prisoner in his cell. And, when he ate lunch with a group of fellow clerks in a cheap restaurant across the way, he wondered, as they went back, why they were spared the lockstep.

In this mood he left the office at half-past four, and passing the place where he usually ate, inexpensively, he entered a luxurious up-town hotel. There he read the papers until half-past six; then dined in a grill room which permitted informal dress.

Coming out later, he met Barry coming in, linked arm in arm with two radiant youths of his own kind and class. Musketeers of modernity, they found their adventures on the city streets, in cafes and cabarets, instead of in field and forest and on the battle-field.

Barry, with a flower in his buttonhole, welcomed Roger uproariously. "Here's Whittington," he said. "You ought to hear his poem, fellows, about a little cat. He had us all hypnotized the other night."

Roger glanced at him sharply. His exaggerated manner, the looseness of his phrasing, the flush on his cheeks were in strange contrast to his usual frank, clean boyishness.

"Come on, Poole," Barry urged, "we'll motor out in Jerry's car to the Country Club, and you can give it to us out there—about Whittington and the little cat."

Roger declined, and Barry took quick offense. "Oh, well, if you don't want to, you needn't," he said; "four's a crowd, anyhow—come on, fellows."

Roger, vaguely troubled, watched him until he was lost in the crowd, then sighed and turned his steps homeward.

As Roger ascended to his Tower, the house seemed strangely silent. Pittiwitz was asleep beside the pot of pink hyacinths. She sat up, yawned, and welcomed him with a little coaxing note. When he had settled himself in his big chair, she came and curled in the corner of his arm, and again went to sleep.

Deep in his reading, he was roused an hour later by a knock at his door.

He opened it, to find Mary on the threshold.

"May I come in?" she asked, and she seemed breathless. "It is Susan's night out, and Aunt Isabelle is at the opera with some old friends. Barry expected to be here with me, but he hasn't come. And I sat in the dining-room—and waited," she shivered, "until I couldn't stand it any more."

She tried to laugh, but he saw that she was very pale.

"Please don't think I'm a coward," she begged. "I've never been that. But I seemed suddenly to have a sort of nervous panic, and I thought perhaps you wouldn't mind if I sat with you—until Barry—came—"

"I'm glad he didn't come, if it is going to give me an evening with you." He drew a chair to the fire.

They had talked of many things when she asked, suddenly, "Mr. Poole, I wonder if you can tell me—about the examinations for stenographers in the Departments—are they very rigid?"

"Not very. Of course they require speed and accuracy."

She sighed. "I'm accurate enough, but I wonder if I can ever acquire speed."

He stared. "You—?"

She nodded. "I haven't mentioned it to any one. One's family is so hampering sometimes—they'd all object—except Aunt Isabelle, but I want to be prepared to work, if I ever need to earn my living."

"May you never need it," he said, fervently, visions rising of little Miss Terry and her machine-made personality. What had this girl with the fair hair and the shining eyes to do with the blank life between office walls?

"May you never need it," he repeated. "A woman's place is in the home—it's a man's place to fight the world."

"But if there isn't a man to fight a woman's battles?"

"There will always be some one to fight yours."

"You mean that I can—marry? But what if I don't care to marry merely to be—supported?"

"There would have to be other things, of course," gravely.

"What, for example?"

"Love."

"You mean the 'honor and obey' kind? But don't want that when I marry. I want a man to say to me, 'Come, let us fight the battle together. If it's defeat, we'll go down together. If its victory, we'll win.'"

This was to him a strange language, yet there was that about it which thrilled him.

Yet he insisted, dogmatically, "There are men enough in the world to take care of the women, and the women should let them."

"No, they should not. Suppose I should not marry. Must I let Barry take care of me, or Constance—and go on as Aunt Isabelle has, eating the bread of dependence?"

"But you? Why, one only needs to look at you to know that there'll be a live-happy-ever-after ending to your romance."

"That's what they thought about Aunt Isabelle. But she lost her lover, and she couldn't love again. And if she had had an absorbing occupation, she would have been saved so much humiliation, so much heart-break."

She told him the story with its touching pathos. "And think of it," she ended, "right here in our garden by the fountain, she saw him for the last time."

Chilled by the ghostly breath of dead romance, they sat for a while in silence, then Mary said: "So that's why I'm trying to learn something—that will have an earning value. I can sing and play a little, but not enough to make—money."

She sighed, and he set himself to help her.

"The quickest way," he said, "to acquire speed, is to have some one read to you."

"Aunt Isabelle does sometimes, but it tires her."

"Let me do it. I should never tire."

"Oh, wouldn't you mind? Could we practice a little—now?"

And so it began—the friendship in which he served her, and loved the serving.

He read, slowly, liking to see, when he raised his eyes, the slim white figure in the big chair, the firelight on the absorbed face.

Thus the time slipped by, until with a start, Mary looked up.

"I don't see what is keeping Barry."

Then Roger told her what he had been reluctant to tell. "I saw him down-town. I think he was on his way to the Country Club. He had been dining with some friends."

"Men friends?"

"Yes. He called one of them Jerry."

He saw the color rise in her face. "I hate Jerry Tuckerman, and Barry promised Constance he'd let those boys alone."

Her voice had a sharp note in it, but he saw that she was struggling with a gripping fear.

This, then, was the burden she was bearing? And what a brave little thing she was to face the world with her head up.

"Would you like to have me call the Country Club—I might be able to get your brother on the wire."

"Oh; if you would."

But he was saved the trouble. For, even while they spoke of him, Barry came, and Mary went down to him.

A little later, there were stumbling steps upon the stairs, and a voice was singing—a strange song, in which each verse ended with a shout.

Roger, stepping out into the dark upper hall, looked down over the railing. Mary, a slender shrinking figure; was coming with her brother up the lower flight. Barry had his arm around her, but her face was turned from him, and her head drooped.

Then, still looking down, Roger saw her guide those stumbling steps to the threshold of the boy's room. The door opened and shut, and she was alone, but from within there still came the shouted words of that strange song.

Mary stood for a moment with her hands clenched at her sides, then turned and laid her face against the closed door, her eyes hidden by her upraised arm.

CHAPTER VIII

In Which Little-Lovely Leila Sees a Picture in an Unexpected
Place; and in Which Perfect Faith Speaks Triumphantly
Over the Telephone.

Whatever Delilah Jeliffe might lack, it was not originality. The
apartment which she chose for her winter in Washington was
like any other apartment when she went into it, but the
changes which she made—the things which she added and the
things which she took away, stamped it at once with her own
individuality.

The peacock screen before the fireplace, the cushions of
sapphire and emerald and old gold on the couch, the mantel
swept of all ornament except a seven-branched candlestick;
these created the first impression. Then one's eyes went to an
antique table on which a crystal ball, upborne by three bronze
monkeys, seemed to gather to itself mysteriously all the glow of
firelight and candlelight and rich color. At the other end of the
table was a low bowl, filled always with small saffron-hued
roses.

In this room, one morning, late in Lent, Leila Dick sat,
looking as out of place as an English daisy in a tropical jungle.

Leila did not like the drawn curtains and the dimness. Outside
the sun was shining, gloriously, and the sky was a deep and
lovely blue.

Temple Bailey

She was glad when Lilah sent for her.

"You are to come right to her room," the maid announced.

"Heavens, child," said the Delilah-beauty, who was combing her hair, "I didn't promise to be up with the birds."

"The birds were up long ago," Leila perched herself on an old English love-seat. "We're to have lunch before we go to Fort Myer, and it is almost one now."

Lilah yawned, "Is it?" and went on combing her hair with the air of one who has hours before her. She wore a silken negligee of flamingo red which matched her surroundings, for this room was as flaming as the other was subdued. Yet the effect was not that of crude color; it was, rather, that of color intensified deliberately to produce a contrast. Delilah's bedroom was high noon under a blazing sun, the sitting-room was midnight under the stars.

With her black hair at last twisted into wonderful coils, Delilah surveyed her face reflectively in the mirror, and having decided that she needed no further aid from the small jars on her dressing table, she turned to her friend.

"What shall I wear, Leila?"

"If I told you," was the calm response, "you wouldn't wear it."

Delilah laughed. "No, I wouldn't. I simply have to think such things out for myself. But I meant what kind of clothes—dress up or motor things?"

"Porter will take us out in his car. You'll need your heavy coat, and something good-looking underneath, for lunch, you know."

"Is Mary Ballard going?"

"Of course. We shouldn't get Porter's car if she weren't."

"Mary wasn't with us the day we had tea with him in the Park."

"No, but she was asked. Porter never leaves her out."

"Are they engaged?"

"No, Mary won't be."

"She'll never get a better chance," Delilah reflected. "She isn't pretty, and she's rather old style."

Leila blazed. "She's beautiful—"

"To you, duckie, because you love her. But the average man wouldn't call Mary Ballard beautiful."

"I don't care—the un-average one would. And Mary Ballard wouldn't look at an ordinary man."

"No man is ordinary when he is in love."

"Oh, with you," Leila's tone was scornful, "love's just a game."

Lilah rose, crossed the room with swift steps, and kissed her. "Don't let me ruffle your plumage, Jenny Wren," she said; "I'm a screaming peacock this morning."

"What's the matter?"

"I'm not the perfect success I planned to be. Oh, I can see it. I've been here for three months, and people stare at me, but they don't call on me—not the ones I want to know. And it's because I am too—emphasized. In New York you have to be emphatic to be anything at all. Otherwise you are lost in the crowd. That's why Fifth Avenue is full of people in startling clothes. In the mob you won't be singled out simply for your pretty face—there are too many pretty faces; so it is the woman who strikes some high note of conspicuousness who attracts attention. But you're like a flock of cooing doves, you Washington girls. You're as natural and frank and unaffected as a—a covey of partridges. I believe I am almost jealous of your Mary Ballard this morning."

"Not because of Porter?"

"Not because of any man. But there are things about her which I can't acquire. I've the money and the clothes and the individuality. But there's a simplicity about her, a directness, that comes from years of association with things I haven't had. Before I came here, I thought money could buy anything. But it can't. Mary Ballard couldn't be anything else. And I—I can be anything from a siren to a soubrette, but I can't be a lady— not the kind that you are—and Mary Ballard."

Saying which, the tropic creature in flamingo red sat down beside the cooing dove, and continued:

"You were right just now, when you said that the un-average man would love Mary Ballard. Porter Bigelow loves her, and he tops all the other men I've met. And he'd never love me. He will laugh with me and joke with me, and if he wasn't in love with Mary, he might flirt with me—but I'm not his kind— and he knows it."

She sighed and shrugged her shoulders. "There are other fish in the sea, of course, and Porter Bigelow is Mary's. But I give you my word, Leila Dick, that when I catch sight of his blessed red head towering above the others—like a lion-hearted Richard, I can't see anybody else."

For the first time since she had known her, Leila was drawn to the other by a feeling of sympathetic understanding.

"Are you in love with him, Lilah?" she asked; timidly.

Lilah stood up, stretching her hands above her head. "Who knows? Being in love and loving—perhaps they are different things, duckie."

With which oracular remark she adjourned to her dressing-room, where, in long rows, her lovely gowns were hung.

Leila, left alone, picked up a magazine on the table beside her glanced through it and laid it down; picked a bonbon daintily out of a big box and ate it; picked up a photograph—

"Mousie," said Lilah, coming back, several minutes later, "what makes you so still? Did you find a book?"

No, Leila had not found a book, and the photograph was back where she had first discovered it, face downward under the box of chocolates. And she was now standing by the window, her veil drawn tightly over her close little hat, so that one might not read the trouble in her telltale eyes. The daisy drooped now, as if withered by the blazing sun.

But Delilah saw nothing of the change. She wore a saffron-hued coat, which matched the roses in the other room, and her leopard skins, with a small hat of the same fur.

As she surveyed herself finally in the long glass, she flung out the somewhat caustic remark:

"When I get down-stairs and look at Mary Ballard, I shall feel like a Beardsley poster propped up beside a Helleu etching."

After lunch, Porter took Aunt Isabelle and Barry and the three girls to Fort Myer. The General and Mr. Jeliffe met them at the drill hall, and as they entered there came to them the fresh fragrance of the tan bark.

As the others filed into their seats, Barry held Leila back. "We will sit at the end," he said. "I want to talk to you."

Through her veil, her eyes reproached him.

"No," she said; "no."

He looked down at her in surprise. Never before had Little-Lovely Leila refused the offer of his valuable society.

"You sit beside—Delilah," she said, nervously, "She's really your guest."

"She is Porter's guest," he declared. "I don't see why you want to turn her over to me." Then as she endeavored to pass him, he caught her arm.

"What's the matter?" he demanded.

"Nothing," faintly,

"Nothing—" scornfully. "I can read you like a book. What's happened?"

But she merely shook her head and sat down, and then the bugle sounded, and the band began to play, and in came the cavalry—a gallant company, through the sun-lighted door, charging in a thundering line toward the reviewing stand—to stop short in a perfect and sudden salute.

The drill followed, with men riding bareback, men riding four abreast, men riding in pyramids, men turning somersaults on their trained and intelligent steeds.

One man slipped, fell from his horse, and lay close in the tan bark, while the other horses went over him, without a hoof touching, so that he rose unhurt, and took his place again in the line.

Leila hid her eyes in her muff. "I don't like it," she said. "I've never liked it. And what if that man had been killed?"

"They don't get killed," said Barry easily. "The hospital is full of those who get hurt, but it is good for them; it teaches them to be cool and competent when real danger comes."

And now came the artillery, streaming through that sun-lighted entrance, the heavy wagons a featherweight to the strong, galloping horses. Breathless Leila watched their manoeuvres, as they wheeled and circled and crisscrossed in spaces which seemed impossibly small—horses plunging, gun-wagons rattling, dust flying—faster, faster— Again she shut her eyes.

But Mary Ballard, cheeks flushed, eyes dancing, turned to Porter. "Don't you love it?" she asked.

"I love you—" audaciously. "Mary, you and I were born in the wrong age. We belong to the days of King Arthur. Then I could have worn a coat of mail and have stormed your castle, and I shouldn't have cared if you hurled defiance from the top turret. I'd have known that, at last, you'd be forced to let down the drawbridge; and I would have crossed the moat and taken you prisoner, and you'd have been so impressed with my strength and prowess that you would—"

"No, I wouldn't," said Mary quickly.

"Wait till I finish," said Porter, coolly. "I'd have shut you up in a tower, and every night I'd have come and sung beneath your window, and at last you'd have dropped a red rose down to me."

They were laughing together now, and Delilah on the other side of Porter demanded, "What's the joke?"

"There isn't any," said Porter; "it is all deadly earnest—for me, if not for Mary."

And now a horse was down; there was a quick bugle-note, silence. Like clockwork, everything had stopped.

People were asking, "Is anybody hurt?"

Barry looked down at Leila. Then he leaned toward her father. "I'm going to take this child outside," he said; "she's as white as a sheet. She doesn't like it. We will meet you all later."

Leila's color came back in the sunshine and air and she insisted that Barry should return to the hall.

"I don't want you to miss it," she said, "just because I am so silly. I can stay in Porter's car and wait."

"I don't want to see it—it's an old story to me."

So they walked on toward Arlington, entering at last the gate which leads into that wonderful city of the nation's Northern dead, which was once the home of Southern hospitality. In a sheltered corner they sat down and Barry smiled at Little-Lovely Leila.

"Are you all right now, kiddie?"

"Yes," but she did not smile.

He bent down and peered through her veil. "Take it off and let me look at your eyes."

With trembling hands, she took out a pin or two and let it fall.

"You've been crying."

"Oh, Barry," the words were a cry—the cry of a little wounded bird.

He stopped smiling. "Blessed one, what is it?"

"I can't tell you."

"You must."

"No."

A low-growing magnolia hid them from the rest of the world; he put masterful hands on her shoulders and turned her face toward him—her little unhappy face.

"Now tell me."

She shook herself free. "Don't, Barry."

He flushed suddenly and sensitively. "I know I'm not much of a fellow."

She answered with a dignity which seemed to surmount her usual childishness, "Barry, if a man wants a woman to believe in him, he's got to make himself worthy of it."

"Well," defiantly, "what have I done?"

"Don't you know?"

"No-o."

"Then I'll tell you. Yes, I *will* tell you," with sudden courage. "I was at Delilah's this morning, and I saw your picture, and what you had written on it—"

He stared at her, with a sense of surging relief. If it was only that he had to explain about—Lilah. A smile danced in his eyes.

"Well?"

"I know you like to—play the game—but I didn't think you'd go as far as that—"

"How far?"

"Oh, you know."

"I don't."

"*Barry!*"

"I don't. I wish you'd tell me what you mean, Leila."

"I will." Her eyes were not reproachful now, they were blazing. She had risen, and with her hands tucked into her muff, and her veil blowing about her flushed cheeks, she made her accusation. "You wrote on that picture, 'To the One Girl— Forever.' Is that the way you think of Delilah, Barry?"

"No. It is the way I think of you. And how did that picture happen to be in Delilah's possession? I sent it to you."

"To me?"

"Yes, I took it over to you yesterday, and left it with one of the maids—a new one. I intended, to go in and give it to you, but when she said you had callers, I handed her the package—"

"And I thought—oh, Barry, what else could I think?"

She was so little and lovely in her tender contrition, that he flung discretion to the winds. "You are to think only one thing," he said, passionately, "that I love you—not anybody else, not ever anybody else. I haven't dared put it into words before. I haven't dared ask you to marry me, because I haven't anything to offer you yet. But I thought you—knew—"

Her little hand went out to him. "Oh, Barry," she whispered, "do you really feel that way about me?"

"Yes. More than I have said. More than I can ever say."

He drew her down beside him on the bench. "Our world won't want us to get married, Leila; they will say that I am such a boy. But you will believe in me, dear one?"

"Always, Barry."

"And you love me?"

"Oh, you know it."

"Yes, I know it," he said, in a moved voice, as he raised her hands and kissed them, "I know it—thank God."

After the drill, Porter took the whole party back to Delilah's for tea. And when her guests had gone, and the black-haired beauty went to her flamingo room to dress for dinner, she found a note on her pincushion.

"I have taken Barry's picture, because he meant it for me; it was a mistake, your getting it. He left it with the new maid one day when you were at our house, and she handed it to you instead of to me—she mixed up our names, just as the maids used to mix them up at school. And I know you won't mind my taking it, because with you it is just a game to play at love—with Barry. But it is my life, as you said that day in the Park. And to-day Barry told me that it is his life, too. And I am very happy. But this is our secret, and please let it be your secret until we let the rest of the world know—"

Delilah, reading the childish scrawl, smiled and shook her head. Then she went to the telephone and called up Leila.

"Duckie," she said, "I'll dance at your wedding. Only don't love him too much—no man is worth it."

Then, triumphant from the other end of the line, came the voice of Perfect Faith—"Oh, Barry's worth it. I've known him all my life, Lilah, and I've never had a single doubt."

CHAPTER IX

In Which Roger Sallies Forth in the Service of a Damsel in Distress, and in Which He Meets Dragons Along the Way.

In the weeks which followed the trip to Fort Myer, Mary found an astonishing change in her brother. For the first time in his life he seemed to be taking things seriously. He stayed at home at night and studied. He gave up Jerry Tuckerman and the other radiant musketeers. She did not know the reason for the change but it brought her hope and happiness.

Barry saw Leila often, but, as yet, no one but Delilah Jeliffe knew of the tie between them.

"I ought to tell Dad," Leila had said, timidly; "he'd be very happy. It is what he has always wanted, Barry."

"I must prove myself a man first," Barry told her, "I've squandered some of my opportunities, but now that I have you to work for, I feel as strong as a lion."

They were alone in the General's library. "It is because you trust me, dear one," Barry went on, "that I am strong."

She slipped her little hand into his. "Barry—it seems so queer to think that I shall ever be—your wife."

"You had to be. It was meant from the—beginning."

"Was it, Barry?"

"Yes."

"And it will be to the end. Oh, I shall always love you, dearly, dearly—"

It was idyllic, their little love affair—their big love affair, if one judged by their measure. It was tender, sweet, and because it was their secret, because there was no word of doubt or of distrust from those who were older and wiser, they brought to it all the beauty of youth and high hope.

Thus the spring came, and the early summer, and Barry passed his examinations triumphantly, and came home one night and told Mary that he was going to marry Leila Dick. As he told her his blue eyes beseeched her, and loving him, and hating to hurt him, Mary withheld the expression of her fears, and kissed him and cried a little on his shoulder, and Barry patted her cheek, and said awkwardly: "I know you think I'm not worthy of her, Mary. But she will make a man of me."

Alone, afterward, Mary wondered if she had been wise to acquiesce—yet surely, surely, love was strong enough to lift a man up to a woman's ideal—and Leila was such a—darling.

She put the question to Roger Poole that night. In these warmer days she and Roger had slipped almost unconsciously into close intimacy. He read to her for an hour after dinner, when she had no other engagements, and often they sat in the old garden, she with her note-book on the arm of the stone bench—he at the other end of the bench, under a bush of roses of a hundred leaves. Sometimes Aunt Isabelle was with them, with her fancy work, sometimes they were alone; but always when the hour was over, he would close his book and ascend to his tower, lest he might meet those who came later. There were many nights that he thus escaped Porter Bigelow—nights when in the moonlight he heard the murmur of voices, mingled with the splash of the fountain; and there were other nights when gay groups danced upon the lawn to the music played by Mary just within the open window.

Yet he thanked the gods for the part which he was allowed to play in her life. He lived for that one hour out of the twenty-four. He dared not think what a day would be if he were deprived of that precious sixty minutes.

Now and then, when she had been very sure that no one would come, he had stayed with her in the moonlight, and the little bronze boy had smiled at him from the fountain, and there had been the fragrance of the roses, and Mary Ballard in white on the stone bench beside him, giving him her friendly, girlish confidences; she discussed problems of genteel poverty, the delightful obstinacies of Susan Jenks, the dominance of Aunt Frances. She gave him, too, her opinions—those startling untried opinions which warred constantly with his prejudices.

And now to-night—his advice.

"Do you think love can change a man's nature? Make a weak man strong, I mean?"

He laid down his book. "You ask that as if I could really answer it."

"I think you can. You always seem to be able to put yourself in the other person's place, and it—helps."

"Thank you. And now in whose place shall put myself?"

"The girl's," promptly.

He considered it. "I should say that the man should be put to the test before marriage."

"You mean that she ought to wait until she is sure that he is made over?"

"Yes."

"Oh, I feel that way. But what if the girl believes in him? Doesn't dream that he is weak—trusts him absolutely, blindly? Should any one try to open her eyes?"

"Sometimes it is folly to be wise. Perhaps for her he will always be strong."

"Then what's the answer?"

"Only this. That the man himself should make the test. He should wait until he knows that he is worthy of her."

She made a little gesture of hopelessness, just the lifting of her hands and letting them drop; then she spoke with a rush of feeling.

"Mr. Poole—it is Barry and Leila. Ought I to let them marry?"

He smiled at her confidence in her ability to rule the destinies of those about her.

"I fancy that you won't have anything to do with it. He is of age, and you are only his sister. You couldn't forbid the banns, you know."

"But if I could convince him—"

"Of what?" gravely. "That you think him a boy? Perhaps that would tend to weaken his powers."

"Then I must fold my hands?"

"Yes. As things are now—I should wait."

He did not explain, and she did not ask, for what she should wait. It was as if they both realized that the test would come, and that it would come in time.

And it did come.

It was while Leila was on a trip to the Maine coast with her father.

July was waning, and already an August sultriness was in the air. Those who were left in town were the workers—every one who could get away was gone. Mary, with the care of her house on her hands, refused Aunt Frances' invitation for a month by the sea, and Aunt Isabelle declined to leave her.

"I like it better here, even with the heat," she told her niece, "than running around Bar Harbor with Frances and Grace."

Barry wrote voluminous letters to Leila, and received in return her dear childish scrawls. But the strain of her absence began to tell on him. He began to feel the pull toward old pleasures and distractions. Then one day Jerry Tuckerman arrived on the scene. The next night, he and Barry and the other radiant musketeers motored over to Baltimore by moonlight. Barry did not come home the next day, nor the next, nor the next. Mary grew white and tense, and manufactured excuses which did not deceive Aunt Isabelle. Neither of the tired pale women spoke to each other of their vigils. Neither of them spoke of the anxiety which consumed them.

Then one night, after a message had come from the office, asking for an explanation of Barry's absence; after she had called up the Country Club; after she had called up Jerry Tuckerman and had received an evasive answer; after she had exhausted all other resources, Mary climbed the steps to the Tower Rooms.

And there, sitting stiff and straight in a high-backed chair, with her throat dry, her pulses throbbing, she laid the case before Roger Poole.

"There is no one else—I can speak to—about it. But Barry's been away for nearly a week from the office and from home—

and nobody knows where he is. And it isn't the first time. It began before father died, and it nearly broke his heart. You see, he had a brother—whose life was ruined because of this. And Constance and I have done everything. There will be months when he is all right. And then there'll be a week—away. And after it, he is dreadfully depressed, and I'm afraid." She was shivering, though the night was hot.

Roger dared not speak his sympathy. This was not the moment.

So he said, simply, "I'll find him, and when I find him," he went on, "it may be best not to bring him back at once. I've had to deal with such cases before. We will go into the country for a few days, and come back when he is completely—himself."

"Oh, can you spare the time?"

"I haven't taken any vacation, and—so there are still thirty days to my credit. And I need an outing."

He prepared at once to go, and when he had packed a little bag, he came down into the garden. There was moonlight and the fragrance and the splashing fountain. Roger was thrilled by the thought of his quest. It was as if he had laid upon himself some vow which was sending him forth for the sake of this sweet lady. As Mary came toward him, he wished that he might ask for the rose she wore, as his reward. But he must not ask. She gave him her friendship, her confidence, and these were very precious things. He must never ask for more—and so he must not ask for a rose.

And now he was standing just below her on the terrace steps, looking up at her with his heart in his eyes.

"I'll find him," he said, "don't worry."

She reached out and touched his shoulder with her hand.

"How good you are," she said, wistfully, "to take all of this trouble for us. I feel that I ought not to let you do it—and yet—we are so helpless, Aunt Isabelle and I."

There was nothing of the boy about her now. She was all clinging dependent woman. And the touch of her hand on his shoulder was the sword of the queen conferring knighthood. What cared he now for a rose?

So he left her, standing there in the moonlight, and when he reached the bottom of the hill, he turned and looked back, and she still stood above him, and as she saw him turn, she waved her hand.

In days of old, knights fought with dragons and cut off their heads, only to find that other heads had grown to replace those which had been destroyed.

And it was such dragons of doubt and despair which Roger Poole fought in the days after he had found Barry.

The boy had hidden himself in a small hotel in the down-town district of Baltimore. Following one clue and then another, Roger had come upon him. There had been no explanations. Barry had seemed to take his rescue as a matter of course, and to be glad of some one into whose ears he could pour the litany of his despair.

"It's no use, Poole. I've fought and fought. Father helped me. And I promised Con. And I thought that my love for Leila would make me strong. But there's no use trying. I'll be beaten. It is in the blood. I had an uncle who drank himself to death. And back of him there was a grandfather."

They had been together for two days. Barry had agreed to Roger's plans for a trip to the country, and now they were under the trees on the banks of one of the little brackish rivers which flow into the Chesapeake. They had fished a little in the early morning, then had brought their boat in, for Barry had grown tired of the sport. He wanted to talk about himself.

"It's no use," he said again; "it's in the blood."

Roger was propped against a tree, his hat off, his dark hair blown back from his fine thin face.

"Our lives," he said, "are our own. Not what our ancestors make them."

"I don't believe it," Barry said, flatly. "I've fought a good fight, no one can say that I haven't. And I've lost. After this do you suppose that Mary will let me marry Leila? Do you suppose the General will let me marry her?"

"Will you let yourself marry her?"

Barry's face flamed. "Then you think I'm not worthy?"

"It is what you think, Ballard, not what I think."

Barry pulled up a handful of grass and threw it away, pulled up another handful and threw it away. Then he said, doggedly, "I'm going to marry her, Poole; no one shall take her away from me."

"And you call that love?"

"Yes. I can't live without her."

Roger with his eyes on the dark water which slipped by the banks, taking its shadows from the darkness of the thick branches which bent above it said quietly, "Love to me has always seemed something bigger than that—it has seemed as if love—great love took into consideration first the welfare of the beloved."

There was a long silence, out of which Barry said tempestuously, "It will break her heart if anything comes between us. I'm not saying that because am a conceited donkey. But she is such a constant little thing."

Roger nodded. "That's all the more reason why you've got to pull up now, Ballard."

"But I've tried."

"I knew a man who tried—and won."

"How?" eagerly.

"I met him in the pine woods of the South. I was down there to recover from a cataclysm which had changed—my life. This man had a little shack next to mine. Neither of us had much money. We lived literally in the open. We cooked over fires in front of our doors. We hunted and fished. Now and then we went to town for our supplies, but most of our things we got from the schooner-men who drove down from the hills. My neighbor was married. He had a wife and three children. But he had come alone. And he told me grimly that he should never go back until he went back a man."

"Did he go back?"

"Yes. He conquered. He looked upon his weakness not merely as a moral disease, but as a physical one. And it was to be cured like any other disease by removing the cause. The first step was to get away from old associations. He couldn't resist temptation, so he had come where he was not tempted. His occupation in the city had been mental, here it was largely physical. He chopped wood, he tramped the forest, he whipped the streams. And gradually he built up a self which was capable of resistance. When he went back he was a different man, made over by his different life. And he has cast out his—devil."

The boy was visibly impressed.

"His way might not be your way," Roger concluded, "but the fact that he fought a winning battle should give you hope."

The next day they went back. Mary met them as if nothing had happened. The basket of fish which they had brought to be cooked by Susan Jenks furnished an unembarrassing topic of conversation. Then Barry went to his room, and Mary was alone with Roger.

She had had a letter from him, and a message by telephone; thus her anxiety had been stilled. And she was very grateful— so grateful that her voice trembled as she held out her hands to him.

"How shall I ever thank you?" she said.

He took her hands in his, and stood looking down at her.

He did not speak at once, yet in those fleeting moments Mary had a strange sense of a question asked and answered. It was as if he were calling upon her for something she was not ready to give—as if he were drawing from her some subconscious admission, swaying her by a force that was compelling, to reveal herself to him.

And, as she thought these things, he saw a new look in her eyes, and her breath quickened.

He dropped her hands.

"Don't thank me," he said. "Ask me again to do something for you. That shall be my reward."

CHAPTER X

In Which a Scarlet Flower Blooms in the Garden; and in Which a Light Flares Later in the Tower.

In September everybody came back to town, Porter Bigelow among the rest.

He telephoned at once to Mary, "I'm coming up."

She was radiant. "Constance and Gordon arrived Monday, and I want you for dinner. Leila will be here and the General and Aunt Frances and Grace from New York."

His growl came back to her. "And that means that I won't have a minute alone with you."

"Oh, Porter—please. There are so many other girls in the world—and you've had the whole summer to find one."

"The summer has been a howling wilderness. But mother has put me through my paces at the resorts. Mary, I've learned such a lot of new dances to teach you."

"Teach them to Grace."

He groaned. "You know what I think of Grace Clendenning."

"Porter, she's beautiful. She wears little black frocks with wide white collars and cuffs and looks perfectly adorable. To-night she's going to wear a black tulle gown and a queer flaring black tulle head-dress, and with her red hair—you won't be able to drag your eyes from her."

"I've enough red hair of my own," Porter informed her, "without having to look at Grace's."

"I'll put you opposite her at dinner. Come and see, and be conquered."

Roger Poole was also invited to the home-coming dinner. Mary had asked nobody's advice this time. Of late Roger and Barry had been much together, and it was their friendship which Mary had exploited, when Constance, somewhat anxiously, had asked, on the day preceding the dinner, if she thought it was wise to include the lonely dweller in the Tower Rooms.

"He's really very nice, Constance. And he has been a great help to Barry."

It was the first time that they had spoken of their brother. And now Constance's words came with something of an effort. "What of Barry, Mary?"

"He is more of a man, Con. He is trying hard for Leila's sake."

"Gordon thinks they really ought not to be engaged."

The sisters were in Mary's room, and Mary at her little desk was writing out the dinner list for Susan Jenks. She looked up and laid down her pen. "Then you've told Gordon?"

"Yes. And he says that Barry ought to go away."

"Where?"

"Far enough to give Leila a chance to get over it."

"Do you think she would ever get over it, Con?"

"Gordon thinks she would."

Mary's head went up. "I am not asking what Gordon thinks. What do you think?"

"I think as Gordon does." Then as Mary made a little impatient gesture, she added, "Gordon is very wise. At first it seemed to me that he was—harsh, in his judgment of Barry. But he knows so much of men—and he says that here, in town, among his old associations—Barry will never be different. And it isn't fair to Leila."

Mary knew that it was not fair to Leila. She had always known it. Yet she was stubbornly resentful of the fact that Gordon Richardson should be, as it were, the arbiter of Barry's destiny.

"Oh, it is all such a muddle, Con," she said, and put the question aside. "We won't talk about it just now. There is so much else to say—and it is lovely to have you back, dearest— and you are so lovely."

Constance was curled up on Mary's couch, resting after her journey. "I am so happy, Mary. No woman knows anything about it, until she has had it for herself. A man's strength is so wonderful—and Gordon's care of me—oh, Mary, if there were only another man in the world for you like Gordon I should be perfectly content."

It was a fervent gentle echo of Aunt Frances' demand upon her, and Mary suppressing her raging jealousy of the man who had stolen her sister, asked somewhat wistfully, "Can you talk about me, for a minute, and forget that you have a husband?"

"I don't need to forget Gordon," was the serene response. "I can keep him in the back of my mind."

Mary picked up her pen, and underscored "*Soup*"; then:

"Constance, darling," she said, "would you feel dreadfully if I went to work?"

"What kind of work, Mary?"

"In one of the departments,—as stenographer."

"But you don't know anything about it."

"Yes, I do, I've been studying ever since you went away."

"But why, Mary?"

"Because—oh, can't you see, Constance? I can't be sure of—Barry—for future support. And I won't go with Aunt Frances. And this house is simply eating up the little that father left us. When you married, I thought the rental of the Tower Rooms would keep things going, but it won't. And I won't sell the house. I love every old stick and stone of it. And anyhow, must I sit and fold my hands all the rest of my life just because I am a woman?"

"But Mary, dear, you will marry—there's Porter."

"Constance, I couldn't think of marriage that way—as a chance to be taken care of. Oh, Con, I want to wait—for love."

"Dearest, of course. But you can live with us. Gordon would never consent to your working—he thinks it is dreadful for a woman to have to fight the world."

Mary shook her head. "No, it wouldn't be fair to you. It is never fair for an outsider to intrude upon the happiness of a home. If your duet is ever to be a trio, it must not be with my big blundering voice, which could make only a discord, but a little piping one."

She looked up to meet Constance's shy, self-conscious eyes.

Mary flew to her, and knelt beside the couch. "Darling, darling?"

And now the list was forgotten and Susan Jenks coming up for it was made a party to that tremulous secret, and the fate of the dinner was threatened until Mary, coming back to realities, kissed her sister and went to her desk, and held herself sternly to the five following courses of the family dinner which was to please the palates of those fresh from Paris and London and from castles by the sea; and which was to test to the utmost the measure of Susan's culinary skill.

At dinner the next night, Gordon Richardson looked often and intently at Roger Poole, and when, under the warmth of the September moon, the men drifted out into the garden to smoke, he said, "I've just placed you."

Roger nodded. "I thought you'd remember. You were one of the younger boys at St. Martin's—you haven't changed much, but I couldn't be sure."

Gordon hesitated. "I thought I heard from someone that you entered the Church."

"I had a church in the South—for three years."

Gordon tried to keep the curiosity out of his voice.

"And you gave it up?"

"Yes. I gave it up."

That was all. Not a word of the explanation for which he knew Gordon was waiting. Nothing but the bare statement, "I gave it up."

They talked a little of St. Martin's after that, of their boyish experiences. But Roger was conscious that Gordon was weighing him, and asking of himself, "Why did he give it up?"

The two men were sitting on the stone bench where Roger had so often sat with Mary. The garden was showing the first signs of the season's blight. Fading leaf and rustling vine had replaced the unspringing greenness and the fragrant growth of the summer. There were, to be sure, dahlias and chrysanthemums and cosmos. But the glory of the garden was gone.

Then into the garden came Mary!

She was wrapped in a thin silken, scarlet cloak that belonged to Constance. As she passed through the broad band of light made by the street lamp. Roger had a sudden memory of the flame-like blossoming of a certain slender shrub in the spring. It had been the first of the flowers to bloom, and Mary had picked a branch for the vase on his table in the Tower sitting-room.

"Constance wants you, Gordon," Mary said, as she came nearer; "some one has called up to arrange about a dinner date, and she can't decide without you."

She sat down on the stone bench, and Roger, who had risen at her approach, stood under the hundred-leaved bush from which all the roses were gone.

"Do you know," he said, without warning or preface, "that it seemed to me that, as you came into the garden, it bloomed again."

Never before had he spoken thus. And he said it again. "When you came, it was as if the garden bloomed."

He sat down beside her. "Is any one going to claim you right away? Because if not, I have something I want to say."

"Nobody will claim me. At least I hope nobody will. Grace Clendenning is telling Porter about the art of woman's dress. She takes clothes so seriously, you know. And Porter is interested in spite of himself. And Barry and Leila are on the terrace steps, looking at the moon over the river, and Aunt Frances and Aunt Isabelle and General Dick are in the house because of the night air, so there's really no one in the garden but you and me."

"Just you—and—me—" he said, and stopped.

She was plainly puzzled by his manner. But she waited, her arms wrapped in her red cloak.

At last he said, "Your brother-in-law and I went to school together."

"Gordon?"

"Yes. St. Martin's. He was younger than I, and we were not much together. But I knew him. And after he had puzzled over it, he knew me."

"How interesting."

"And he asked me something about myself, which I have never told you; which I want to tell you now."

He was finding it hard to tell, with her eyes upon him, bright as stars.

"Your brother said he had heard that I had gone into the Church—that I had a parish. And what he had heard was true. Until five years ago, I was rector of a church in the South."

"*You?*" That was all. Just a little breathed note of incredulity.

"Yes. I wanted to tell you before he should have a chance to tell, and to think that I had kept from you something which you should have been told. But I am not sure, even now, that it should be told."

"But on Christmas Eve, you said that you did not believe—"

"I do not."

"And was that the reason you gave it up?"

"No. It is a long story. And it is not a pleasant one. Yet it seems that I must tell it."

The wind had risen and blew a mist from the fountain. The dead leaves rustled.

Mary shivered.

"Oh, you are cold," Roger said, "and I am keeping you."

"No," she said, mechanically, "I am not cold. I have my cloak. Please go on."

But he was not to tell his story then, for a shaft of strong light illumined the roadway, and a big limousine stopped at the foot of the terrace steps. They heard Delilah Jeliffe's high laugh; then Porter's voice in the garden. "Mary, are you there?"

"Yes."

"Grace Clendenning and her mother are going, and Delilah and Mr. Jeliffe have motored out to show you their new car."

There was deep disapproval in his voice. Mary rose reluctantly as he joined them. "Oh, Porter, must I listen to Delilah's chatter for the rest of the evening?"

"You made me listen to Grace's. This is your punishment."

"I don't want to be punished. And I am very tired, Porter."

This was a new word in Mary Ballard's vocabulary, and Porter responded at once to its appeal.

"We will get rid of Delilah presently, and then Gordon and

Constance will go with us for a spin around the Speedway. That will set you up, little lady."

Roger stood silent by the fountain. Through the veil of mist the little bronze boy seemed to smile maliciously. During all the years in which he had ridden the dolphin, he had seen men and women come and go beneath the hundred-leaved bush. And he had smiled on all of them, and by their mood they had interpreted his smiles.

Roger's mood at this moment was one of impotent rebellion at Porter's air of proprietorship, and it was with this air intensified that, as Mary shivered again Porter drew her wrap about her shoulders, fastening the loop over the big button with expert fingers and said, carelessly, "Are you coming in with us, Poole?"

"No. Not now."

Above the head of the little bronze boy, level glance met level glance, as in the moonlight the men surveyed each other.

Then Mary spoke.

"Mr. Poole, I am so sorry not to hear the rest of the—story."

"You shall hear it another time."

She hesitated, looking up at him. It was as if she wanted to speak but could not, with Porter there to listen.

So she smiled, with eyes and lips. Just a flash, but it warmed his heart.

Yet as she went away with Porter, and passed once more through the broad band of the street lamp's light which made of her scarlet cloak a flaming flower, he looked after her wistfully, and wondered if when she had heard what he had to tell she would ever smile at him like that again.

Delilah, fresh from a triumphal summer, was in the midst of a laughing group on the porch.

As Mary came up, she was saying: "And we have taken a dear old home in Georgetown. No more glare or glitter. Everything is to be subdued to the dullness of a Japanese print—pale gray and dull blue and a splash of black. This gown gives the keynote."

She was in gray taffeta, with a girdle of soft old blue, and a string of black rose-beads. No color was on her cheeks—there was just the blackness of her hair and the whiteness of her fine skin.

"It's great," Barry said,

Delilah nodded. "Yes. It has taken me several years to find out some things." She looked at Grace and smiled. "It didn't take you years, did it?"

Grace smiled back. The two women were as far apart as the poles. Grace represented the old Knickerbocker stock, Lilah, a later grafting. Grace studied clothes because it pleased her to make fashions a fine art. Delilah studied to impress. But each one saw in the other some similarity of taste and of mood, and the smile that they exchanged was that of comprehension.

Aunt Frances did not approve of Delilah. She said so to Grace going home.

"My dear, they live on the West Side—in a big house on the Drive. My calling list stops east of the Park."

Grace shrugged. "Mother," she said, "I learned one thing in Paris—that the only people worth knowing are the interesting people, and whether they live on the Drive or in Dakota, I don't care. And we've an awful lot of fossils in our set."

Mrs. Clendenning shifted the argument. "I don't see why

General Dick allows Leila to be so much with Miss Jeliffe."

"They were at school together, and the General and Mr. Jeliffe are old friends."

Her mother shrugged. "Well, I hope that if we stay here for the winter that they won't be forced upon us. Washington is such a city of climbers, Grace."

Grace let the matter drop there. She had learned discretion. She and her mother viewed life from different angles. To attempt to reconcile these differences would mean, had always meant, strife and controversy, and in these later years, Grace had steered her course toward serenity. She had refused to be blown about by the storms of her mother's prejudices. In the midst of the conventionality of her own social training, she had managed to be untrammeled. In this she was more like Mary than the others of her generation. And she loved Mary, and wanted to see her happy.

"Mother," she asked abruptly, "who is this Roger Poole?"

Mrs. Clendenning told her that he was a lodger in the Tower Rooms—a treasury clerk—a mere nobody.

Grace challenged the last statement. "He's a brilliant man," she said. "I sat next to him at dinner. There's a mystery some-where. He has an air of authority, the ease of a man of the world."

"He is in love with Mary," said Mrs. Clendenning, "and he oughtn't to be in the house."

"But Mary isn't in love with him—not yet."

"How do you know?"

In the darkness Grace smiled. How did she know? Why, Mary in love would be lighted up by a lamp within! It would burn in her cheeks, flash in her eyes.

"No, Mary's not in love," she said.

"She ought to marry Porter Bigelow."

"She ought not to marry Porter. Mary should marry a man who would utilize all that she has to give. Porter would not utilize it."

"Now what do you mean by that?" said Mrs. Clendenning, impatiently. "Don't talk nonsense, Grace."

"Mary Ballard," Grace analyzed slowly, "is one of the women who if she had been born in another generation would have gone singing to the lions for the sake of an ideal; she would have led an army, or have loaded guns behind barricades. She has courage and force, and the need of some big thing in her life to bring out her best. And Porter doesn't need that kind of wife. He doesn't want it. He wants to worship. To kneel at her feet and look up to her. He would require nothing of her. He would smother her with tenderness. And she doesn't want to be smothered. She wants to lift up her head and face the beating winds."

Mrs. Clendenning, helpless before this burst of eloquence on the part of her usually restrained daughter, asked, tartly, "How in the world do you know what Porter wants or Mary needs?"

"Perhaps," said Grace, slowly, "it is because I am a little like Mary. But I am older, and I've learned to take what the world gives. Not what I want. But Mary will never be content with compromise, and she will always go through life with her head up."

Mary's head was up at that very moment, as with cheeks flaming and eyes bright, she played hostess to her guests, while in the back of her brain were beating questions about Roger Poole.

Freed from the somewhat hampering presence of Mrs. Clendenning, Delilah was letting herself go, and she drew even from grave Gordon Richardson the tribute of laughter.

"It was an artist that I met at Marblehead," she said, "who showed me the way. He told me that I was a blot against the sea and the sky, with my purples and greens and reds and yellows. I will show you his sketches of me as I ought to be. They opened my eyes; and I'll show you my artist too. He's coming down to see whether I have caught the idea."

And now she moved down the steps. "Father will be furious if I keep him waiting any longer. He's crazy over the car, and when he drives, it is a regular Tam O'Shanter performance. I won't ask any of you to risk your necks with him yet, but if you and the General are willing to try it, Leila, we will take you home."

"I haven't fought in fifty battles to show the white feather now," said the General, and Leila chirruped, "I'd love it," and presently, with Barry in devoted attendance, they drove off.

Mary, waiting on the porch for Porter to telephone for his own car, which was to take them around the Speedway, looked eagerly toward the fountain. The moon had gone under a cloud, and while she caught the gleam of the water, the hundred-leaved bush hid the bench. Was Roger Poole there? Alone?

She heard Porter's voice behind her. "Mary," he said, "I've brought a heavy wrap. And the car will be here in a minute."

Aunt Isabelle had given him the green wrap with the fur. She slipped into it silently, and he turned the collar up about her neck.

"I'm not going to have you shivering as you did in that thin red thing," he said.

She drew away. It was good of him to take care of her, but she didn't want his care. She didn't want that tone, that air of possession. She was not Porter's. She belonged to herself. And to no one else. She was free.

With the quick proud movement that was characteristic of her, she lifted her head. Her eyes went beyond Porter, beyond the porch, to the Tower Rooms where a light flared, suddenly. Roger Poole was not in the garden; he had gone up without saying "Good-night."

CHAPTER XI

In Which Roger Writes a Letter; and in Which a Rose Blooms Upon the Pages of a Book.

In the Tower Rooms, Midnight—

It is best to write it. What I might have said to you in the garden would have been halting at best. How could I speak it all with your clear eyes upon me—all the sordid history of those years which are best buried, but whose ghosts to-night have risen again?

If in these months—this year that I have lived in these rooms, I have seemed to hide that which you will now know, it was not because I wanted to set myself before you as something more than I am. Not that I wished to deceive. It was simply that the thought of the old life brought a surging sense of helplessness, of hopelessness, of rebellion against fate, Having put it behind me, I have not wished to talk about it—to think about it—to have it, in all its tarnished tragedy, held up before your earnest, shining eyes.

For you have never known such things as I have to tell you, Mary Ballard. There has been sorrow in your life, and, I have seen of late, suffering for those you love. But, as yet, you have not doffed an ideal. You have not bowed that brave young head of yours. You have never yet turned your back upon the things which might have been.

As I have turned mine. I wish sometimes that you might have known me before the happening of these things which I am to tell you. But I wish more than all, that I might have known you. Until I came here, I did not dream that there was such a woman in the world as you. I had thought of women first, as a chivalrous boy thinks, later, as a disillusioned man. But of a woman like a young and ardent soldier, on fire to fight the winning battles of the world—of such a woman I had never dreamed.

But this year has taught me. I have seen you pushing away from you the things which would have charmed most women I have seen you pushing away wealth, and love for the mere sake of loving. I have seen you willing to work that you might hold undimmed the ideal which you had set for your womanhood. Loving and love-worthy, you have not been willing to receive unless you could give, give from the fulness of that generous nature of yours. And out of that generosity, you have given me your friendship.

And now; as I write the things which your clear eyes are to read, I am wondering whether that friendship will be withdrawn. Will you when you have heard of my losing battle, find anything in me that is worthy—will there be anything saved out of the wreck of your thought of me?

Well, here it is, and you shall judge:

I will skip the first years, except to say that my father was one of the New York Pooles who moved South after the Civil War. My mother was from Richmond. We were prosperous folk, with an unassailable social position. My mother, gracious and charming, is little more than a memory; she died when I was a child. My father married again, and died when I was in college. There were three children by this second marriage, and when the estate was settled, only a modest sum fell to my share.

I had been a lonely little boy—at college I was a dreamy, idealistic chap, with the saving grace of a love of athletics. Your brother-in-law will tell you something of my successes on our school team. That was my life—the day in the open, the nights among my books.

As time went on, I took prizes in oratory—there was a certain commencement, when the school went wild about me, and I was carried on the shoulders of my comrades.

There seemed open to me the Church and the law. Had I lived in a different environment, there would have been also the stage. But I saw only two outlets for my talents, the Church, toward which my tastes inclined, and the law, which had been my father's profession.

At last I chose the Church. I liked the thought of my scholarly future—of the power which my voice might have to sway audiences and to move them.

I am putting it all down, all of my boyish optimism, conceit—whatever you may choose to call it.

Yet I am convinced of this, and my success of a few years proved it, that had nothing interfered with my future, I should have made an impression on ever-widening circles.

But something came to interfere.

In my last years at the Seminary, I boarded at a house where I met daily the daughter of the landlady. She was a little thing, with yellow hair and a childish manner. As I look back, I can't say that I was ever greatly attracted to her. But she was a part of my life for so long that gradually there grew up between us a sort of good fellowship. Not friendship in the sense that I have understood it with you; there was about it nothing of spiritual or of mental congeniality. But I played the big brother. I took her to little dances; and to other college affairs. I gave both to herself and to her widowed mother such little pleasures as it is possible for a man to give to two rather lonely women. There were other students in the house, and I was not conscious that

I was doing anything more than the rest of them.

Then there came a day when the yellow-haired child—shall I call her Kathy?—wanted to go to a pageant in a neighboring town. It was to last two days, and there was to be a night parade, and floats and a carnival. Many of the students were going, and it was planned that Kathy and I should take a morning train on the first day, so that we might miss nothing. Kathy's mother would come on an afternoon train, and they would spend the night at a certain quiet hotel, while I was to go with a lot of fellows to another.

Well, when that afternoon train arrived, the mother was not on it. Nor did she come. Without one thought of unconventionality, I procured a room for Kathy at the place where she and her mother would have stopped. Then I left her and went to the other hotel to join my classmates. But carnival-mad; they did not come in at all, and went back on an express which passed through the town in the early morning.

When Kathy and I reached home at noon, we found her mother white and hysterical. She would listen to no explanations. She told me that I should have brought Kathy back the night before—that she had missed her train and thus her appointment with us. And she told me that I was in honor bound to marry Kathy.

As I write it, it seems such melodrama. But it was very serious then. I have never dared analyze the mother's motives. But to my boyish eyes her anxiety for her daughter's reputation was sincere, and I accepted the responsibility she laid upon me.

Well, I married her. And she put her slender arms about my neck and cried and thanked me.

She was very sweet and she was my—wife—and when I was given a parish and had introduced her to my people, they loved her for the white gentleness which seemed purity, and for acquiescent amiability which seemed—goodness.

I have myself much to blame in this—that I did not love her. All these years I have known it. But that I was utterly unawakened I did not know. Only in the last few months have I learned it.

Perhaps she missed what I should have given her. God knows. And He only knows whether, if I had adored her, worshiped her, things would have been different.

I was very busy. She was not strong. She was left much to herself. The people did not expect any great efforts on her part—it was enough that she should look like a saint—that she should lend herself so perfectly to the ecclesiastical atmosphere.

And now comes the strange, the almost unbelievable part. One morning when we had been married two years, I left the house to go to the office of one of my most intimate friends in the parish—a doctor who lived near us, who was unmarried, and who had prescribed now and then for my wife. As I went out, Kathy asked me to return to him a magazine which she handed me. It was wrapped and tied with a string. I had to wait in the doctor's office, and I unwrapped the magazine and untied the string, and between the leaves I found a note to—my friend.

Why do people do things like that? She might have telephoned what she had to say; she might have written it, and have sent it through the mails. But she chose this way, and let me carry to another man the message of her love for him.

For that was what the note told. There was no doubt, and I walked out of the office and went home. In other times with other manners, I might have killed him. If I had loved her, I might; I cannot tell. But I went home.

She seemed glad that I knew. And she begged that I would divorce her and let her marry him.

Dear Clear Eyes, who read this, what do you think of me? Of this story?

And what did I think? I who had dreamed, and studied and preached, and had never—lived? I who had hated the sordid? I who had thought myself so high?

As I married her, so I gave her a divorce. And as I would not have her name and mine smirched, I separated myself from her, and she won her plea on the ground of desertion.

Do you know what that meant in my life? It meant that I must give up my church. It meant that I must be willing to bear the things which might be said of me. Even if the truth had been known, there would have been little difference, except in the sympathy which would have been vouchsafed me as the injured party. And I wanted no man's pity.

And so I went forth, deprived of the right to lift up my voice and preach—deprived of the right to speak to the thousands who had packed my church. And now—what meaning for me had the candles on the altar, what meaning the voices in the choir? I had sung too, in the light of the holy candles, but it was ordained that my voice must be forever still.

I fought my battle out one night in the darkness of my church. I prayed for light and I saw none. Oh, Clear Eyes, why is light given to a man whose way is hid? I went forth from that church convinced that it was all a sham. That the lights meant nothing; that the music meant less, and that what I had preached had been a poetic fallacy.

Some of the people of my church still believe in me. Others, if you should meet them, would say that she was a saint, and that I was the sinner. Well, if my sin was weakness, I confess it. I should, perhaps, never have married her; but having married her, could I have held her mine against her will?

She married him. And a year after, she died. She was a frail little thing, and I have nothing harsh to say of her. In a sense she was a victim, first of her mother's ambition, next of my lack of love, and last of all, of his pursuit.

Perhaps I should not have told you this. Except my Bishop, who asked for the truth, and to whom I gave it, and whose gentleness and kindness are never-to-be-forgotten things— except for him, you are the only one I have ever told; the only one I shall ever tell.

But I shall tell you this, and glory in the telling. That if I had a life to offer of honor and of achievement, I should offer it now to you. That if I had met you as a dreaming boy, I would have tried to match my dreams to yours.

You may say that with the death of my wife things have changed. That I might yet find a place to preach, to teach—to speak to audiences and to sway them.

But any reentrance into the world means the bringing up of the old story—the question—the whispered comment. I do not think that I am a coward. For the sake of a cause, I could face death with courage. But I cannot face questioning eyes and whispering lips.

So I am dedicated for all my future to mediocrity. And what has mediocrity to do with you, who have "never turned your back, but marched face forward"?

And so I am going away. Not so quickly that there will be comment. But quickly enough to relieve you of future embarrassment in my behalf.

I do not know that you will answer this. But I know that whatever your verdict, whether I am still to have the grace of your friendship or to lose it forever, I am glad to have lived this one year in the Tower Rooms. I am glad to have known the one woman who has given me back—my boyish dreams of all women.

And now a last line. If ever in all the years to come you should have need of me, I am at your service. I shall count nothing too hard that you may ask. I am whimsically aware that in the midst of all this darkness and tragedy my offer is that of the Mouse to the Lion. But there came a day when the Mouse paid its debt. Ask me to pay mine, and I will come—from the ends of the earth.

This was the letter which Mary found the next morning on her desk in the little office room into which Roger had been shown on the night of the wedding. She recognized his firm script and found herself trembling as she touched the square white envelope.

But she laid the letter aside until she had given Susan her orders, until she had given other orders over the telephone, until she had interviewed the furnace man and the butcher's boy, and had written and mailed certain checks.

Then she took the letter with her to her own room, locked the door and read it.

Constance, knocking a little later, was let in, and found her sister dressed and ready for the street.

"I've a dozen engagements," Mary said. She was drawing on her gloves and smiling. She was, perhaps, a little pale, but that the Mary of to-day was different from the Mary if yesterday was not visible from outward signs.

"I am going first to the dressmaker, to see about having that lovely frock you bought me fitted for Delilah's tea dance; then I'll meet you at Mrs. Carey's luncheon. And after that will be our drive with Porter, and the private view at the Corcoran, then two teas, and later the dinner at Mrs. Bigelow's. I'm afraid it will be pretty strenuous for you, Constance."

"I sha'n't try to take in the teas. I'll come home and lie down before I have to dress for dinner."

As she followed out her programme for the day, Mary was conscious that she was doing it well. She made conscientious plans with her dressmaker, she gave herself gayly to the light chatter of the luncheon; during the drive she matched Porter's exuberant mood with her own, she viewed the pictures and made intelligent comments.

After the view, Constance went home in Porter's car, and Mary was left at a house on Dupont Circle. Porter's eyes had begged that she would let him come with her, but she had refused to meet his eyes, and had sent him off.

As she passed through the glimmer of the golden rooms, she bowed and smiled to the people that she knew, she joked with Jerry Tuckerman, who insisted on looking after her and getting her an ice. And then, as soon as she decently could, she got away, and came out into the open air, drawing a long breath, as one who has been caged and who makes a break for freedom.

She did not go to the other tea. All day she had lived in a dream, doing that which was required of her and doing it well. But from now until the time that she must go home and dress for dinner, she would give herself up to thoughts of Roger Poole.

She turned down Connecticut Avenue, and walking lightly and quickly came at last to the old church, where all her life she had worshiped. At this hour there was no service, and she knelt for a moment, then sat back in her pew, glad of the sense of absolute immunity from interruption.

And as she sat there in the stillness, one sentence from his letter stood out.

"And now what meaning for me had the candles on the altar, what meaning the voices in the choir? I had sung, too, in the light of the candles, but it was ordained that my voice must be forever still."

This to Mary was the great tragedy—his loss of courage, his

loss of faith—his acceptance of a passive future. Resolutely she had conquered all the shivering agony which had swept over her as she had read of that sordid marriage and its sequence. Resolutely she had risen above the faintness which threatened to submerge her as the whole of that unexpected history was presented to her; resolutely she had fought against a pity which threatened to overwhelm her.

Resolutely she had made herself face with clear eyes the conclusion; life had been too much for him and he had surrendered to fate.

To say that his letter in its personal relation to herself had not thrilled her would be to underestimate the warmth of her friendship for him; if there was more than friendship, she would not admit it. There had been a moment when, shaken and stirred by his throbbing words, she had laid down his letter and had asked herself, palpitating, "has love come to me—at last?" But she had not answered it. She knew that she would never answer it until Roger Poole found a meaning in life which was, as yet, hidden from him.

But how could she best help him to find that meaning? Dimly she felt that it was to be through her that he would find it. And he was going away. And before he went, she must light for him some little beacon of hope.

It was dark in the church now except for the candle on the altar.

She knelt once more and hid her face in her hands. She had the simple faith of a child, and as a child she had knelt in this same pew and had asked confidently for the things she desired, and she had believed that her prayers would be answered.

It was late when she left the church. And she was late in getting home. All the lower part of the house was lighted, but there was no light in the Tower Rooms. Roger, who dined down-town, would not come until they were on their way to

Mrs. Bigelow's.

As she passed through the garden, she saw that on a bush near the fountain bloomed a late rose. She stooped and picked it, and flitting in the dusk down the path, she entered the door which led to the Tower stairway.

And when, an hour later, Roger Poole came into the quiet house, weary and worn from the strain of a day in which he had tried to read his letter with Mary's eyes, he found his room dark, except for the flicker of the fire.

Feeling his way through the dimness, he pulled at last the little chain of the electric lamp on his table. The light at once drew a circle of gold on the dark dull oak. And within that circle he saw the answer to his letter.

Wide open and illumined, lay John Ballard's old Bible. And across the pages, fresh and fragrant as the friendship which she had given him, was the late rose which Mary had picked in the garden.

CHAPTER XII

In Which Mary and Roger Have Their Hour; and in Which a Tea-Drinking Ends in What Might Have Been a Tragedy.

To Mary, possessed and swayed by the letter which she had received from Roger, it seemed a strange thing that the rest of the world moved calmly and unconsciously forward.

The letter had come to her on Saturday. On Sunday morning everybody went to church. Everybody dined afterward, unfashionably, at two o'clock, and later everybody motored out to the Park.

That is, everybody but Mary!

She declined on the ground of other things to do.

"There'll be five of you anyhow with Aunt Frances and Grace," she said, "and I'll have tea for you when you come back."

So Constance and Gordon and Aunt Isabelle had gone off, and with Barry at Leila's, Mary was at last alone.

Alone in the house with Roger Poole!

Her little plans were all made, and she went to work at once to execute them.

It was a dull afternoon, and the old-fashioned drawing-room, with its dying fire, and pale carpet, its worn stuffed furniture and pallid mirrors looked dreary.

Mary had Susan Jenks replenish the fire. Then she drew up to it one of the deep stuffed chairs and a lighter one of mahogany, which matched the low tea-table which was at the left of the fireplace. She set a tapestry screen so that it cut off this corner from the rest of the room and from the door.

Gordon had brought, the night before, a great box of flowers, and there were valley lilies among them. Mary put the lilies on the table in a jar of gray-green pottery. Then she went up-stairs and changed the street costume which she had worn to church for her old green velvet gown. When she came down, the fire was snapping, and the fragrance of the lilies made sweet the screened space—Susan had placed on the little table a red lacquered tray, and an old silver kettle.

Susan had also delivered the note which Mary had given her to the Tower Rooms.

Until Roger came down Mary readjusted and rearranged everything. She felt like a little girl who plays at keeping house. Some new sense seemed waked within her, a sense which made her alive to the coziness and comfort and seclusion of this cut-off corner. She found herself trying to see it all through Roger Poole's eyes.

When he came at last around the corner of the screen, she smiled and gave him her hand.

"This is to be our hour together. I had to plan for it. Did you ever feel that the world was so full of people that there was no corner in which to be—alone?"

As he sat down in the big chair, and the light shone on his face, she saw how tired he looked, as if the days and the nights since she had seen him, had been days and nights of vigil.

She felt a surging sense of sympathy, which set her trembling as she had trembled when she had touched his letter as it had laid on her desk, but when she spoke her voice was steady.

"I am going to make you a cup of tea—then we can talk."

He watched her as she made it, her deft hands unadorned, except by the one quaint ring, the whiteness of her skin set on by her green gown, the whiteness of her soul symbolized by the lilies.

He leaned forward and spoke suddenly. "Mary Ballard," he said, "if I ever reach paradise, I shall pray that it may be like this, with the golden light and the fragrance, and you in the midst of it."

Earnestly over the lilies, she looked at him. "Then you believe in Paradise?"

"I should like to think that in some blessed future state I should come upon you in a garden of lilies."

"Perhaps you will." She was smiling, but her hand shook.

She felt shy, almost tongue-tied. She made him his tea, and gave him a cup; then she spoke of commonplaces, and the little kettle boiled and bubbled and sang as if there were no sorrow or sadness in the whole wide world.

She came at last timidly to the thing she had to say.

"I don't quite know how to begin about your letter. You see when I read it, it wasn't easy for me at first to think straight. I hadn't thought of you as having any such background to your life. Somehow the outlines I had filled in were—different. I am not quite sure what I had thought—only it had been nothing like—this."

"I know. You could not have been expected to imagine such

a past."

"Oh, it is not your past which weighs so heavily—on my heart; it is your future."

Her eyes were full of tears. She had not meant to say it just that way. But it had come—her voice breaking on the last words.

He did not speak at once, and then he said: "I have no right to trouble you with my future."

"But I want to be troubled."

"I shall not let you. I shall not ask that of your friendship. Last night when I came back to my rooms I found a rose blooming upon the pages of a book. It seemed to tell me that I had not lost your friendship; and you have given me this hour. This is all I have a right to ask of your generosity."

She moved the jar of lilies aside, so that there might be nothing between them. "If I am your friend, I must help you," she said, "or what would my friendship be worth?"

"There is no help," he said, hurriedly, "not in the sense that I think you mean it. My past has made my future. I cannot throw myself into the fight again. I know that I have been called all sorts of a coward for not facing life. But I could face armies, if it were anything tangible. I could do battle with a sword or a gun or my fists, if there were a visible adversary. But whispers—you can't kill them; and at last they—kill you."

"I don't want you to fight," she said, and now behind the whiteness of her skin there was a radiance. "I don't want you to fight. I want you to deliver your message."

"What message?"

"The message that every man who stands in the pulpit must

have for the world, else he has no right to stand there."

"You think then that I had no message?"

"I think," and now her hand went out to him across the table, as if she would soften the words, "I think that if you had felt yourself called to do that one thing, that nothing would have swayed you from it—there are people not in the churches, who never go to church, who want what you have to give—there are the highways and hedges. Oh, surely, not all of the people worth preaching to are the ones in the pews."

She flung the challenge at him directly.

And he flung it back to her, "If I had had such a woman as you in my life—"

"Oh, don't, *don't*." The radiance died. "What has any woman to do with it? It is you—yourself, who must stand the test."

After the ringing words there was dead silence. Roger sat leaning forward, his eyes not upon her, but upon the fire. In his white face there was no hint of weakness; there was, rather, pride, obstinacy, the ruggedness of inflexible purpose.

"I am afraid," he said at last, "that I have not stood the test."

Her clear eyes met his squarely. "Then meet it now."

For a moment he blazed. "I know now what you think of me, that I am a man who has shirked."

"You know I do not think that."

He surrendered. "I do know it. And I need your help."

Shaken by their emotion, they became conscious that this was indeed their hour. She told him all that she had dreamed he might do. Her color came and went as she drew the picture of

his future. Some of the advice she gave was girlish, imprac-
ticable, but through it all ran the thread of her faith to him.
She felt that she had the solution. That through service he was
to find—God.

It was a wonderful hour for Roger Poole. An hour which was
to shine like a star in his memory. Mary's mind had a largeness
of vision, the ability to rise above the lesser things in order to
reach the greater, which seemed super-feminine. It was not
until afterward when he reviewed what they had said, that he
was conscious that she had placed the emphasis on what he
was to do. Not once had she spoken of what had been done—
not once had she spoken of his wife.

"You mustn't bury yourself. You must find a way to reach first
one group and then another. And after a time you'll begin to
feel that you can face the world."

He winced. As she put it into words, he began to see himself as
others must have seen him. And the review was not a pleasant
one.

In a sense that hour with Mary Ballard in the screened space
by the fire was the hour of Roger Poole's spiritual awakening.
He realized for the first time that he had missed the meaning
of the candles on the altar, the voices in the choir; he had
missed the knowledge that one must spend and be spent in the
service of humanity.

"I must think it over," he said. "You mustn't expect too much
of me all at once."

"I shall expect—everything."

As she spoke and smiled, and it seemed to him that his old
garment of fear slipped from him—as if he were clothed in the
shining armor of her confidence in him.

They had little time to talk after that, for it was not long before they heard without the bray of a motor horn.

Roger rose at once.

"I must go before they come," he said.

But she laid her hand upon his arm. "No," she said, "you are not to go. You are never going to run away from the world again. Set aside the screen, please—and stay."

Porter, picked up on the way, came in with the others, to behold that glowing corner, and those two together.

With his red crest flaming, he advanced upon them.

"Somebody said 'tea.' May I have some, Mary?"

"When the kettle boils." She had risen, and was holding out her hand to him.

As the two men shook hands, Porter was conscious of some subtle change in Roger. What had come over the man—had he dared to make love to Mary?

And Mary? He looked at her.

She was serenely filling her tea ball. She had lighted the lamp beneath her kettle, and the blue flame seemed to cast her still further back among the shadows of her corner.

Grace Clendenning and Aunt Frances had come back with the rest for tea. Grace's head, with Porter's, gave the high lights of the scene. Barry had nicknamed them the "red-headed wood-peckers," and the name seemed justified.

While Porter devoted himself to Grace, however, he was acutely conscious of every movement of Mary's. Why had she given up her afternoon to Roger Poole? He had asked if he might come, and she had said, "after four," and now it was after four, and the hour which she would not give him had been granted to this lodger in the Tower Rooms.

It has been said before that Porter was not a snob, but to him Mary's attitude of friendliness toward this man, who was not one of them, was a matter of increasing irritation. What was there about this tall thin chap with the tired eyes to attract a woman? Porter was not conceited, but he knew that he possessed a certain value. Of what value in the eyes of the world was Roger Poole—a government clerk, without ambition, handsome in his dark way, but pale and surrounded by an air of gloom?

But to-night it was as if the gloom had lifted. To-night Roger shone as he had shone on the night of the Thanksgiving party—he seemed suddenly young and splendid—the peer of them all.

It came about naturally that, as they drank their tea, some one asked him to recite.

"Please "—it was Mary who begged.

Porter jealously intercepted the look which flashed between them, but could make nothing of it.

"The Whittington one is too long," Roger stated, "and I haven't Pittiwitz for inspiration—but here's another."

Leaning forward with his eyes on the fire, he gave it.

It was a man's poem. It was in the English of the hearty times of Ben Jonson and of Kit Marlowe—and every swinging line rang true.

> "What will you say when the world is dying?
> What when the last wild midnight falls,
> Dark, too dark for the bat to be flying
> Round the ruins of old St. Paul's?

What will be last of the lights to perish?
What but the little red ring we knew,
Lighting the hands and the hearts that cherish
A fire, a fire, and a friend or two!"

CHORUS:

"Up now, answer me, tell me true.
What will be last of the stars to perish?
—The fire that lighteth a friend or two."

As the last brave verse was ended, Gordon Richardson said, "By Jove, how it comes back to me—you used to recite Poe's 'Bells' at school."

Roger laughed. "Yes. I fancy I made them boom toward the end."

"You used to make me shiver and shake in my shoes."

Aunt Frances' voice broke in crisply, "What do you mean, Gordon; were you at school with Mr. Poole?"

"Yes. St. Martin's, Aunt Frances."

The name had a magic effect upon Mrs. Clendenning; the boys of St. Martin's were of the elect.

"Poole?" she said. "Are you one of the New York Pooles?"

Roger nodded. "Yes. With a Southern grafting—my mother was a Carew."

He was glad now to tell it. Let them follow what clues they would. He was ready for them. Henceforth nothing was to be hidden.

"I am going down next week," he continued, "to stay for a

time with a cousin of my mother's—Miss Patty Carew. She lives still in the old manor house which was my grand-father's—she hadn't much but poverty and the old house for an inheritance, but it is still a charming place."

Aunt Frances was intent, however, on the New York branch of his family tree.

"Was your grandfather Angus Poole?"

"Yes."

Grace was wickedly conscious of her mother's state of mind. No one could afford to ignore any descendant of Angus Poole. To be sure, a second generation had squandered the fortune he had left, but his name was still one to conjure with.

"I never dreamed—" said Aunt Frances.

"Naturally," said Roger, and there was a twinkle in his eyes. "I am afraid I'm not a credit to my hard-headed financier of a grandfather."

It seemed to Mary that for the first time she was seeing him as he might have been before his trouble came upon him. And she was swept forward to the thought of what he might yet be. She grew warm and rosy in her delight that he should thus show himself to her people. She looked up to find Porter's accusing eyes fixed on her; and in the grip of a sudden shyness, she gave herself again to her tea-making.

"Surely some of you will have another cup?"

It developed that Aunt Frances would, and that the water was cold, and that the little lamp was empty of alcohol.

Mary filled it, and, her hand shaking from her inward excitement, let the alcohol overflow on the tray and on the kettle frame. She asked for a match and Gordon gave her one.

Then, nobody knew how it happened! The flames seemed to sweep up in a blue sheet toward the lace frills in the front of Mary's gown. It leaped toward her face. Constance screamed. Then Roger reached her, and she was in his arms, her face crushed against the thickness of his coat, his hands snatching at her frills.

It was over in a moment. The flames were out. Very gently, he loosed his arms. She lay against his shoulder white and still. Her face was untouched, but across her throat, which the low collar had left exposed, was a hot red mark. And a little lock of hair was singed at one side, her frills were in ruins.

He put her into a chair, and they gathered around her—a solicitous group. Porter knelt beside her. "Mary, Mary," he kept saying, and she smiled weakly, as his voice broke on "Contrary Mary."

Gordon had saved the table from destruction. But the flame had caught the lilies, crisping them, and leaving them black. Constance was shaken by the shock, and Aunt Frances kept asking wildly, "How did it happen?"

"I spilled the alcohol when I filled it," Mary said. "It was a silly thing to do—if I had had on one of my thinner gowns—" She shuddered and stopped.

"I shall send you an electric outfit to-morrow," Porter announced. "Don't fool with that thing again, Mary."

Roger stood behind her chair, with his arms folded on the top and said nothing. There was really nothing for him to say, but there were many things to think. He had saved that dear face from flame or flaw, the dear eyes had been hidden against his shoulder—his fingers smarted where he had clutched at her burning frills.

Porter Bigelow might take possession of her now, he might give her electric outfits, he might call her by her first name, but it had not been Porter who had saved her from the flames; it had not been Porter who had held her in his arms.

CHAPTER XIII

In Which the Whole World is at Sixes and Sevens, and in Which Life is Looked Upon as a Great Adventure.

It had been decided that, for a time at least, Gordon and Constance should stay with Mary. In the spring they would again go back to London. Grace Clendenning and Aunt Frances were already installed for the winter at their hotel.

The young couple would occupy the Sanctum and the adjoining room, and Mary was to take on an extra maid to help Susan Jenks.

In all her planning, Mary had a sense of the pervasiveness of Gordon Richardson. With masculine confidence in his ability, he took upon himself not only his wife's problems, but Mary's. Mary was forced to admit, even while she rebelled, that his judgments were usually wise. Yet, she asked herself, what right had an outsider to dictate in matters which pertained to herself and Barry? And what right had he to offer her board for Constance? Constance, who was her very own?

But when she had indignantly voiced her objection to Gordon, he had laughed. "You are like all women, Mary," he had said, "and of course I appreciate your point of view and your hospitality. But if you think that I am going to let my wife stay here and add to your troubles and expense without giving adequate compensation, you are vastly mistaken. If you won't let us pay, we won't stay, and that's all there is to it."

Here was masculine firmness against which Mary might rage impotently. After all, Constance was Gordon's wife, and he could carry her off.

"Of course," she said, yielding stiffly, "you must do as you think best."

"I shall," he said, easily, "and I will write you a check now, and you can have it to settle any immediate demands upon your exchequer. I shall be away a good deal, and I want Constance to be with you and Aunt Isabelle. It is a favor to me, Mary, to have her here. You mustn't add to my obligations by making me feel too heavily in your debt."

He smiled as he said it, and Gordon had a nice smile. And presently Mary found herself smiling back.

"Gordon," she said, in a half apology, "Porter calls me Contrary Mary. Maybe I am—but you see, Constance was my sister before she was your wife."

He leaned back in his chair and looked at her. "And you've had twenty years more of her than I—but please God, Mary, I am going to have twenty beautiful years ahead of me to share with her—I hope it may be three times twenty."

His voice shook, and in that moment Mary felt nearer to him than ever before.

"Oh, Gordon," she said, "I'm a horrid little thing. I've been jealous because you took Constance away from me. But now I'm glad you—took her, and I hope I'll live to dance at your— golden wedding." And then, most unexpectedly, she found herself sobbing, and Gordon was patting her on the back in a big-brotherly way, and saying that he didn't blame her a bit, and that if anybody wanted to take Constance away from him, they'd have to do it over his dead body.

Then he wrote the check, and Mary took it, and in the

knowledge of his munificence, felt the relief from certain financial burdens.

Before he left her, Gordon, hesitating, referred gravely to another subject.

"And it will be better for you to have Constance here if Barry goes away."

"Barry?" breathlessly.

"Yes. Don't you think he ought to go, Mary?"

"No," she said, stubbornly; "where could he go?"

"Anywhere away from Leila. He mustn't marry that child. Not yet—not until he has proved himself a man."

The blow hit her heavily. Yet her sense of justice told her that he was right.

"I can't talk about it," she said, unsteadily; "Barry is all I have left."

He rose. "Poor little girl. We must see how we can work it out. But we've got to work it out. It mustn't drift."

Left alone, Mary sat down at her desk and faced the future. With Roger gone, and Barry going—

And the Tower Rooms empty!

She shivered. Before her stretched the darkness and storms of a long winter. Even Constance's coming would not make up for it. And yet a year ago Constance had seemed everything.

She crossed the hall to the dining-room and looked out of the window. The garden was dead. The fountain had ceased to play. But the little bronze boy still flung his gay defiance to wind and weather.

Pittiwitz, following her, murmured a mewing complaint. Mary picked her up; since Roger's going the gray cat had kept away from the emptiness of the upper rooms.

With the little purring creature hugged close, Mary reviewed her worries—the world was at sixes and sevens. Even Porter was proving difficult. Since the Sunday when Roger had saved her from the fire, Porter had adopted an air of possession. He claimed her at all times and seasons; she had a sense of being caught in a web woven of kindness and thoughtfulness and tender care, but none the less a web which held her fast and against her will.

Whimsically it came to her that the four men in her life were opposed in groups of two: Gordon and Porter stood arrayed on the side of logical preferences; Barry and Roger on the side of illogical sympathies.

Gordon had conveyed to her, in rather subtle fashion, his disapproval of Roger. It was only in an occasional phrase, such as "Poor Poole," or "if all of his story were known." But Mary had grasped that, from the standpoint of her brother-in-law, a man who had failed to fulfil the promise of his youth might be dismissed as a social derelict.

As for Barry—the situation with regard to him had become acute. His first disappearance after the coming of Constance had resulted in Gordon's assuming the responsibility of the search for him. He had found Barry in a little town on the upper Potomac, ostensibly on a fishing trip, and again there was a need for fighting dragons.

But Gordon did not fight with the same weapons as Roger Poole. His arguments had been shrewd, keen, but unsympathetic. And the result had been a strained relation between him and Barry. The boy had felt himself misunderstood. Gordon had sat in judgment. Constance had tearfully agreed with Gordon, and Mary, torn between her sense of Gordon's rightness, and her own championship of Barry, had been strung to the point of breaking.

She turned from the window, and went up-stairs slowly. In the Sanctum, Constance and Aunt Isabelle were sewing. At last Aunt Isabelle had come into her own. She spent her days in putting fine stitches into infinitesimal garments. There was about her constantly the perfume of the sachet powder with which she was scenting the fine lawn and lace which glorified certain baskets and bassinets. When she was not sewing she was knitting—little silken socks for a Cupid's foot, little warm caps, doll's size; puffy wool blankets on big wooden needles.

The Sanctum had taken on the aspect of a bower. Here Constance sat enthroned—and in her gentleness reminded Mary more and more of her mother. Here was always the sweetness of the flowers with which Gordon kept his wife supplied; here, too, was an atmosphere of serene waiting for a supreme event.

Mary, entering with Pittiwitz in her arms, tried to cast away her worries on the threshold. She must not be out of tune with this symphony. She smiled and sat down beside Constance. "Such lovely little things," she said; "what can I do?"

It seemed that there was a debate on, relative to the suitability of embroidery as against fine tucks.

Mary settled it. "Let me have it," she said; "I'll put in a few tucks and a little embroidery—I shall be glad to have my fingers busy."

"You're always so occupied with other things," Constance complained, gently. "I don't see half enough of you."

"You have Gordon," Mary remarked.

"You say that as if it really made a difference."

"It does," Mary murmured. Then, lest she trouble Constance's gentle soul, she added bravely, "But Gordon's a dear. And you're a lucky girl."

"I know I am." Constance was complacent. "And I knew you'd recognize it, when you'd seen more of Gordon."

Mary felt a rising sense of rebellion. She was not in a mood to hear a catalogue of Gordon's virtues. But she smiled, bravely. "I'll admit that he is perfect," she said; "we won't quarrel over it, Con, dear."

But to herself she was saying, "Oh, I should hate to marry a perfect man."

All the morning she sat there, her needle busy, and gradually she was soothed by the peace of the pleasant room. The world seemed brighter, her problems receded.

Just before luncheon was announced came Aunt Frances and Grace.

They brought gifts, wonderful little things, made by the nuns of France—sheer, exquisite, tied with pale ribbons.

"We are going from here to Leila's," Aunt Frances informed them; "we ordered some lovely trousseau clothes and they came with these."

Trousseau clothes? Leila's? Mary's needle pricked the air for a moment.

"They haven't set the day, you know, Aunt Frances; it will be a long engagement."

"I don't believe in long engagements," Aunt Frances' tone was final; "they are not wise. Barry ought to settle down."

Nobody answered. There was nothing to say, but Mary was

oppressed by the grim humor of it all. Here was Aunt Frances bearing garments for the bride, while Gordon was planning to steal the bridegroom.

She stood up. "You better stay to lunch," she said; "it is Susan Jenks' hot roll day, and you know her rolls."

Aunt Frances peeled off her long gloves. "I hoped you'd ask us, we are so tired of hotel fare."

Grace laughed. "Mother is of old New York," she said, "and better for her are hot rolls and chops from her own kitchen range, than caviar and truffles from the hands of a hotel chef— in spite of all of our globe trotting, she hasn't caught the habit of meals with the mob."

Grace went down with Mary, and the two girls found Susan Jenks with the rolls all puffy and perfect in their pans.

"There's plenty of them," she said to Mary, "an' if the croquettes give out, you can fill up on rolls."

"Susan," Grace said, "when Mary gets married will you come and keep house for me?"

Susan smiled. "Miss Mary ain't goin' to git married."

"Why not?"

"She ain't that kind. She's the kind that looks at a man and studies about him, and then she waves him away and holds up her head, and says, 'I'm sorry, but you won't do.'"

The two girls laughed. "How did you get that idea of me, Susan?" Mary asked.

"By studyin' you," said Susan. "I ain't known you all your life for nothin'.

"Now Miss Constance," she went on, as she opened the oven and peeped in, "Miss Constance is just the other way. 'Most any nice man was bound to git her. An' it was lucky that Mr. Gordon was the first."

"And what about me?" was Grace's demand.

"Go 'way," said Susan, "you knows yo'se'f, Miss Grace. You bats your eyes at everybody, and gives your heart to nobody."

"And so Mary and I are to be old maids—oh, Susan."

"They don't call them old maids any more," Susan said, "and they ain't old maids, not in the way they once was. An old maid is a woman who ain't got any intrus' in life but the man she can't have, and you all is the kin' that ain't got no intrus' in the men that want you."

They left her, laughing, and when they reached the dining-room they sat down on the window-seat; where Mary had gazed out upon the dead garden and the bronze boy.

"And now," said Grace, "tell me about Roger Poole."

"There isn't much to tell. He's given up his position in the Treasury, and he's gone down to his cousin's home for a while. He's going to try to write for the magazines; he thinks that stories of that section will take."

"He's in love with you, Mary. But you're not in love with him—and you mustn't be."

"Of course not. I'm not going to marry, Grace."

Grace gave her a little squeeze. "You don't know what you are going to do, darling; no woman does. But I don't want you to fall in love with anybody yet. Flit through life with me for a time. I'll take you to Paris next summer, and show you my world."

"I couldn't, unless I could pay my own way."

"Oh, Mary, what makes you fight against anybody doing anything for you?"

"Porter says it is my contrariness—but I just can't hold out my hands and let things drop into them."

"I know—and that's why you won't marry Porter Bigelow."

Mary flashed at her a surprised and grateful glance. "Grace," she said, solemnly, "you're the first person who has seemed to understand."

"And I understand," said Grace, "because to me life is a Great Adventure. Everything that happens is a hazard on the highway—as yet I haven't found a man who will travel the road with me; they all want to open a gate and shut me in and say, 'Stay here.'"

Mary's eyes were shining. "I feel that, too."

Grace kissed her. "You'd laugh, Mary, if I told the dream which is at the end of my journey."

"I sha'n't laugh—tell me."

There was a rich color in Grace's cheeks. In her modish frock of the black which she affected, and which was this morning of fine serge set on by a line of fur at hem and wrist, and topped by a little hat of black velvet which framed the vividness of her glorious hair, she looked the woman of the world, so that her words gained strength by force of contrast.

"Nobody would believe it," she prefaced, "but, Mary Ballard, some day when I'm tired of dancing through life, when I am weary of the adventures on the road, I'm going to build a home for little children, and spend my days with them."

So the two girls dreamed dreams and saw visions of the future. They sang and soared, they kissed and confided.

"Whatever comes, life shall never be commonplace," Mary declared, and as the bell rang and she went to the table, she felt that now nothing could daunt her—the hard things would be merely a part of a glorious pilgrimage.

Susan's hot rolls were pronounced perfect, and Susan, serenely conscious of it, banished the second maid to the kitchen and waited on the table herself.

Here were five women of one clan. She understood them all, she loved them all. She gave even to Aunt Frances her due. "They all holds their heads high," she had confided on one occasion to Roger Poole, "and Miss Frances holds hers so high that she almost bends back, but she knows how to treat the people who work for her, and she's always been mighty good to me."

Mary's mood of exaltation lasted long after her guests had departed. She found herself singing as she climbed the stairs that night to her room. And it was with this mood still upon her that she wrote to Roger Poole.

Her letter, penned on the full tide of her new emotion, was like wine to his thirsty soul. It began and ended formally, but every line throbbed with hope and courage, and responding to the note which she had struck, he wrote back to her.

CHAPTER XIV

In Which Mary Writes From the Tower Rooms; and in Which Roger Answers From Among the Pines.

The Tower Rooms.

Dear Mr. Poole:

I have taken your rooms for mine, and this is my first evening in them. Pittiwitz is curled up under the lamp. She misses you and so do I. Even now, it seems as if your books ought to be on the table; and that I ought to be talking to you instead of writing.

I liked your letter. It seemed to tell me that you were hopeful and at home. You must tell me about the house and your Cousin Patty—about everything in your life—and you must send me your first story.

Here everything is the same. Constance will be with me until spring, and we are to have a quiet Thanksgiving and a quiet Christmas with just the family, and Leila and the General. Porter Bigelow goes to Palm Beach to be with his mother. I don't know why we always count him in as one of the family except that he never waits for an invitation, and of course we're glad to have him. Mother and father used to feel sorry for him; he was always a sort of "Poor-little-rich-boy" whose money cut him out from lots of good times that families have who don't live in such formal fashion as Mr. and Mrs. Bigelow seem to enjoy.

As soon as Constance leaves, I am going to work. I haven't told any one, for when I hinted at it, Constance was terribly upset, and asked me to live with her and Gordon. Grace wants me to go to Paris with her; Barry and Leila have stated that I can have a home with them.

But I don't want a home with anybody. I want to live my own life, as I have told you. I want to try my wings. I don't believe you quite like the idea of my working. Nobody does, not even Grace Clendenning, although Grace seems to understand me better than any one else.

Grace and I have been talking to-day about life as a great adventure. And it seems to me that we have the right idea. So many people go through life as just something to be endured, but I want to make things happen, or rather, if big things don't happen, I want to see in the little things something that is interesting. I don't believe that any life need be common-place. It is just the way we look at it. I'm copying these words which I read in one of your books; perhaps you've seen them, but anyhow it will tell you better than I what I mean.

"But life is a great adventure, and the worst of all fears is the fear of living. There are many forms of success, many forms of triumph. But there is no other success that in any way approaches that which is open to most of the many men and women who have the right idea. These are the men and the women who see that it is the intimate and homely things that count most. They are the men and women who have the courage to strive for the happiness which comes only with labor and effort and self-sacrifice, and only to those whose joy in life springs in part from power of work and sense of duty."

Aren't those words like a strong wind blowing from the sea? I just love them. And I know you will. I am so glad that I can talk to you of such things. Everybody has to have a friend who can understand—and that's the fine thing about our friendship—that we both have things to overcome, and that our letters can be reports of progress.

Of course the things which I have to overcome are just little fussy woman things—but they are big to me because I am breaking away from family traditions. All the women our household have followed the straight and narrow path of conventional living. Even Grace does it, although she rebels inwardly—but Aunt Frances keeps her to it. Once Grace tried to be an artist, and she worked hard in Paris, until Aunt Frances swooped down and carried her off—Grace still speaks of that time in Paris as her year out of prison. You see she worked hard and met people who worked, too, and it interested her. She had a studio apartment, and was properly chaperoned by a little widow who went with her and shared her rooms.

But Aunt Frances popped in on them suddenly one day and found a Bohemian party. There wasn't anything wrong about it, Grace says, but you know Aunt Frances! She has never ceased to talk about the frumpy crowd she met there. She hated the students in their velvet coats and the women with their poor queer clothes. And Grace loved them. But she's given up the idea of ever living there again. She says you can't do a thing twice and have it the same. I don't know. I only know that Grace may seem frivolous on the outside, but that underneath she is different. She has taken up advanced ideas about women, and she says that I have them naturally, and that she didn't expect such a thing in Washington where everybody stops to think what somebody else is going to say. But I haven't arrived at the point where I am really interested in Suffrage and things like that. Grace says that I must begin to look beyond my own life, and perhaps when I get some of my own problems settled, I will. And then I shall be taking up the problems of the girls in factories and the girls in laundries and the girls in the big shops, as Grace is. She says that she may live like a bond-slave herself, but she'd like to help other women to be free.

And now I must tell you about Delilah Jeliffe. She had a house-warming last week. The old house in Georgetown is a dream. Delilah hasn't a superfluous or gorgeous thing in it. Everything is keyed to the old-family note. Some of the things are even shabby. She has done away with flamingo colors, and her monkeys with the crystal ball and the peacock screen. She has little stools in her drawing-room with faded covers of canvas work, and she has samplers and cracked portraits, and the china doesn't all match. There isn't a sign of "new richness" in the place. She keeps colored servants, and doesn't wear rings, and her gowns are frilly flowing white things which make her look like one of those demure grandmotherly young persons of the early sixties.

Her little artist is a charming blond who doesn't come up to her shoulders, and Delilah hangs on every word he says. For the moment he obscures all the other men on her horizon. He made sketches of the way every room in her house ought to look. And what seems to be the result of years of formal pleasant living really is the result of the months of hunting and hard work which he and Delilah have put in. He even indicates the flowers she shall wear, and those which are to bloom next summer in her garden. She affects heliotrope, and on the night of her house-warming she carried a tight bunch of it with a few pink rosebuds.

Really, in her new role Delilah is superb. And, people are beginning to notice her and to call on her. Even in this short time she has been invited to some very good houses. She has a new way with her eyes, and drops her lashes over them, and is very still and lovely.

Do you remember her leopard skins of last year? Well, now she wears moleskins—a queer dolman-shaped wrap of them, and a little hat with a dull blue feather, and she drapes a black lace veil over the hat and looks like a duchess.

Grace Clendenning says that Delilah and her artist will achieve a triumph if they keep on. They aren't trying to storm society, they are trying to woo it, and out of it the artist gets the patronage of the people whom he meets through Delilah. Perhaps it will end by Delilah's marrying him. But Grace says not. She says that Delilah simply squeezes people dry, like so many oranges, and when she has what she wants, she throws them aside.

Yet Grace and Delilah get along very well together. Grace has always made a study of clothes, because it is the only way in which she can find an outlet for her artistic tastes. And she is interested in Delilah's methods. She says that they are masterly.

But I am forgetting to tell you what Delilah said of you. It was on the night of her house-warming. She asked about you, and when I said that you had gone south to get atmosphere for some stories you were writing, she said:

"Do you know it came to me yesterday, while I was in church, where I had seen him. It was the same text, and that was what brought it back. He was *preaching*, my dear. I remember that I sat in the front pew and looked up at him, and thought that I had never heard such a voice; and now, tell me why he has given it up, and why he is burying himself in the South?"

At first I didn't know just what to say, and then I thought it best to tell the truth. So I looked straight at her, and said: "He made a most unhappy marriage, and gave up his life-work. But now his wife is dead, and some day he may preach again." Was it wrong for me to say that? I do hope you are going to preach; somehow I feel that you will. And anyhow while people need never know the details of your story, they will have to know the outlines. It seemed to me that the easiest way was to tell it and have it over.

Of course Gordon has asked some questions, and I have told what I thought should be told. I hope that you won't feel that I have been unwise. I thought it best to start straight, and then there would be nothing to hide.

And now may I tell you a little bit about Barry? They want him to go away—back to England with Gordon and Constance. You see Gordon looks at it without sentiment. Gordon's sentiment stops at Constance. He thinks that Barry should simply give Leila up, go away, and not come back until he can show a clear record.

Of course I know that Gordon is right. But I can't bear it—that's why I haven't been able to face things with quite the courage that I thought I could. But since my talk with Grace, I am going to look at it differently. I shall try to feel that Barry's going is best, and that he must ride away gallantly, and come back with trumpets blowing and flags flying.

And that's the way you must some day come into your own.—I like to think about it. I like to think about victory and conquest, instead of defeat and failure. Somehow thinking about a thing seems to bring it, don't you think?

Oh, but this is such a long letter, and it is gossipy, and scrappy. But that's the way we used to talk, and you seemed to like it.

And now I'll say "Good-night." Pittiwitz waked up a moment ago, and walked across this sheet, and the blot is where she stepped on a word. So that's her message. But my message is Psalms 27:14. You can look it up in father's Bible—I am so glad you took it with you. But perhaps you don't have to look up verses; you probably know everything by heart. Do you?

Sincerely ever,

MARY BALLARD.

Among the Pines.

My good little friend:

I am not going to try to tell you what your letter meant to me.

It was the bluebird's song in the spring, the cool breeze in the desert, sunlight after storm—it was everything that stands for satisfaction after a season of discomfort or of discontent.

Yet, except that I miss the Tower Rooms, and miss, too, the great happiness I found in pursuing our friendship at close range, I should have no reason here either for discomfort or lack of content—if I feel the world somewhat barren, it is not because of what I have found, but because of what I have brought with me.

I like to think of you in the Tower Rooms. You always belonged there, and I felt like a usurper when I came and discovered that all of your rosy belongings had been moved down-stairs and my staid and stiff things were in their place. It is queer, isn't it, the difference in the atmosphere made by a man and by a woman. A man dares not surround himself with pale and pretty colors and delicate and dainty things, lest he be called effeminate—perhaps that's why men take women into their lives, so that they may have the things which they crave without having their masculinity questioned.

Yet the atmosphere which seems to fit you best is not merely one of rosiness and prettiness; it is rather that of sunshine and out-of-doors. When you talk or write to me I have the sensation of being swept on and on by your enthusiasms—I seem to fly on strong wings—the quotation which you gave is the utterance of some one else, but you unerringly selected, and passed it on to me, and so in a sense made it your own. I am going to copy it and illumine it, and keep it where I can see it at all times.

I find that I do not travel as fast as you toward my future. I have shut myself up for many years. I have been so sure that all the wine of life was spilled, that the path ahead of me was dreary, that I cannot see myself at all with trumpets blowing, with flags flying and the rest of it. Perhaps I shall some day— and at least I shall try, and in the trying there will be something gained. Some day, perhaps, I shall reach the upper air where you soar—perhaps I shall "mount as an eagle."

Your message—! Dear child—do you know how sweet you are? I don't know all the verses—but that one I do know. Yet I had let myself forget, and you brought it back to me with all its strong assurance.

Your decision that it was best to tell what there is to tell, to let nothing be hidden, is one which I should have made long ago. Only of late have I realized that concealment brings in its train a thousand horrors. One lives in fear, dreading that which must inevitably come. Yet I do not think I must be blamed too much. I was beaten and bruised by the knowledge of my overthrow. I only wanted to crawl into a hole and be forgotten.

Even now, I find myself unfolding slowly. I have lived so long in the dark, and the light seems to blind my eyes!

It is strange that I should have remembered Delilah Jeliffe, but not strange that she should have remembered me; for I stood alone in the pulpit, but she was one of a crowd. Since your letter, I have been thinking back, and I can see her as she sat reading in the front pew, big and rather fine with her black hair and her bold eyes. I think that perhaps the thing which made me remember her was the fleeting thought that her type stood usually for the material in woman, and I wondered if in her case outward appearances were as deceptive as they were in my wife—with her saint's eyes, and her distorted moral vision. Perhaps I was intuitively right, and that beneath Delilah Jeliffe's exterior there is a certain fineness, and that these funny fads of dress and decorations are merely in some way her striving toward the expression of her real self.

What you tell me of your talk with your cousin Grace interests me very much. I fancy she is more womanly than she is willing to admit. Yet she should marry. Every woman should marry, except you—who are going to be my friend! There peeps out my selfishness—but I shall let it stand.

No, I don't like the idea that you must work. I don't want you to try your wings. I want you to sit safe in your nest in the top of the Tower, and write letters to me!

Labor, office drudgery, are things which sap the color from a woman's cheeks, and strength from her body. She grows into a machine, and you are a bird, to fly and light on the nearest branch and sing!

But now you will want to know something of my life, and of the house and of Cousin Patty.

The house has suffered from the years of poverty since the War. Yet it has still about it something of the dignity of an ancient ruin. It is a big frame structure with the Colonial pillars which belong to the period of its building. Many of the rooms are closed. My own suite is on the second floor— Cousin Patty's opposite, and adjoining her rooms those of an old aunt who is a pensioner.

There is little of the old mahogany which once made the rooms stately, and little of the old silver to grace the table. Cousin Patty's poverty is combined, happily, with common sense. She has known the full value of her antiques, and has preferred good food to family traditions. Yet there are the old portraits and in her living-room a few choice pieces. Here we have an open fire, and here we sit o' nights.

Cousin Patty is small, rather white and thin, and she is fifty-five. I tell you her age, because in a way it explains many things which would otherwise puzzle you. She was born just before the war. She knew nothing of the luxury of the days of slavery. She has twisted and turned and economized all of her life. She has struggled with all the problems which beset the South in Reconstruction times, and she has come out if it all, sweet and shrewd, and with a point of view about women which astonishes me, and which gives us a chance for many sprightly arguments. Her black hair is untouched with gray, she wears it parted and in a thick knot high on her head. Her gowns are invariably of black silk, well cut and well made. She makes them herself, and gets her patterns from New York! Can you see her now?

Our arguments are usually about women, and their position in the world to-day. You know I am conservative, clinging much to old ideals, old fashions, to the beliefs of gentler times—but Cousin Patty in this backwater of civilization has gone far ahead of me. She believes that the hope of the South is in its women. "They read more than the men," she says, "and they have responded more quickly to the new social ideals."

But of our arguments more in another letter—this will serve, however, to introduce you to some of the astonishing mental processes of this little marooned cousin of mine.

For in a sense she is marooned. Once upon a time when Cotton was king, and slave labor made all things possible, there was prosperity here, but now the land is impoverished. So Cousin Patty does not depend upon the land. She read in some of her magazines of a woman who had made a fortune in wedding cake. She resolved that what one woman could do could be done by another. Hence she makes and sells wedding cake, and while she has not made a fortune she has made a living. She began by asking friends for orders; she now gets orders from near and far.

So all day there is the good smell of baking in the house, and the sound of the whisking of eggs. And every day little boxes have to be filled. Will you smile when I tell you that I like the filling of the little boxes? And that while we talk o' nights, I busy myself with this task, while Cousin Patty does things with narrow white ribbon and bits of artificial orange blossoms, so that the packages which go out may be as beautiful and bride-y as possible.

It is strange, when one thinks of it, that I came to your house on a wedding night, and here I live in a perpetual atmosphere of wedding blisses.

In the morning I write. In the afternoon I do other things. The weather is not cold—it is dry and sunshiny—windless. I take long walks over the hills and far away. Some of it is desolate country where the boxed pines have fallen, or where an area has been burned but one comes now and then upon groves of shimmering and shining young trees,—is there any tree as beautiful as a young pine with the sunshine on it?

It is rare to find a grove of old pines, yet there are one or two estates where for years no trees have been cut or burned, and beneath these tall old singing monarchs I sit on the brown needles, and write and write—to what end I know not.

I have not one finished story to show you, though the beginnings of many. The pen is not my medium. My thoughts seem to dry up when I try to put them on paper. It is when I talk that I grow most eloquent. Oh, little friend, shall I ever make the world listen again?

I am going to tell you presently of those who have listened, down here—such an audience—and in such an amphitheater!

My walks take me far afield. The roads are sandy, and I do not always follow them, preferring, rather, the dunes which remind me so much of those by the sea. Once upon a time this ground was the ocean's bed—I have the feeling always that just beyond the low hills I shall glimpse the blue.

Now and then I meet some darkey of the old school with his cheery greeting; now and then on the highroad a schooner wagon sails by. These wagons give one the queer feeling of being set back to pioneer days,—do you remember the Pike's Peak picture at the Capitol with all the eager faces turned toward the setting sun?

Now and then I run across a hunting party from one of the big hotels which are getting to be plentiful in this healthy region, but these people with their sporting clothes and their sophistication always seem out of place among the pines.

And now, since you have written to me of life as a journey on the highroad, I will tell you of my first adventure.

There's a schooner-man who comes from the sandhills on his way to the nearest resort with his chickens and eggs. It is a three days' journey, and he camps out at night, sleeping in his wagon, building his fire in the open.

One day he passed me as I sat tired by the wayside, and offered to give me a lift toward home. I accepted, and rode beside him. And thus began an acquaintance which interests me, and evidently pleases him.

He is tall and loosely put together, this knight of the Sandy Road, but with the ease of manner which seems to belong to his kind. There's good blood in these sand-hill people, and it shows in a lack of self-consciousness which makes one feel that they would meet a prince or an emperor without embarrassment. Yet there's nothing of forwardness, nothing of impertinence. It is a drawing-room manner, preserved in spite of generations of illiteracy and degeneration.

He is not an unpicturesque object. Given a plumed hat, a doublet and hose, and he would look the part, and his manner would fit in with it. Given good English, his voice would never betray him for what he is. For another thing that these people have preserved is a softness of voice and an inflection which is Elizabethan rather than twentieth century American.

Having grown to know him fairly well, I fished for an invitation to visit his home. I wanted to see where this gentlemanly backwoodsman spent the days which were not lived on the road.

I carried a rug with me, and slept for the first night under the open sky. Have you ever seen a southern sky when it was studded with stars? If not, there's something yet before you. There's no whiteness or coldness about these stars, they are pure gold, and warm with light.

My schooner-man slept in his wagon, covered with an old quilt. His mules were picketed close by, the dog curled himself beside his master, each getting warmth from the other.

We cooked supper and breakfast over the coals—chickens broiled for our evening meal, ham and eggs for the morning. We gave the dog the bones and the crusts. I took bread with me, for Cousin Patty warned me that I must not depend upon my squire for food. Cooking among these people is a lost art. Cousin Patty believes that the regeneration of the poor whites of the South will be accomplished through the women. "When they learn to cook," she says, "the men won't need whiskey. When the whiskey goes, they'll respect the law."

A mile before we reached the end of our journey, we were met by the children of my schooner-squire. Five of them—two boys, two girls, and a baby in the arms of the oldest girl. They all had the gentle quiet and ease of the father—but they were unkempt little creatures, uncombed, unwashed, in sad-colored clothes. That's the difference between the negro and the white man of this region. The negro is cheerful, debonair, he sings, he dances, and he wears all the colors of the rainbow. An old black woman who carries home my wash wore the other day a purple petticoat with a scarlet skirt looped above it, an old green sweater, and, tied over her head, a pink wool shawl. Against the neutral background of sandy hill she was a delight to the eye. The whites on the other hand seem like little animals, who have taken on the color of the landscape that they may be hidden.

But to go back to my sad children. It seemed to me that in them I was seeing the South with new eyes, perhaps because I have been away just long enough to get the proper perspective. And my life has been, you see, lived in the Southern cities, where one touches rarely the primitive.

The older boys are, perhaps, ten and twelve, blue-eyed and tow-headed. I saw few signs of affection or intelligence. They did not kiss their father when he came, except the small girl, who ran to him and was hugged; the others seemed to practice a sort of incipient stoicism, as if they were too old, too settled, for demonstration.

The mother, as we entered, was like her children. None of them has the initiative or the energy of the man. They are subdued by the changeless conditions of their environment; his one adventure of the week keeps him alert and alive.

It is a desolate country, charred pines sticking up straight from white sand. It might be made beautiful if for every tree that they tapped for turpentine they would plant a new one.

But they don't know enough to make things beautiful. The Moses of this community will be some man who shall find new methods of farming, new crops for this soil, who will show the people how to live.

And now I come to a strange fairy-tale sort of experience—an experience with the children who have lived always among these charred pines.

All that evening as I talked, their eyes were upon me, like the eyes of little wild creatures of the wood—a blank gaze which seemed to question. The next day when I walked, they went with me, and for some distance I carried the baby, to rest the arms of the big girl, who is always burdened.

It was in the afternoon that we drifted to a little grove of young pines, the one bit of pure green against the white and gray and black of that landscape. The sky was of sapphire, with a buzzard or two blotted against the blue.

Here with a circle of the trees surrounding us, the children sat down with me. They were not a talkative group, and I was overcome by a sense of the impossibility of meeting them on any common ground of conversation. But they seemed to expect something—they were like a flock of little hungry birds waiting to be fed—and what do you think I gave them? Guess. But I know you have it wrong.

I recited "Flos Mercatorum," my Whittington poem!

It was done on an impulse, to find if there was anything in them which would respond to such rhyme and rapture of words.

I gave it in my best manner, standing in the center of the circle. I did not expect applause. But I got more than applause. I am not going to try to describe the look that came into the eyes of the oldest boy—the nearest that I can come to it is to say that it was the look of a child waked from a deep sleep, and gazing wide-eyed upon a new world.

He came straight toward me. "Where—did you—git—them words?" he asked in a breathless sort of way.

"A man wrote them—a man named Noyes."

"Are they true?"

"Yes."

"Say them again."

It was not a request. It was a command. And I did say them, and saw a soul's awakening.

Oh, there are people who won't believe that it can be done like that—in a moment. But that boy was ready. He had dreamed and until now no one had ever put the dreams into words for him. He cannot read, has probably never heard a fairy tale— the lore of this region is gruesome and ghostly, rather than lovely and poetic.

Perhaps, 'way back, five, six generations, some ancestor of this lad may have drifted into London town, perhaps the bells sang to him, and subconsciously this sand-hill child was illumined by that inherited memory. Somewhere in the back of his mind bells have been chiming, and he has not known enough to call them bells. However that may be, my verses revealed to him a new heaven and a new earth.

Without knowing anything, he is ready for everything. Perhaps there are others like him. Cousin Patty says there are girls. She insists that the girls need cook-books, not poetry, but I am not sure.

I shall go again to the pines, and teach that boy first by telling him things, then I shall take books. I haven't been as interested in anything for years as I am in that boy.

So, will you think of me as seeing, faintly, the Vision? Your eyes are clearer than mine. You can see farther; and what you see, will you tell me?

And now about Barry. I know how hard it is to have him leave you, and that under all your talk of trumpets blowing and flags flying, there's the ache and the heart-break. I cannot see why such things should come to you. The rest of us probably deserve what we get. But you—I should like to think of you always as in a garden—you have the power to make things bloom. You have even quickened the dry dust of my own dead life, so that now in it there's a little plot of the pansies of my thoughts of you, and there's rosemary, for remembrance, and there's the little bed of my interest in that boy—what seeds did you plant for it?

It is raining here to-night. I wonder it the rain is beating on the windows of the Tower Rooms, and if you are snug within, with Pittiwitz purring and the fire snapping, and I wonder if throughout all that rain you are sending any thought to me.

Perhaps I shouldn't ask it. But I do ask for another letter. What the last was to me I have told you. I shall live on the hope of the next.

Faithfully and gratefully always,

ROGER POOLE.

CHAPTER XV

In Which Barry and Leila Go Over the Hills and Far Away; and in Which a March Moon Becomes a Honeymoon.

The news that Barry must go away had been a blow to Leila's childish dreams of immediate happiness. She knew that Barry was bitter, that he rebelled against the plans which were being made for him, but she did not know that Gordon had told the General frankly and flatly the reason for this delay in the matrimonial arrangements.

The General, true to his ancient code, had protested that "a man could drink like a gentleman," that Barry's good blood would tell. "His wild oats aren't very wild—and every boy must have his fling."

Gordon had listened impatiently, as to an ancient and outworn philosophy. "The business world doesn't take into account the wild oats of a man, General," he had said. "The new game isn't like the old one,—the convivial spirit is not the popular one among men of affairs. And that isn't the worst of it, with Barry's temperament there's danger of a breakdown, moral and physical. If it were not for that, he could come into your office and practice law, as you suggest. But he's got to get away from Washington. He's got to get away from old associations, and you'll pardon me for saying it, he's got to get away from Leila. She loves him, and is sorry for him, even though we've kept from her the knowledge of his fault. She thinks we are all against him and her sympathy weakens him. It was the same

with her mother, Constance tells me. She wouldn't believe that
her boy could be anything but perfect, and John Ballard wasn't
strong enough to counteract her influence. Mary was the only
one, and now that it has come to an actual crisis, even Mary
blames me for trying to do what I know is best for Barry. I
want to take him over to the other side, cut him away from all
that hampers him here, and bring him back to you stronger in
fiber and more of a man."

The General shook his head. "Perhaps," he said, "but I can't
bear to think of the hurt heart of my little Leila."

"They should never have been engaged," Gordon said, "but it
won't make matters any better to let things go on. If Leila
doesn't marry Barry, she won't have to bear the burdens he
will surely bring to her. She'd better be unhappy with you to
take care of her, than tied to him and unhappy."

"But I'm an old man, and she is such a child. Life for me is so
short, and for her so long."

"We must do what seems best for the moment, and let the
future take care of itself. Barry's only a boy. They are neither of
them ready for marriage—a few years of waiting won't hurt
them."

It was in this strain that Gordon talked to Barry.

"It won't hurt you to wait."

"Wait for what?" Barry flamed; "until Leila wears her heart
out? Until you teach her that I'm not—fit? Until somebody
else comes along and steals her, while I'm gone?"

"Is that the opinion you have of her constancy?"

"No," Barry said, huskily, "she's as true as steel. But I can't see
the use of this, Gordon. If I marry Leila, she'll make a man of
me."

"She hasn't changed you during these last months," Gordon stated, inexorably, "and you mustn't run the risk of making her unhappy. It is a mere business proposition that I am putting before you, Barry. You must be able to support a wife before you marry one, and Washington isn't the place for you to start. In a business like ours, a man must be at his best. You are wasting your time here, and you've acquired the habit of sociability, which is just a habit, but it grows and will end by paralyzing your forces. A man who's always ready to be with the crowd isn't the man that's ready for work, and he isn't the man who's usually onto his job. I am putting this not from any moral or spiritual ideal, but from the commercial. The man who wins out isn't the one with his brain fuddled; he's the one with his brain clear. Business to-day is too keen a game for any one to play who isn't willing to be at it all the time."

Thus practical common sense met the boy at every turn. And he was forced at last for pride's sake to consent to Gordon's plans for him. But he had gone to Mary, raging. "Is he going to run our lives?"

"He is doing it for your good, Barry."

"Why can't I go South with Roger Poole?—if I must go away? He told me of a man who stayed in the woods with him."

"That would simply be temporary, and it would delay matters. Gordon's idea is that in this way you'll be established in business. If you went South you'd be without any remunerative occupation."

"Doesn't Poole make a living down there?"

"He hasn't yet. He's to try story-writing."

"Are you corresponding with him, Mary?"

Resenting his catechism, she forced herself to say, quietly, "We write now and then."

"What does Porter think of that?"

"Porter hasn't anything to do with it."

"He has, too. You know you'll marry him, Mary."

"I shall not. I haven't the least idea of marrying Porter."

"Then why do you let him hang around you?"

"Barry," she was blazing, "I don't let him hang around. He comes as he has always come—to see us all."

"Do you think for a moment that he'd come if it weren't for you? He isn't craving my society, or Aunt Isabelle's, or Susan Jenks'."

Barry was glad to blame somebody else for something—he was aware of himself as the blackest sheep in the fold, but let those who had other sins hear them.

He flung himself away from her—out of the house. And for days he did not come home. They kept the reason of his absence from Leila, and as far as they could from Constance. But Mary went nearly wild with anxiety, and she found in Gordon a strength and a resourcefulness on which she leaned.

When Barry came back, he offered no further objections to their plans. Yet they could see that he was consenting to his exile only because he had no argument with which to meet theirs. He refused to resign from the Patent Office until the last moment, as if hoping for some reprieve from the sentence which his family had pronounced. He was moody, irritable, a changed boy from the one who had hippity-hopped with Leila on Constance's wedding night.

Even Leila saw the change. "Barry, dear," she said one evening as she sat beside him in her father's library, "Barry—is it because you hate to leave—me?"

He turned to her almost fiercely. "If I had a penny of my own, Leila, I'd pick you up, and we'd go to the ends of the earth together."

And she responded breathlessly, "It would be heavenly, Barry."

He dallied with temptation. "If we were married, no one could take you away from me."

"No one will ever take me away."

"I know. But they might try to make you give me up."

"Why should they?"

"They'll say that I'm not worthy—that I'm a poor idiot who can't earn a living for his wife."

"Oh, Barry," she whispered, "how can any one say such things?" She knelt on a little stool beside him, and her brown hair curled madly about her pink cheeks. "Oh, Barry," she said again, "why not—why not get married now, and show them that we can live on what you make, and then you needn't go—away."

He caught at that hope. "But, sweetheart, you'd be—poor."

"I'd have you."

"I couldn't take you to our old house. It—belongs to Mary. Father knew that Constance was to be married, so he tried to provide for Mary until she married; after that the property will be divided between the two girls. He felt that I was a man, and he spent what money he had for me on my education."

"I don't want to live in Mary's house. We could live with Dad."

"No," sharply. Barry had been hurt when the General had

seemed to agree so entirely with Gordon. He had expected the offer of a place in the General's office, and it had not come.

"If we marry, darling," he said, "we must go it alone. I won't be dependent on any one."

"We could have a little apartment," her eyes were shining, "and Dad would furnish it for us, and Susan Jenks could teach me to cook and she could tell me your favorite things, and we'd have them, and it would be like a story book. Barry, please."

He, too, thought it would be like a story book. Other people had done such things and had been happy. And once at the head of his own household he would show them that he was a man.

Yet he tried to put her away from him. "I must not. It wouldn't be right."

But as the days went on, and the time before his departure grew short, he began to ask himself, "Why not?"

And it was thus, with Romance in the lead, with Love urging them on, and with Ignorance and Innocence and Impetuosity hand in hand, that, at last, in the madness of a certain March moon, Leila and Barry ran away.

Leila had a friend in Rockville—an old school friend whom she often visited. Barry knew Montgomery County from end to end. He had fished and hunted in its streams, he had motored over its roads, he had danced and dined at its country houses, he had golfed at its country clubs, he had slept at its inns and worshiped in its churches.

So it was to Montgomery County and its county seat that they looked for their Gretna Green, and one night Leila kissed her father wistfully, and told him that she was going to see Elizabeth Dean.

"Just for Saturday, Dad. I'll go Friday night, and come back in time for dinner Saturday."

"Why not motor out?"

"The train will be easier. And I'll telephone you when I get there."

She took chances on the telephoning—for had he called her up, he would have found that she did not reach Rockville on Friday night, nor was she expected by Elizabeth Dean until Saturday in time for lunch.

There was thus an evening and a night and the morning of the next day in which Little-Lovely Leila was to be lost to the world.

She took the train for Rockville, but stopped at a station half-way between that town and Washington, and there Barry met her. They had dinner at the little station restaurant—a wonderful dinner of ham and eggs and boiled potatoes, but the wonderfulness had nothing to do with the food; it had to do rather with Little-Lovely Leila's shining eyes and blushes, and Barry's abounding spirits. He was like a boy out of school. He teased Leila and wrote poetry on the fly-specked dinner card, reading it out loud to her, reveling in her lovely confusion.

When they finished, Leila telephoned to her father that she had arrived at Rockville and was safe. If her voice wavered a little as she said it, if her eyes filled at the trustfulness of his affectionate response, these things were soon forgotten, as Barry caught up her little bag, and they left the station, and started over the hills in search of happiness.

The way was rather long, but they had thought it best to avoid trolley or train or much-traveled roads, lest they be recognized. And so it came about that they crossed fields, and slipped through the edges of groves, and when the twilight fell Little-Lovely Leila danced along the way, and Barry danced, too, until the moon came up round and gold above the blackness of the distant hills.

Once they came to a stream that was like silver, and once they passed through a ghostly orchard with budding branches, and once they came to a farmhouse where a dog barked at them, and the dog and the orchard and the budding trees and the stream all seemed to be saying:

"*You are running away—you are running away.*"

And now they had walked a mile, and there was yet another.

"But what's a mile?" said Barry, and Little-Lovely Leila laughed.

She wore a frock of pale yellow, with a thick warm coat of the same fashionable color. Her hat was demurely tied under her little chin with black velvet ribbons. She was like a primrose of the spring—and Barry kissed her.

"May I tell Dad, when I get home to-morrow night?" she asked.

"We'll wait until Sunday. April Fool's Day, Leila. We'll tell him, and he will think it's a joke. And when he sees how happy we are, he will know we were right."

So like children they refused to let the thought of the future mar the joy of the present.

Once they rested on a fallen log in a little grove of trees. The wind had died down, and the air was warm, with the still warmth of a Southern spring. Between the trees they could see a ribbon of white road which wound up to a shadowy church.

"The minister's house is next to the church," Barry told her; "in a half hour from now you'll be mine, Leila. And no one can take you away from me."

In the wonder of that thought they were silent for a time, then:

"How strange it will seem to be married, Barry."

"It seems the most natural thing in the world to me. But there will be those who will say I shouldn't have let you."

"I let myself. It wasn't you. Did you want my heart to break at your going, Barry?"

For a moment he held her in his arms, then he kissed her, gently, and let her go. When they came back this way, she would be his wife.

The old minister asked few questions. He believed in youth and love; the laws of the state were lenient. So with the members of his family for witnesses, he declared in due time that this man and woman were one, and again they went forth into the moonlight.

And now there was another little journey, up one hill and down another to a quaint hostelry—almost empty of guests in this early season.

A competent little landlady and an old colored man led them to the suite for which Barry had telephoned. The little landlady smiled at Leila and showed the white roses which Barry had sent for her room, and the old colored man lighted all the candles.

There was a supper set out on the table in their sitting-room, with cold roast chicken and hot biscuits, a bottle of light wine, and a round cake with white frosting.

Leila cut the cake. "To think that I should have a wedding cake," she said to Barry.

So they made a feast of it, but Barry did not open the bottle of wine until their supper was ended. Then he poured two glasses.

"To you," he whispered, and smiled at his bride.

Then before his lips could touch it, he set the glass down hastily, so that it struck against the bottle and broke, and the wine stained the white cloth.

Leila looking up, startled, met a strange look. "Barry," she whispered, "Barry, dear boy."

He rose and blew out the candles.

"Let me tell you—in the dark," he said. "You've got to know, Leila."

And in the moonlight he told her why they had wanted him to go away.

"It is because I've got to fight—devils."

At first she did not understand. But he made her understand.

She was such a little thing in her yellow gown. So little and young to deal with a thing like this.

But in that moment the child became a woman. She bent over him.

"My husband," she said, "nothing can ever part us now, Barry."

So love taught her what to say, and so she comforted him.

The next morning Elizabeth Dean met Leila Dick at the station. That she was really meeting Leila Ballard was a thing, of course, of which she had no knowledge. But Leila was acutely conscious of her new estate. It seemed to her that the motor horn brayed it, that the birds sang it, that the cows mooed it, that the dogs barked it, "*Leila Ballard, Leila Ballard, Leila Ballard, wife of Barry—you're not Leila Dick, you're not, you're not, you're not.*"

"I never knew you to be so quiet," Elizabeth said at last, curiously. "What's the matter?"

Leila brought herself back with an effort. "I like to listen," she said, "but I am usually such a chatterbox that people won't believe it."

Somehow she managed to get through that day. Somehow she managed to greet and meet the people who had been invited to the luncheon which was given in her honor. But while in body she was with them, in spirit she was with Barry. Barry was her husband—her husband who loved her and needed her in his life.

His confession of the night before had brought with it no deadening sense of hopelessness. To her, any future with Barry was rose-colored.

But it had changed her attitude toward him in this, that she no longer adored him as a strong young god who could stand alone, and whom she must worship because of his condescension in casting his eyes upon her.

He needed her! He needed little Leila Dick! And the thought gave to her marriage a deeper meaning than that of mere youthful raptures.

He had put her on the train that morning reluctantly, and had promised to call her up the moment she reached town.

So her journey toward Washington on the evening train was an hour of anticipation. To those who rode with her, she seemed a very pretty and self-contained young person making a perfectly proper and commonplace trip on the five o'clock express—in her own mind, she was set apart from all the rest by the fact of her transcendant romance.

Her father met her at the station and put her into a taxi. All the way home she sat with her hand in his.

"Did you have a good time?" he asked.

"Heavenly, Dad."

They ate dinner together, and she talked of her day, wishing that there was nothing to keep from him, wishing that she might whisper it to him now. She had no fear of his disapproval. Dad loved her.

No call had come from Barry. She finished dinner and wandered restlessly from room to room.

When nine o'clock struck, she crept into the General's library, and found him in his big chair reading and smoking.

She sat on a little stool beside him, and laid her head against his knee. Presently his hand slipped from his book and touched her curls. And then both sat looking into the fire.

"If your mother had lived, my darling," the old man said, "she would have made things easier for you."

"About Barry's going away?"

"Yes."

"It seems silly for him to go, Dad. Surely there's something here for him to do."

"Gordon thinks that the trip will bring out his manhood, make him less of a boy."

"I don't think Gordon understands Barry."

"And you do, baby? I'm afraid you spoil him."

"Nobody could spoil Barry."

"Don't love him too much."

"As if I could."

"I'm not sure," the old man said, shrewdly, "that you don't. And no man's worth it. Most of us are selfish pigs—we take all we can get—and what we give is usually less than we ask in return."

But now she was smiling into the fire. "You gave mother all that you had to give, Dad, and you made her happy."

"Yes, thank God," and now there were tears on the old cheeks; "for the short time that I had her—I made her happy."

When Barry came, he found her curled up in her father's arms. Over her head the General smiled at this boy who was some day to take her from him.

But Barry did not smile. He greeted the General, and when Leila came to him, tremulously self-conscious, he did not meet her eyes, but he took her hand in his tightly, while he spoke to her father.

"You won't mind, General, if I carry Leila off to the other room. I've a lot of things to say to her."

"Of course not. I was in love once myself, Barry."

They went into the other room. It was a long and formal parlor with crystal chandeliers and rose-colored stuffed furniture and gilt-framed mirrors. It had been furnished by the General's mother, and his little wife had loved it and had kept it unchanged.

It was dimly lighted now, and Leila in her white dinner gown and Barry tall and slender in his evening black were reflected by the long mirrors mistily.

Barry took her in his arms, and kissed her. "My wife, my wife," he said, again and again, "my wife."

At first she yielded gladly, meeting his rapture with her own. But presently she became aware of a wildness in his manner, a broken note in his whispers.

So she released herself, and stood back a little from him, and asked, breathing quickly, "Barry, what has happened?"

"Everything. Since I left you this morning I've lost my place. I found the envelope on my desk this morning—telling of my discharge. They said that I'd been too often away without sufficient excuse, and so they have dropped me from the rolls. And you see that what Gordon said was true. I can't earn a living for a wife. Now that I have you, I can't take care of you—it is not much of a fellow that you've married, Leila."

Oh, the little white face with the shining eyes!

Then out of the stillness came her cry, like a bird's note, triumphant. "But I'm your wife now, and nothing can part us, Barry."

He caught up her hands in his. "Dearest, dearest—don't you see that I can't ever tell them of our marriage until I can show them—"

"Show them what, Barry?"

"That I can take care of you."

"Do you mean that I mustn't even tell Dad, Barry?"

"You mustn't tell any one, not until I come back."

Every drop of blood was drained from her face.

"Until you come back. Are you going—away?"

"I promised Gordon to-day that I would."

She swayed a little, and he caught her. "I had to promise, Leila. Don't you see? I haven't a penny, and I can't confess to them that I've married you. I wanted to tell him that you were mine—that all your sweetness and dearness belonged to me. I wanted to shout it to the world. But I haven't a penny, and I'm proud, and I won't let Gordon think I've been a—fool."

"But Dad would help us."

"Do you think I'd beg him to give me what he hasn't offered, Leila? I've got to show them that I'm not a boy."

She struggled to bring herself out of the strange numbness which gripped her. "If I could only tell Dad."

"Surely it can be our own sweet secret, dearest."

She laid her cheek against his arm, in a dumb gesture of surrender, and her little bare left hand crept up and rested like a white rose petal against the blackness of his coat.

He laid his own upon it. "Poor little hand without a wedding ring," he said.

And now the numbness seemed to engulf her, to break—

"Hush, Leila, dear one."

But she could not hush. That very morning they had slipped the wedding ring over a length of narrow blue ribbon, and Barry had tied it about her neck. To-morrow, he had promised, she should wear it for all the world to see.

But she was not to wear it. It must be hidden, as she had hidden it all day above her heart.

"Leila, you are making it hard for me."

It was the man's cry of selfishness, but hearing it, she put her own trouble aside. He needed her, and her king could do no wrong.

So she set herself to comfort him. In the month that was left to them they would make the most of their happiness. Then perhaps she could get Dad to bring her over in the summer, and he should show her London, and all the lovely places, and there would be the letters; she would write everything—and he must write.

"You little saint," he said when he left her, "you're too good for me, but all that's best in me belongs to you—my precious."

She went to the door with him and said "good-night" bravely.

Then she shut the door and shivered. When at last she made her way through the hall to the library, she seemed to be pushing against some barrier, so that her way was slow.

On the threshold of that room she stopped.

"Dad," she said, sharply.

"My darling."

He sprang to his feet just in time and caught her.

She lay against his heart white and still. The strain of the last two days had been too great for her, and Little-Lovely Leila had fainted dead away.

CHAPTER XVI

In Which a Long Name is Bestowed Upon a Beautiful Baby; and in Which a Letter in a Long Envelope Brings Freedom to Mary.

The christening of Constance's baby brought together a group of feminine personalities, which, to one possessed with imagination, might have stood for the evil and beneficent fairies of the old story books.

The little Mary-Constance Ballard Richardson, in spite of the dignity of her hyphenated name, was a wee morsel. Swathed in fine linen, she showed to the unprejudiced eye no signs of great beauty. With a wrinkly-red skin, a funny round nose, a toothless mouth—she was like every other normal baby of her age, but to her family and friends she was a rare and unmatched object.

Even Aunt Frances succumbed to her charms. "I must say," she remarked to Delilah Jeliffe, as they bent over the bassinet, "that she is remarkable for her age."

Delilah shrugged. "I'm not fond of them. They're so red and squirmy."

Leila protested hotly. "Delilah, she's lovely—such little perfect hands."

"Bird's claws!"

Mary took up the chant. "Her skin's like a rose leaf."

And Grace: "Her hair is going to be gold, like her mother's."

"Hair?" Delilah's tone was incredulous. "She hasn't any."

Aunt Frances expertly turned the small morsel on its back. "What do you call that?" she demanded, indignantly.

Above the fat crease of the baby's neck stuck out a little feathery duck's-tail curl—bright as a sunbeam.

"What do you call that?" came the chorus of worshipers.

Delilah gave way to quiet, mocking laughter. "That isn't hair," she said; "it is just a sample of yellow silk."

Porter, coming up, was treated to a repetition of this remark.

"Let us thank the Gods that it isn't red," was his fervent response.

Grace's hands went up to her own lovely hair.

"Oh," she reproached him.

Porter apologized. "I was thinking of my carroty head. Yours is glorious."

"Artists paint it," Grace agreed pensively, "and it goes well with the right kind of clothes."

Delilah looked from one to the other.

"You two would make a beautiful pair of saints on a stained glass window," she said reflectively, "with a spike of lilies and halos back of your heads."

"Most women are ready for halos," Porter said, "and wings,

but I can't see myself balancing a spike of lilies."

"Nor I," Grace rippled; "you'd better make it hollyhocks, Delilah—do you know the old rhyme

"'A beau never goes
Where the hollyhock blows'?'"

"You've never lacked men in your life," Delilah told her, shrewdly, "but with that hair you won't be one of the comfortable married kind—it will be either a *grande passion* or a career for you. If you don't find your Romeo, you'll be Mother Superior in a convent, the head of a deaconess home, or a nurse on a battle-field."

Grace's eyes sparkled. "Oh, wise Delilah, you haven't drifted so very far away from my dreams. Where did you get your wisdom?"

"I'm learning things from Colin Quale. We study types together. It's great fun for me, but he's perfectly serious."

Colin Quale was Delilah's artist. "Why didn't you bring him?" Constance asked.

"Because he doesn't belong in this family group; and anyhow I had something for him to do. He's making a sketch of the gown I am to wear at the White House garden party. It will keep him busy for the afternoon."

"Delilah," Leila looked up from her worship of Mary-Constance, "I don't believe you ever see in people anything but the way they look."

"I don't, duckie. To me—you are a sort of family art gallery. I hang you up in my mind, and you make a rather nice little collection."

Barry, coming in, caught up her words, with something of his old vivacity.

"The baby belongs to the Dutch school—with that nose."

There was a chorus of protest.

"She looks like you," Delilah told him. "Except for her nose, she's a Ballard. There's nothing of her father in her, except her beautiful disposition."

She flashed a challenging glance at Gordon. He stiffened. Such women as Delilah Jeliffe might have their place in the eternal scheme of femininity, but he doubted it.

"She is a Ballard even in that," he said, formally; "it is Constance whose disposition is beyond criticism, not mine."

"And now that you've carried off Constance, you're going to take Barry," Delilah reproached him.

Leila dropped the baby's hand.

"Yes," Gordon discussed the subject with evident reluctance, "he's going over with me, to learn the business—he may never have a better opportunity."

The light went out of Barry's eyes. He left the little group, wandered to the window, and stood looking out.

"Mary will go next," Delilah prophesied. "With Constance and Barry on the other side, she won't be able to keep away."

Mary shook her head. "What would Aunt Isabelle and Susan Jenks and Pittiwitz do without me?"

"What would I do without you?" Porter demanded, boldly. "Don't put such ideas in her head, Delilah; she's remote enough as it is."

But Mary was not listening. Barry had slipped from the room, and presently she followed him. Leila had seen him go, and had looked after him longingly, but of late she had seemed timid in her public demonstrations; it was as if she felt when she was under the eye of others that by some sign or look she might betray her secret.

Mary found Barry down-stairs in the little office, his head in his hands.

"Dear boy," she said, and touched his bright hair with hesitating fingers.

He reached up and caught her hand.

"Mary," he said, brokenly, "what's the use? I began wrong— and I guess I'll go on wrong to the end."

And now she spoke with earnestness, both hands on his shoulders.

"Oh, Barry, boy—if you fight, fight with all your weapons. And don't let the wrong thoughts go on molding you into the wrong thing. If you think you are going to fail, you'll fail. But if you think of yourself as conquering, triumphant—if you think of yourself as coming back to Leila, victorious, why you'll come that way; you'll come strong and radiant, a man among men, Barry."

It was this convincing optimism of Mary Ballard's which brought to weaker natures a sense of actual achievement. To hear Mary say, "You can do it," was to believe in one's own powers. For the first time in his life Barry felt it. Hitherto, Mary had seemed rather worrying when it came to rules of conduct—rather unreasonable in her demands upon him. But now he was caught up on the wings of her belief in him.

"Do you think I can?" a light had leaped into his tired eyes.

"I know you can, dear boy," she bent and kissed him.

"You'll take care of Leila," he begged, and then, very low, "I'm afraid I've made an awful mess of things, Mary."

"You mustn't think of that—just think, Barry—of the day when you come back! How all the wedding bells will ring!"

But he thought of a wedding where there had been no bells. He thought of Little-Lovely Leila, in her yellow gown on the night of the mad March moon.

"You'll take care of her," he said again, and Mary promised.

And now the Bishop arrived, and certain old friends of the family. As Barry and Mary made their way up-stairs, they met Susan with the mail. There was one long letter for Mary, which she tore open with eagerness, glanced at it, and tucked it into her girdle, then went on with winged feet.

Porter, glancing at her as she came in, was struck by the radiance of her aspect. How lovely she was with that flush on her cheek, and with her sweet shining eyes!

With due formality and with the proper number of godfathers and godmothers, little Mary-Constance Ballard Richardson was officially named.

During the ceremony, Leila sat by her father's side, her hand in his. In these days the child clung to the strong old soldier. When she had come back to consciousness on the night that she had fainted on the threshold of the library, he had asked, "My darling, what is it?"

And she had cried, "Oh, Dad, Dad," and had wept in his arms. But she had not told him that she was Barry's wife. It was because of Barry's going, she had admitted; it seemed as if her heart would break.

The General talked the situation over with Mary. "How will she stand it, when he is really gone?"

"It will be better when the parting is over, and she settles down to other things."

Yet that day, after the christening, Mary wondered if what she had said was true. What would life hold for Leila when Barry was gone?

Her own life without Roger Poole was blank. Reluctantly, she was forced to admit it. Constance, the baby, Porter, these were the shadows, Roger was the substance.

The letters which had passed between them had shown her depths in him which had hitherto been unrevealed. Comparing him with Porter Bigelow, she realized that Porter could never say the things which Roger said; he could not think them.

And while in the eyes of the world Roger was a defeated man, and Porter a successful one, yet there was this to think of, that Porter's qualities were negative rather than positive. With all of his opportunities, he was narrowing his life to the pursuit of pleasure and his love for her. Roger had shirked responsibility toward his fellow man by withdrawal; Porter was shirking by indifference.

So she found herself, as many another woman has found herself, fighting the battle of the less fortunate. Roger wanted her, yet pressed no claim. Porter wanted her and meant to have her.

He had shown of late his impatience at the restraint which she had put upon him. He had encroached more and more upon her time—demanded more and more. He had been kept from saying the things which she did not want him to say only by the fact that she would not listen.

She knew that he was expecting things which could never be—and that by her silence she was giving sanction to his expectations. Yet she found herself dreading to say the final word which would send him from her.

The friendship between a man and a woman has this poignant quality—it has no assurance of permanence. For, if either marries, the other must suffer loss; if either loves, the other must put away that which may have become a prized association. As her friend, Mary valued Porter highly. She had known him all her life. Yet she was aware that she was taking all and returning nothing; and surely Porter had the right to ask of life something more than that.

She sighed, and going to her desk, took out of it the letter which she had received in the morning mail.

She knew that the moment that she announced the contents of that letter would be a dramatic one. Even if she did it quietly, it would have the effect of a bomb thrown into the midst of a peaceful circle. She had a fancy that it would be best to tell Porter first. He was to come back to dinner, so she dressed and went down early.

He found her in the garden. There were double rows of hyacinths in the paths now, with tulips coming up between, and beyond the fountain was an amethyst sky where the young moon showed.

She rose to greet him, her hands full of fragrant blossoms.

He held her hand tightly. "How happy you look, Mary."

"I am happy."

"Because I'm here? If you could only say that once truthfully."

"It is always good to have you,"

"But you won't tell a lie, and say you're happier, because of my coming? Oh, Contrary Mary!"

She shook her head. "If I said nice things to you, you'd misunderstand."

"Perhaps. But why this radiance?"

"Good news."

"From whom?"

"A man."

"What man?" with rising jealousy.

"One who has given me the thing I want."

He was plainly puzzled.

"I don't know what you mean."

"A letter came this morning—a lovely letter in a long envelope."

She took a paper out of a magazine which lay on the stone bench by her side. "Read that," she said.

He read and his face went perfectly white, so that it showed chalkily beneath his red hair.

"Mary," he said, "what have you done this for? You know I'm not going to let you."

"You haven't anything to do with it."

"But I have. It is ridiculous. You don't know what you are doing. You've never been tied to an office desk—you've never fought and struggled with the world."

"Neither have you, Porter."

"Well, if I haven't, is it my fault?" he demanded, "I was born into the world with this millstone of money around my neck, and a red head. Dad sent me to school and to college, and he set me up in business. There wasn't anything left for me to do but to keep straight, and I've done that for you."

"I know," she was very sweet as she leaned toward him, "but, Porter, sometimes, lately, I've wondered if that's all that is expected of us."

"All? What do you mean?"

"Aren't we expected to do something for others?"

"What others?"

She wanted to tell him about Roger Poole and the boy in the pines. Her eyes glowed. But her lips were silent.

"What others, Mary?"

"The people who aren't as fortunate as we are."

"What people?"

Mary was somewhat vague. "The people who need us—to help."

"Marry me, and you can be Lady Bountiful—dispensing charity."

"It isn't exactly charity." She had again the vision of Roger Poole and the boy. "People don't just want our money—they want us to—understand."

He was not following her. "To think that you should want to go out in the world—to work. Tell me why you are doing it."

"Because I need an outlet for my energies—the girl of limited income in these days is as ineffective as a jellyfish, if she hasn't some occupation."

"You could never be a jellyfish. Mary, listen, listen. I need you, dear. I've kept still for a year—Mary!"

"Porter, I can't."

And now he asked a question which had smouldered long in his breast.

"Is there any one else?"

Was there? Her thoughts leaped at once to Roger. What did he mean to her? What could he ever mean? He had said himself that he could expect nothing. Perhaps he had meant that she must expect nothing.

"Mary, is it—Roger Poole?"

Her eyes came up to meet his; they were like stars. "Porter, I don't—know."

He took the blow in silence. The shadows were on them now. In all the beauty of the May twilight, the little bronze boy grinned at love and at life.

"Has he asked you, Mary?"

"No. I'm not sure that he wants to marry me—I'm not sure that I want to marry him—I only know that he is different." It was like Mary to put it thus, frankly.

"No man could know you without wanting to marry you. But what has he to offer you—oh, it is preposterous."

She faced him, flaming. "It isn't preposterous, Porter. What has any man to offer any woman except his love? Oh, I know you men—you think because you have money—but if—if—both of you loved me—you'd stand before me on your merits as men—there would be nothing else in it for me but that."

"I know. And I'm willing to stand on my merits." The temper which belonged to Porter's red head was asserting itself. "I'm willing to stand on my merits. I offer you a past which is clean—a future of devotion. It's worth something, Mary—in the years to come when you know more of men, you'll understand that it is worth something."

"I know," she said, her hand on his, "it is worth a great deal. But I don't want to marry anybody." It was the old cry reiterated. "I want to live the life I have planned for a little while—then if Love claims me, it must be *love*—not just a comfortable getting a home for myself along the lines of least resistance. I want to work and earn, and know that I can do it. If I were to marry you, it would be just because I couldn't see any other way out of my difficulties, and you wouldn't want me that way, Porter."

He did want her. But he recognized the futility of wanting her. For a little while, at least, he must let her have her way. Indeed, she would have it, whether he let her or not. But Roger Poole should not have her. He should not. All that was primitive in Porter rose to combat the claims which she made for his rival.

"I knew there'd be trouble when you let the Tower Rooms," he said heavily at last; "a man like that always appeals to a girl's sense of romance."

The Tower Rooms! Mary saw Roger as he had stood in them for the first time amid all the confusion of Constance's flight from the home nest. That night he had seemed to her merely a person who would pay the rent—yet the money which she had received from him had been the smallest part.

She drifted away on the tide of her dreams, and Porter felt

sharply the sense of her utter detachment from him.

"Mary," he said, tensely, "Mary, oh, my little Contrary Mary—you aren't going to slip out of my life. Say that you won't."

"I'm not slipping away from you," she said, "any more than I am slipping away from my old self. I don't understand it, Porter. I only know that what you call contrariness is a force within me which I can't control. I wish that I could do the things which you want me to do, I wish I could be what Gordon and Constance and Barry and even Aunt Frances want—but there's something which carries me on and on, and seems to say, 'There's more than this in the world for you'— and with that call in my ears, I have to follow."

He rose, and his head was up. "All my life, I have wanted just one thing which has been denied me—and that one thing is you. And no other man shall take you from me. I suppose I've got to set myself another season of patience. But I can wait, because in the end I shall get what I want—remember that, Mary."

"Don't be too sure, Porter."

"I am so sure," lifting the hand which was weighted with the heavy ring, "I am so sure, that I will make a wager with fortune, that the day will come when this ring shall be our betrothal ring, I'll give you others, Mary, but this shall be the one which shall bind you to me."

She snatched her hand away. "You speak as if you were— sure," she said.

"I am. I'm going to let you work and do as you please for a little while, if you must. But in the end I'm going to marry you, Mary."

At dinner Mary announced the contents of her letter in the

long envelope. "I have received my appointment as stenographer in the Treasury, and I'm to report for duty on the twentieth."

It was Aunt Frances who recovered first from the shock. "Well, if you were my child—"

Grace, with little points of light in her eyes, spoke smoothly, "If Mary were your child, she would be as dutiful as I am, mother. But you see she isn't your child."

Aunt Frances snorted—"Dutiful."

Gordon was glowering. "It is rank foolishness."

Mary flared. "That's your point of view, Gordon. You judge me by Constance. But Constance has always been feminine and sweet—and I've never been particularly feminine, nor particularly sweet."

Barry followed up her defense. "I guess Mary knows how to take care of herself, Gordon."

"No woman knows how to take care of herself," Gordon was obstinate, "when it comes to the fight with economic conditions. I should hate to think of Constance trying to earn a living."

"Gordon, dear," Constance's voice appealed, "I couldn't—but Mary can—only I hate to see her do it."

"I don't," said Grace, stoutly. "I envy her."

Aunt Frances fixed her daughter with a stern eye. "Don't encourage her in her foolishness, Grace," she said; "each of you should marry and settle down with some nice man."

"But what man, mother?" Grace, leaning forward, put the question, with an irritating air of doubt.

"There are a half dozen of them waiting."

"Nice boys! But a man. Find me one, mother, and I'll marry him."

"The trouble with you and Mary," Porter informed her, "is that you don't want a man. You want a hero."

Grace nodded. "With a helmet and plume, and riding on a steed—that's my dream—but mother refuses to let me wander in Arcady where such knights are found."

"I think," Constance remarked happily, "that now and then they are found in every-day life, only you and Mary won't recognize them."

From the other side her husband smiled at her. "She thinks I'm one," he said, and his fine young face was suffused by faint color. "She thinks I'm one. I hope none of you will ever undeceive her."

Under the table Leila's little hand was slipped into Barry's big one. She could not proclaim to the world that she had found her knight, and loved him.

Aunt Frances, very stiff and straight in her jetted dinner gown, resumed, "I wish it were possible to give girls a dose of common sense, as you give them cough syrup."

"*Mother!*"

But Aunt Frances, mounted on her grievance, rode it through the salad course. She had wanted Grace to marry—her beauty and her family had entitled her to an excellent match. But Grace was single still, holding her own against all her mother's arguments, maintaining in this one thing her right to independent action.

Isabelle, straining her ears to hear what it was all about, asked

Mary, late that night, "What upset Frances at dinner?"

Mary told her.

"Do you think I'm wrong, Aunt Isabelle?" she asked.

The gentle lady sighed, "If you feel that it is right, it must be right for you. But you're trying to be all head, dear child. And there's your heart to reckon with."

Mary flushed "I know. But I don't want my heart to speak— yet."

Aunt Isabelle patted her hand. "I think it has—spoken," she said softly.

Mary clung to her. "How did you know?"

"We who have dull ears have often clear eyes—it is one of our compensations, Mary."

CHAPTER XVII

In Which an Artist Finds What All His Life He Has Been Looking For; and in Which He Speaks of a Little Saint in Red.

It might have been by chance that Delilah Jeliffe driving in her electric through a broad avenue on the afternoon following the christening of Constance's baby, met Porter Bigelow, and invited him to go home with her for a cup of tea.

There were certain things which Delilah wanted of Porter. Perhaps she wanted more than she would ever get. But to-day she had it in her mind to find out if he would go with her to the White House garden party.

Colin Quale was little and blond. Because of his genius, his presence had added distinction to her entrances and exits. But at the coming function, she knew that she needed more than the prestige of genius—among the group of distinguished guests who would attend, the initial impression would mean much. Porter's almost stiff stateliness would match the gown she was to wear. His position, socially, was impregnable; he had wealth, and youth, and charm. He would, in other words, make a perfectly correct background for the picture which she designed to make of herself.

The old house at Georgetown, to which they came finally, was set back among certain blossoming shrubs and bushes. A row of tulips flamed on each side of the walk. Small and formal cedars pointed their spired heads toward the spring sky.

In the door, as they ascended the steps, appeared Colin Quale.

"Come in," he said, "come in at once. I want you to see what I have done for you."

He spoke directly to Delilah. It was doubtful if he saw Porter. He was blind to everything except the fact that his genius had designed for Delilah Jeliffe a costume which would make her fame and his.

They followed him through the wide hall to the back porch in which he had set up his easel. There, where a flowering almond bush flung its branches against a background of green, he had worked out his idea.

A water-color sketch on the easel showed a girl in white—a girl who might have been a queen or an empress. Her gown partook of the prevailing mode, but not slavishly. There was distinction in it, and color here and there, which Colin explained.

"It must be of sheer white, with many flowing flounces, and with faint pink underneath like the almond bloom. And there must be a bit of heavenly blue in the hat, and a knot of green at the girdle—and a veil flung back—you see?—there'll be sky and field and flowers and a white cloud—all the delicate color and bloom—"

Still explaining, he was at last induced to leave the picture, and have tea. While Delilah poured, Porter watched the two, interested and diverted by enthusiasms which seemed to him somewhat puerile for a man who could do real things in the world of art.

Yet he saw that Delilah took the little man very seriously, that she hung on his words of advice, and that she was obedient to his demands upon her.

"She'll marry him some day," he said to himself, and Delilah seemed to divine his thought, for when at last Colin had rushed back to his sketch, she settled herself in her low chair, and told Porter of their first meeting.

"I'll begin at the beginning," she said; "it is almost too funny to be true, and it could not possibly have happened to any one but me and Colin.

"It was last summer when I was on the North Shore. Father and I stayed at a big hotel, but I was crazy to get acquainted with the cottage colony.

"But somehow I didn't seem to make good—you see that was in my crude days when I wanted to be a cubist picture instead of a daguerreotype. I liked to be startling, and thought that to attract attention was to attract friends—but I found that I did not attract them.

"One night in August there was a big dance on at one of the hotels, and I wanted a gown which should outshine all the others—the ball was to be given for the benefit of a local chanty, and all the cottage colony would attend. I sent an order for a gown to my dressmaker, and she shipped out a strange and wonderful creation. It was an imported affair—you know the kind—with a bodice of a string of jet and a wisp of lace—with a tulle tunic, and a skirt of gold brocade that was so tight about my feet that it had the effect of Turkish trousers. For my head she sent a strip of gold gauze which was to be swathed around and around my hair in a sort of nun's coif, so that only a little knot could show at the back and practically none in front. It was the last cry in fashions. It made me look like a dream from the Arabian Nights, and I liked it."

She laughed, and, in spite of himself, Porter laughed with her.

"I wore it to the dance, and it was there that I met Colin Quale. I wish I could make you see the scene—the great ballroom, and all the other women staring at me as I came in—and the men, smiling.

"I was in my element. I thought, in those days, that the test of charm was to hold the eyes of the multitude. To-day I know that it is to hold the eyes of the elect, and it is Colin who has taught me.

"I had danced with a dozen other men when he came up to claim me. I scarcely remembered that I had promised him a dance. When he was presented to me I had only been aware of a pale little man with eye-glasses and nervous hands who had stared at me rather too steadily.

"We danced in silence for several minutes and he danced divinely.

"He stopped suddenly. 'Let's get out of here,' he said. 'I want to talk to you.'

"I looked at him in amazement. 'But I want to dance.'

"'You can always dance,' he said, quietly, 'but you cannot always talk to me.'"

"There was nothing in his manner to indicate the preliminaries of a flirtation. He was perfectly serious and he evidently thought that he was offering me a privilege. Curiosity made me follow him, and he led the way down the hall to a secluded reception room where there was a long mirror, a little table, and a big bunch of old-fashioned roses in a bowl.

"On our way we passed a row of chairs, where some one had left a wrap and a scarf. Colin snatched up the scarf—it was a long wide one of white chiffon. The next morning I returned it to him, and he found the owner. I am not sure what explanation he made for his theft, but it was undoubtedly attributed to the eccentricities of genius!

"Well, when, as I said, we reached the little room, he pulled a chair forward for me, so that I sat directly in front of the mirror.

"I remember that I surveyed myself complacently. To my deluded eyes, my appearance could not be improved. My head, swathed in its golden coif, seemed to give the final perfect touch."

She laughed again at the memory, and Porter found himself immensely amused. She had such a cool way of turning her mental processes inside out and holding them up for others to see.

"As I sat there, stealing glances at myself, I became conscious that my little blond man was studying me. Other men had looked at me, but never with such a cold, calculating gaze— and when he spoke to me, I nearly jumped out of my shoes— his voice was crisp, incisive.

"'Take it off,' he said, and touched the gauze that tied up my head."

"I gasped. Then I drew myself up in an attempt at haughtiness. But he wasn't impressed a bit."

"'I suppose you know that I am an artist, Miss Jeliffe,' he said, 'and from the moment you came into the room, I haven't had a bit of peace. You're spoiling your type—and it affects me as a chromo would, or a crude crayon portrait, or any other dreadful thing.'

"Do you know how it feels to be called a 'dreadful thing' by a man like that? Well, it simply made me shrivel up and have shivers down my spine.

"'But why?' I stammered."

"'Women like you,' he said, 'belong to the stately, the aristocratic type. You can be a *grande dame* or a duchess—and you are making of yourself—what? A soubrette, with your tango skirt and your strapped slippers, and your hideous head-dress—take it off.'"

"'But I can't take it off,' I said, almost tearfully; 'my hair underneath is—awful.'"

"'It doesn't make any difference about your hair underneath—it can't be worse than it is,' he roared. 'I want to see your coloring—take it off.'"

"And I took it off. My hair was perfectly flat, and as I caught a glimpse of myself in the mirror, I wanted to laugh, to shriek. But Colin Quale was as solemn as an owl. 'Ah,' he said, 'I knew you had a lot of it!'"

"He caught up the scarf which he had borrowed and flung it over my shoulders. He gave a flick of his fingers against my forehead and pulled down a few hairs and parted them. He whisked a little table in front of me, and thrust the bunch of roses into my arms."

"'Now look at yourself,' he commanded."

"I looked and looked again. I had never dreamed that I could be like that. The scarf and the table hid every bit of that Paris gown, and showed just a bit of white throat. My plain parted hair and the roses—I looked," and now Delilah was blushing faintly, "I looked as I had always wanted to look—like the lovely ladies in the old English portraits.

"'Do you like it?' Colin asked."

"He knew that I liked it from my eyes, and for the first time since I had met him, he laughed."

"'All my life,' he said, 'I have been looking for just such a woman as you. A woman to make over—to develop. We must be friends, Miss Jeliffe. You must let me know where I can see you again.'"

"Well, I didn't dance any more that night. I wrapped the scarf about my head, and went back to my hotel. Colin Quale went with me. All the way he talked about the sacredness of beauty. He opened my eyes. I began to see that loveliness should be suggested rather than emphasized. And I have told you this because I want you to understand about Colin. He isn't in love with me. I rather fancy that back home in Amesbury or Newburyport, or whatever town it is that he hails from, there's somebody whom he'll find to marry. To him I am a statue to be molded. I am clay, marble, a tube of paint, a canvas ready for his brush. It was the same way with this old house. He wanted a setting for me, and he couldn't rest until he had found it. He has not only changed my atmosphere, he has changed my manner—I was going to say my morals—he brings to me portraits of Romney ladies and Gainsborough ladies—until I seem positively to swim in a sea of stateliness. And what I said just now about manners and morals is true. A woman lives up to the clothes she wears. If you think this change is on the surface, it isn't. I couldn't talk slang in a Gainsborough hat, and be in keeping, so I don't talk slang; and a perfect lady in a moleskin mantle must have morals to match; so in my little mantle I cannot tell a lie."

To see her with lowered lashes, telling it, was the funniest thing in the world, and Porter shouted. Then her lashes were, for a moment, raised, and the old Delilah peeped out, shrewd, impish.

"He wants me to change my name. No, don't misunderstand me—not my last one. But the first. He says that Delilah smacks of the adventuress. I don't think he is quite sure of the Bible story, but he gets his impressions from grand opera—and he knows that the Delilah of the Samson story wasn't nice—not in a lady-like sense. My middle name is Anne. He likes that better."

"Lady Anne? You'll look the part in that garden party frock he is designing for you."

And now she had reached the question toward which she had been working. "Shall you go?"

He shook his head. "I doubt it. It isn't a function from which one will be missed. And the Ballards won't be there. Mary is going over to New York with Constance for a few days before the sailing. I'm to join them on the final day."

"And you won't go to the garden party without Mary?"

He found himself moved, suddenly, to speak out to her.

"She wouldn't go if she were here—not with me."

"Contrary Mary?" she drawled the words, giving them piquant suggestion.

"It isn't contrariness. Her independence is characteristic. She won't let me do things because she wants to do them by herself. But some day she'll let me do them."

He said it grimly, and Delilah flashed a glance at him, then said carefully, "It would be a pity if she should fancy—Roger Poole."

"She won't."

"You can't tell—pity leads to the softer feeling, you know."

"Why should she pity him?"

"There's his past."

"His past? Roger Poole's? What do you know of it, Delilah?"

As he leaned forward to ask the eager question, he knew that by all the rules of the game he should not be discussing Mary with any one. But he told himself hotly that it was for Mary's good. If things had been hidden, they should be revealed—the sooner the better.

Delilah gave him the details dramatically.

"Then his wife is dead?"

"Yes. But before that the scandal lost him his church. Nobody seems to know much of it all, I fancy. Mary only gave me the outline."

"And she knows?"

"Yes. Roger told her."

"The chances are that there's—another side."

He knew that it was a small thing to say. He would not have said it to any one but Delilah. She would not think him small. To her all things would be fair for a lover.

Before he went, that afternoon, he had promised to go with Delilah to the White House garden party.

Hence a week later there floated within the vision of the celebrities and society folk, gathered together on the spacious lawn of the executive mansion, a lovely lady in faint rose-white, with a touch of heavenly blue in her wide hat, from which floated a veil which half hid her down-drooped eyes.

People began at once to ask, "Who is she?"

When it was discovered that her name was Jeliffe, and that she was not a distinguished personage, it did not matter greatly. There was about her an air of distinction—a certain quiet atmosphere of withdrawal from the common herd which had nothing in it of haughtiness, but which seemed to set her apart.

Porter, following in her wake as she swept across the green, thought of the girl in leopard skins, whose unconventionality had shocked him. Surely in this woman was developed a sense of herself as the center of a picture which was almost uncanny. He found himself contrasting Mary's simplicity and lack of pose.

Mary's presence here to-day would have meant much to a few people who knew and loved her; it would have meant nothing to the crowd who stared at Delilah Jeliffe.

Colin Quale was there to enjoy the full triumph of the transformation. He hovered at a little distance from Delilah, worshiping her for the genius which met and matched his own.

"I shall paint her in that," he said to Porter. "It will be my masterpiece. And if you could have seen her on the night I met her—"

"She told me." Porter was smiling.

"It was like one of the old masters daubed by a novice, or like a room whitewashed over rare carvings—everything was hidden which should have been shown, and everything was shown which should have been hidden. It was monstrous.

"There are few women," he went on, "whom I could make over as I have made her over. They have not the adaptability— the temperament. There was one whom I could have transformed. But I was not allowed. She was little and blonde and the wife of a clergyman; she looked like a saint—and she should have worn straight things of clear green or red, or blue. But she wore black. I've sometimes wondered if she was such a saint as she looked. There was a divorce afterward, I believe, and another man. And she died."

Porter, listening idly, came back. "What type was she?"

"Fra Angelico—to perfection. I should have liked to dress her."

"Did you ever tell her that you wanted to do it?"

"Yes. And she listened. It was then that I gained my impression —that she was not a saint. One night there was a little entertainment at the parish house and I had my way. I made of her an angel, in a red robe with a golden lyre—and I painted her afterward. She used to come to my studio, but I'm not sure that Poole liked it."

"Poole?" Porter was tense.

"Her husband. He could not make her happy."

"Was she—the one in fault?"

Colin shrugged. "There are always two stories. As I have said, she looked like a saint."

"I should like to see—the picture." Porter tried to speak lightly. "May I come up some day to your rooms?"

Colin's face beamed.

"I'm getting into new quarters. I shall want your opinion—call me up before you come."

It was Colin who went home with Delilah in Porter's car. Porter pleaded important business, and walked for an hour around the Speedway, his brain in a whirl.

Then Mary knew—Mary *knew*—and it had made no difference in her thought of Roger Poole!

CHAPTER XVIII

In Which Mary Writes of the Workaday World, and
in Which Roger Writes of the Dreams of a Boy.

In the Tower Rooms—June.

I have been working in the office for a week, and it has been
the hardest week of my life. But please don't think that I have
any regrets—it is only that the world has been so lovely
outside, and that I have been shut in.

I am beginning to understand that the woman in the home has
a freedom which she doesn't sufficiently value. She can run
down-town in the morning; or slip out in the afternoon, or
put off until to-morrow something which should have been
done to-day. But men can't run out or slip away or put off—
no matter if the sun is shining, or the birds singing, or the
wind calling, or the open road leading to adventure.

Yet there are compensations, and I am trying to see them. I am
trying to live up to my theories. And I am sustained by the
thought that at last I am a wage-earner—independent of any
one—capable of buying my own bread and butter, though all
masculine help should fail!

Aunt Isabelle is a dear, and so is Susan Jenks. And that's
another thing to think about. What will the wage-earning part
of the world do, when there are no home-keepers left? If it
were not for Aunt Isabelle and Susan, there wouldn't be any

one to trail after me with cushions for my tired back, and cold things for me to drink on hot days, and hot things to drink on cool days.

I begin to perceive faintly the masculine point of view. If I were a man I should want a wife for just that—to toast my slippers before the fire as they do in the old-fashioned stories, to have my dinner piping hot, and to smooth the wrinkles out of my forehead.

That's why I'm not sure that I should make a comfortable sort of wife. I can't quite see myself toasting the slippers. But I can see Constance toasting them, or Leila—but Grace and I—you see, after all, there are home women and the other kind, and I fancy that I'm the other kind.

This, you'll understand, is a philosophy founded on the vast experience of a week in the workaday world—I'll let you know later of any further modification of my theories.

Well, the house seems empty with just the three of us, and Pittiwitz. I miss Constance beyond words, and the beautiful baby. Constance wanted to name her for me, but Gordon insisted that she should be called after Constance, so they compromised on Mary-Constance, such a long name for such a mite.

We all went to New York to see them off. By "all," I mean our crowd—Aunt Frances and Grace, Leila and the General—oh, poor little Leila—Delilah and Colin Quale, Aunt Isabelle and I, Susan Jenks with the baby in her arms until the very last minute—and Porter Bigelow.

At the boat Leila went all to pieces. I could never have believed that our gay little Leila would have taken anything so hard— and it was pitiful to see Barry. But I can't talk about that—I can't think about it.

Porter was dear to Leila. He treated her as if she were his own little sister, and it was lovely. He took her right away from the General, when the ship was leaving the dock.

"Brace up, little girl," he said; "he'll be back before you know it."

He literally carried her to a taxi and put her in, and then began such a day. We did all of the delightful things that one can do in New York on a summer day, beginning with breakfast at a charming inn on Long Island, and ending with a roof garden at night. And that night Leila was so tired that she went to sleep all in a minute, like a child, and forgot to grieve.

Since we came back to Washington, Porter has kept it up, not letting Leila miss Barry any more than possible, and playing big brother to perfection.

It is queer how we misjudge people. If any one had told me that Porter could be so sweet and tender to anybody, I wouldn't have believed it. But perhaps Leila brings out that side of him. Now I am independent, and aggressive, and I make Porter furious, and most of the time we fight.

As I said, the house seems empty—but I am not in it much now. If I had not had my work, I think I should have gone crazy. That's why men don't get silly and hysterical and morbid like women—they are saved by the day's work. I simply have to forget my troubles while I transcribe my notes on the typewriter.

Of course you know what life in the Departments is without my telling you. But to me it isn't monotonous or machine-like. I am awfully interested in the people. Of course my immediate work is with the nice old Chief. I'm glad he is old, and gray-haired. It makes me feel comfortable and chaperoned. Do you know that I believe the reason that most girls hate to go out to work is because of the loss of protection. You see we home girls are always in the care of somebody. I've been more than usually independent, but there has always been some one to play propriety in the background. When I was a tiny tot there was my nurse. Later at kindergarten I was sent home in a 'bus with all the other babies, and with a nice teacher to see that we arrived safely. Then there was mother and father and Barry and Constance, some of them wherever I went—and finally, Aunt Isabella.

But in the office, I am not Mary Ballard, Daughter of the Home. I am Mary Ballard, Independent Wage-Earner—stenographer at a thousand a year. There's nobody to stand between me and the people I meet. No one to say, "Here is my daughter, a woman of refinement and breeding; behind her I stand ready to hold you accountable for everything you may do to offend her." In the wage-earning world a woman must stand for what she is—and she must set the pace. So, in the office I find that I must have other manners than those in my home. I can't meet men as frankly and freely. I can't laugh with them and talk with them as I would over a cup of tea at my own little table. If you and I had met, for example, in the office, I should have put up a barrier of formality between us, and I should have said, "Good-morning" when I met you and "Good-night" when I left you, and it would have taken us months to know as much about each other as you and I knew after a week in the same house.

I suppose if I live here for years and years, that I shall grow to look upon my gray-haired chief as a sort of official grandfather, and my fellow-clerks will be brothers and sisters by adoption, but that will take time.

I wonder if I shall work for "years and years"? I am not sure that I should like it. And there you have the woman of it. A man knows that his toiling is for life; unless he grows rich and takes to golf. But a woman never looks ahead and says, "This thing I must do until I die." She always has a sense of possible release.

I am not at all sure that I am a logical person. In one breath I am telling you that I like my work; and in the next I am saying that I shouldn't care to do it all my life. But at least there's this for it, that just now it is a heavenly diversion from the worries which would otherwise have weighed.

What did you do about lunches? Mine are as yet an unsolved problem. I like my luncheon nicely set forth on my own mahogany, with the little scalloped linen doilies that we've always used. And I want my own tea and bread and butter and marmalade, and Susan's hot little made-overs. But here I am expected to rush out with the rest, and feast on impossible soups and stews and sandwiches in a restaurant across the way. The only alternative is to bring my lunch in a box, and eat it on my desk. And then I lose the breath of fresh air which I need more than the food.

Oh, these June days! Are they hot with you? Here they are heavenly. When the windows are open, the sweet warm air blows up from the river and across the White Lot, and we get a whiff of roses from the gardens back of the President's house; and when I reach home at night, the fragrance of the roses in our own garden meets me long before I can see the house. We have wonderful roses this year, and the hundred-leaved bush back of the bench by the fountain is like a rosy cloud. I made a crown of them the other day, and put them on the head of the little bronze boy, and I took a picture which I am sending. Somehow the boy of the fountain has always seemed to me to be alive, and to have in him some human quality, like a faun or a dryad.

Last night I sat very late in the garden, and I thought of what you said to me that night when you tried to tell me about your life. Do you remember what you said—that when I came into it, it seemed to you that the garden bloomed? Well, I came across this the other day, in a volume of Ruskin which father gave me, and which somehow I've never cared to read—but now it seems quite wonderful:

"You have heard it said that flowers flourish rightly only in the garden of some one who loves them. I know you would like that to be true; you would think it a pleasant magic if you could flush your flowers into brighter bloom by a kind look upon them; if you could bid the dew fall upon them in the drought, and say to the south wind, 'Come thou south wind and breathe upon my garden that the spices of it may flow forth.' This you would think a great thing. And do you not think it a greater thing that all this you can do for fairer flowers than these—flowers that have eyes like yours and thoughts like yours, and lives like yours; which, once saved, you save forever.

"Will you not go down among them—far among the moorlands and the rocks—far in the darkness of the terrible streets; these feeble florets are lying with all their fresh leaves torn and their stems broken—will you never go down to them, not set them in order in their little fragrant beds, nor fence them in their shuddering from the fierce wind?"

There's a lot more of it—but perhaps you know it. I think I have always done nice little churchly things, and charitable things, but I haven't thought as much, perhaps, about my fellow man and woman as I might. We come to things slowly here in Washington. We are conservative, and we have no great industrial problems, no strikes and unions and things like that. Grace says that there is plenty here to reform, but the squalor doesn't stick right out before your eyes as it does in some of the dreadful tenements in the bigger cities. So we forget—and I have forgotten. Until your letter came about that boy in the pines.

Everything that you tell me about him is like a fairy tale. I can shut my eyes and see you two in that circle of young pines. I can hear your voice ringing in the stillness. You don't tell me of yourself, but I know this, that in that boy you've found an audience—and he is doing things for you while you are doing them for him. You are living once more, aren't you?

And the little sad children. I was so glad to pick out the books with the bright pictures. Weren't the Cinderella illustrations dear? With all the gowns as pink as they could be and the grass as green as green, and the sky as blue as blue. And the yellow frogs in "The frog he would a wooing go," and the Walter Crane illustrations for the little book of songs.

You must make them sing "Oh, What Have You Got for Dinner, Mrs. Bond?" and "Oranges and Lemons" and "Lavender's blue, Diddle-Diddle."

Do you know what Aunt Isabelle is making for the little girls? She is so interested. Such rosy little aprons of pink and white checked gingham—with wide strings to tie behind. And my contribution is pink hair ribbons. Now won't your garden bloom?

You must tell me how their little garden plots come on. Surely that was an inspiration. I told Porter about them the other night, and he said, "For Heaven's sake, who ever heard of beginning with gardens in the education of ignorant children?"

But you and I begin and end with gardens, don't we? Were the seeds all right, and did the bulbs come up? Aunt Isabelle almost cried over your description of the joy on the little faces when the crocuses they had planted appeared.

I am eager to hear more of them, and of you. Oh, yes, and of Cousin Patty. I simply love her.

There's so much more to say, but I mustn't. I must go to bed, and be fresh for my work in the morning.

Ever sincerely,

MARY BALLARD.

Among the Pines.

I shall have to begin at the last of your letter, and work toward the beginning, for it is of my sad children that I must speak first—although my pen is eager to talk about you, and what your letter has meant to me.

The sad children are no longer sad. Against the sand-hills they are like rose petals blown by the wind. Their pink aprons tied in the back with great bows, and the pink ribbons have transformed them, so that, except for their blank eyes, they might be any other little girls in the world.

I have taught them several of the pretty songs; you should hear their piping voices—and with their picture books and their gardens, they are very busy and happy indeed.

Their mother is positively illumined by the change her young folks. Never in her life has she seen any country but this one of charred pines and sand. I find her bending over the Cinderella book, liking it, and liking the children's little gardens.

"We ain't never had no flower garden," she confided to me. "Jim he ain't had time, and I ain't had time, and I ain't never had no luck nohow."

But the boy still means the most to me. And you have found the reason. It isn't what I am doing for him, it is what he is doing for me. If you could see his eyes! They are a boy's eyes now, not those of a little wild animal. He is beginning to read the simple books you sent. We began with "Mother Goose," and I gave him first "The King of France and Forty Thousand Men." The "Oranges and Lemons" song carried on the Dick Whittington atmosphere which he had liked in my poem, with its bells of Old Bailey and Shoreditch. He'll know his London before I get through with him.

But we've struck even a deeper note. One Sunday I was moved to take out with me your father's old Bible. There's a rose between its leaves, kept for a talisman against the blue devils which sometimes get me in their grip. Well, I took the old Bible out to our little amphitheater in the pines, and read, what do you think? Not the Old Testament stories.

I read the Beatitudes, and my boy listened, and when I had finished, he asked, "What is blessed? And who said that?"

I told him, and brought back to myself in the telling the vision of myself as a boy. Oh, how far I have drifted from the dreams of that boy! And if it had not been for you I should never have turned back. And now this boy in the pines, and the boy who was I are learning together, step by step. I am trying to forget the years between. I am trying to take up life where it was before I was overthrown. I can't quite get hold of things yet as a man, for when I try, I feel a man's bitterness. But the boy believes, and I have shut the man in me away, until the boy grows up.

Does this sound fantastic? To whom else would I dare write such a thing, but to you? But you will understand. I feel that I need make no apology.

Coming now to you and your work. I can bring no optimism to bear, I suppose I should say that it is well. But there is in me too much of the primitive masculine for that. When a man cares for a woman he inevitably wants to shield her. But what would you? Shall a man let the thing which he would cherish be buffeted by the winds?

I don't like to think of you in an office, with all your pretty woman instincts curbed to meet the stern formality of such a life. I don't like to think that any chief, however fatherly, shall dictate to you not only letters but rules of conduct. I don't like to think of you as hustled by a crowd at lunch time. I don't like to think of the great stone walls which shut you in. I don't want your wings clipped for such a cage.

And there is this I must say, that all men do not need wives to toast their slippers or to serve their meals piping hot, or even to smooth the wrinkles, although I confess that there's an appeal in this last. Some of us need wives for inspiration, for spiritual and mental uplift, for the word of cheer when our hearts are weary—for the strength which believes in our strength—one doesn't exactly think of Juliet as toasting slippers, or of Rosalind, or of Portia, yet such women never for one moment failed their lovers.

My Cousin Patty says that work will do you good, and we have great arguments. I have told her of you, not everything, because there are some things which are sacred. But I have told her that life for me, since I have known you, has taken on new meanings.

She glories in your independence and wants to know you. Some day, it is written, I am sure, that you two shall meet. In some things you are much alike—in others utterly different, with the differences made by heredity and environment.

My little Cousin Patty is the composite of three generations. Amid her sweets and spices, she is as domestic as her grandmother, but her mind sweeps on to the future of women in a way which makes me gasp.

Politics are the breath of her life. She comes of a long line of statesmen, and having no father or brother or husband to uphold the family traditions of Democracy, she upholds them herself. She is intensely interested just now in the party nominations. A split among the Republicans gives her hope of the election of the Democratic candidate. She's such a feminine little creature with her soft voice and appealing manner, with her big white aprons covering her up, and curling wisps of black hair falling over her little ears, that the contrasts in her life are almost funny. In our evenings over the little white boxes, we mix questions of State Rights and Free Trade with our bridal decorations, and it seems to me that I shall never again go to a wedding without a vision of my little Cousin Patty among her orange blossoms, laying down the law on current politics.

The negro question in Cousin Patty's mind is that of the Southerner of the better class. It isn't these descendants of old families who hate the negro. Such gentlefolk do not, of course, want equality, but they want fair treatment for the weaker race. Find me a white man who raves with rabid prejudice against the black, and I will show you one whose grandfather belonged not to the planter but to the cracker class, or a Northerner grafting on Southern Stock. Even in slave times there was rancor between the black man and what he called "po' white trash" and it still continues.

The picture of the little bronze boy with his crown of roses lies on my desk. I should like much to sit with you on the bench beneath the hundred-leaved bush. What things I should have to say to you! Things which I dare not write, lest you never let me write again.

You glean the best from everything. That you should take my little talk about gardens, and fit it to what Ruskin has said, is a gracious act. You speak of that night in the garden. Do you remember that you wore a scarlet wrap of thin silk? I could think of nothing as you came toward me, but of some glorious flower of almost supernatural bloom. All about you the garden was dying. But you were Life—Life as it springs up afresh from a world that is dead.

I know how empty the old house seems to you, without Barry, without Constance, without the beautiful baby whom I have never seen. To me it can never seem empty with you in it. Is the saying of such things forbidden? Please believe that I don't mean to force them on you, but I write as I think.

By this post Cousin Patty is sending a box of her famous cake, for you and Aunt Isabelle. There's enough for an army, so I shall think of you as dispensing tea in the garden, with your friends about you—lucky friends—and with the little bronze boy looking on and laughing.

To Mary of the Garden, then, this letter goes with all good wishes.

ROGER POOLE.

CHAPTER XIX

In Which Porter Plants an Evil Seed Which Grows and Flourishes; and in Which Ghosts Rise and Confront Mary.

As has been said, Porter Bigelow was not a snob, and he was a gentleman. But even a gentleman can, when swayed by primal emotions, convince himself that high motives rule, even while performing acts of doubtful honor.

It was thus that Porter proved to himself that his interest in Roger Poole's past was purely that of the protector and friend of Mary Ballard. Mary must not throw herself away. Mary must be guarded against the tragedy of marriage with a man who was not worthy. And who could do this better than he?

In pursuance of his policy of protection he took his way one afternoon in July to Colin's studio.

"I'm staying in town," Colin told him, "because of Miss Jeliffe. Her father is held by the long Session. I'm painting another picture of her, and fixing up these rooms in the interim—how do you like them?"

In his furnishing, Colin had broken away from conventional tradition. Here were no rugs hung from balconies, no rich stuffs and suits of armor. It was simply a cool little place, with a big window overlooking one of the parks. Its walls were tinted gray, and there were a few comfortable rattan chairs, with white linen cushions. A portrait of Delilah dominated the room. He had painted her in the costume which she had worn at the garden party—in all the glory of cool greens and faint pink, and heavenly blue.

Porter surveying the portrait said, slowly, "You said that you had painted—other women?"

"Yes—but none so satisfactory as Miss Jeliffe."

"There was the little saint—in red."

"You remember that? It is just a small canvas."

"You said you'd show it to me."

Colin, rummaging in a second room, called back, "I've found it, and here's another, of a woman who seemed to fit in with a Botticelli scheme. She was the long lank type."

Porter was not interested in the Botticelli woman, nor in Colin's experiments. He wanted to see Roger Poole's wife, so he gave scant attention to Colin's enthusiastic comments on the first canvas which he displayed.

"She has the long face. D'you see? And the thin long body. But I couldn't make her a success. That's the joy of Delilah Jeliffe. She has the temperament of an actress and simply lives in her part. But this woman couldn't. And lobster suppers and lovely lank ladies are not synonymous—so I gave her up."

But Porter was reaching for the other sketch.

With it in his hand, he surveyed the small creature with the angel face. In her dress of pure clear red, with the touch of gold in the halo, and a lyre in her hand, she seemed lighted by divine fire, above the earth, appealing.

"I fancy it must have been the man's fault if marriage with

such a wife was a failure," he ventured.

Colin shrugged. "Who can tell?" he said. "There were moments when she did not seem a saint."

"What do you mean?" Porter's voice was almost irritable.

"It is hard to tell," the little artist reflected—"now and then a glance, a word—seemed to give her away."

"You may have misunderstood."

"Perhaps. But men who know women rarely misunderstand—that kind."

"Did you ever hear Roger Poole preach?" Porter asked, abruptly.

"Several times. He promised to be a great man. It was a pity."

"And you say she married again."

"Yes, and died shortly after."

The subject ended there, and Porter went away with the vision in his mind of Roger's wife, and of what the picture of the little saint in red would mean to Mary Ballard if she could see it.

The thought, having lodged like an evil seed, grew and flourished.

Of late he had seen comparatively little of Mary. He was not sure whether she planned deliberately to avoid him, or whether her work really absorbed her. That she wrote to Roger Poole he knew. She did not try to hide the fact, but spoke frankly of Roger's life in the pines.

The flames of his jealous thought burned high and hot. He

refused to go with his father and mother to the northern coast, preferring to stay and swelter in the heat of Washington where he could be near Mary. He grew restless and pale, unlike himself. And he found in Leila a confidante and friend, for the General, like Mr. Jeliffe, was held in town by the late Congress.

Little-Lovely Leila was Little-Lonely Leila now. Yet after her collapse at the boat, she had shown her courage. She had put away childish things and was developing into a steadfast little woman, who busied herself with making her father happy. She watched over him and waited on him. And he who loved her wondered at her unexpected strength, not knowing that she was saying to herself, "I am a wife—not a child. And I mustn't make it hard for father—I mustn't make it hard for anybody. And when Barry comes back I shall be better fitted to share his life if I have learned to be brave."

She wrote to Barry—such cheerful letters, and one of them sent him to Gordon.

"It would have been better if I had brought her with me," he said, as he read extracts; "she's a little thing, Gordon, but she's a wonder. And she's the prop on which I lean."

"Presently you will be the prop," Gordon responded, "and that's what a husband should be, Barry, as you'll find out when you're married."

When!—if Gordon had only known how Barry dreamed of Leila—in her yellow gown, trudging by his side toward the church on the hill—dancing in the moonlight, a primrose swaying on its stem. How unquestioning had been her faith in him! And he must prove himself worthy of that faith.

And he did prove it by a steadiness which astonished Gordon, and by an industry which was almost unnatural, and he wrote to Leila, "I shall show them, dear heart, and then they'll let me have you."

It was on the night after Leila received this letter that Porter came to take her for a ride.

"Ask Mary to go with us," he said; "she won't go with me alone."

Leila's glance was sympathetic. "Did she say she wouldn't?"

"I asked her. And she said she was—tired. As if a ride wouldn't rest her," hotly.

"It would. You let me try her, Porter."

Leila's voice at the telephone was coaxing. "I want to go, Mary, dear, and Dad is busy at the Capitol, and—"

"But I said I wouldn't."

"Porter won't care, just so he gets you. He's at my elbow now, listening. And he says you are to ask Aunt Isabelle, and sit with her on the back seat if you want to be fussy."

"Leila," Porter was protesting, "I didn't say anything of the kind."

She went on regardless, "Well, if he didn't say it he meant it. And we want you, both of us, awfully."

Leila hanging up the receiver shook her head at Porter. "You don't know how to manage Mary. If you'd stay away from her for weeks—and not try to see her—she'd begin to wonder where you were."

"No she wouldn't." Porter's tone was weighted with woe. "She'd simply be glad, and she'd sit in her Tower Rooms and write letters to Roger Poole, and forget that I was on the earth."

It was out now—all his flaming jealousy. Leila stared at him.

"Oh, Porter," she asked, breathlessly, "do you really think that she cares for Roger?"

"I know it."

"Has she told you?"

"Not—exactly. But she hasn't denied it. And he sha'n't have her. She belongs to me, Leila."

Leila sighed. "Oh, why should love affairs always go wrong?"

"Mine shall go right," Porter assured her grimly. "I'm not in this fight to give up, Leila."

When they took Mary in and Aunt Isabelle, Mary insisted that Leila should keep her seat beside Porter. "I'm dead tired," she said, "and I don't want to talk."

And now Porter, aiming strategically for Colin Quale's studio, took them everywhere else but in the direction of his objective point. But at last, after a long ride, they crossed the park which was faced by Colin's rooms.

"Have you seen Delilah's portrait?" Porter asked, casually.

They had not, and he knew it.

"If Colin's in, why not stop?"

They agreed and found Delilah there, and her father. The night was very hot, the room was faintly illumined by a hanging silver lamp in an alcove. From among the shadows, Delilah rose. "Colin is telephoning to the club for lemonades and things," she said; "he'll be back in a minute."

"We came to see your picture," Mary informed her.

"He is painting me again," Delilah said, "in the moonlight,

like this."

She seated herself in the wide window, so that back of her was the silver haze of the glorious night Her dress of thin fine white was unrelieved.

Colin, coming in, set down his tray hastily and hastened to change the pose of her head. "It will be hard to get just the effect I want," he told them. "It must not be hard black and white, but luminous."

"I want them to see the other picture," Porter said.

Colin switched on the lights. "I'll never do better than this," he said.

"Do you like it, Mary?" Delilah asked. "It is the garden party dress."

"I love it," Mary said. "It isn't just the dress, Delilah. It's you. It's so joyous—as if you were expecting much of life."

"I am," Delilah said. "I'm expecting everything."

"And you'll get it," Colin stated. "You won't wait for any one to hand it to you; you'll simply reach out and take it."

Porter's eyes were searching. "Look here, Quale," he said, at last, "do you mind letting us see the others?—that Botticelli woman and the Fra Angelico—they show your versatility."

Colin hesitated. "They are crude beside this."

But Porter insisted. "They're charming. Trot them out, Quale."

So out they came—the picture of the lank lady with the long face, and the picture of the little saint in red.

It was to the girl in red that they gave the most attention.

"How lovely she is," Mary said, "and how sweet."

But Delilah, observing closely, did not agree with her. "I'm not sure. Some women look like that who are little fiends. You haven't shown me this before, Colin. Who was she?"

Colin evaded. "Some one I knew a long time ago."

Porter was shaken inwardly by the thought that the little blond artist was proving himself a gentleman. He would not proclaim to the world what he had told Porter in confidence.

Porter's instincts, however, were purely primitive. He wanted to shout to the housetops, "That's the picture of Roger Poole's wife. Look at her and see how sweet she is. And then decide if she made her own unhappiness."

But he did not shout. He kept silent and watched Mary. She was still studying the picture attentively. "I don't see how you can say that she could be anything but sweet, Delilah. I think it is the face of a truthful child."

Porter's heart leaped. The time would come when he would tell her that the picture of the little trustful child was the picture of Roger Poole's wife. And then—

Colin had turned off the lights again. They sat now among the shadows and drank cool things and ate the marvelous little cakes which were a specialty of the pastry cook around the corner.

"In a week we'll all be away from here," Delilah said. "I wonder why we are so foolish. If it weren't for the fact that we've got the habit, we'd be just as comfortable at home."

"I shall be at home," Mary said. "I'm not entitled yet to a vacation."

"Don't you hate it?" Delilah demanded frankly.

Mary hesitated. "No, I don't. I can't say that I really like it—but it gave me quite a wonderful feeling to open my first pay envelope."

"Women have gone mad," Porter said. "They are deliberately turning away from womanly things to make machines of themselves."

Delilah, taking up the cudgels for Mary, demanded, "Is Mary turning her back on womanly things any more than I? I am making a business of capturing society—Mary is simply holding down her job until Romance butts into her life."

Colin stopped her. "I wish you'd put your twentieth century mind on your mid-Victorian clothes," he said, "and live up to them—in your language."

Delilah laughed. "Well, I told the truth if I didn't do it elegantly. We are both working for things which we want. Mary wants Romance and I want social recognition."

Leila sighed. "It isn't always what we want that we get, is it?" she asked, and Porter answered with decision, "It is not. Life throws us usually brickbats instead of bouquets."

Colin did not agree. "Life gives us sometimes more than we deserve. It has given me that picture of Miss Jeliffe. And I consider that a pretty big slice of good fortune."

"You're a nice boy, Colin," Delilah told him, "and I like you—and I like your philosophy. I fancy life is giving me as much as I deserve."

The others were silent. Life was not giving Leila or Porter or Mary at that moment the things that they wanted. Porter's demands on destiny were definite. He wanted Mary. Leila wanted Barry. Mary did not know what she wanted; she only knew that she was unsatisfied.

Porter took Leila home first, then drove Mary and Aunt Isabelle back through the park to the old house on the hill.

"I'm coming in," he said, as he helped Mary out of the car.

"But it is so late, Porter."

"I've been here lots of times as late as this. I won't be sent home, Mary, not to-night."

Aunt Isabelle, tired and sleepy, went at once up-stairs. Mary sat on the porch with Porter. Below them lay the city in the white moonlight. For a while they were silent, then Porter said, suddenly:

"Mary, there's something I want to tell you. You may think that I'm interfering in your affairs, but I can't help it. I can't see you doing things which will make you unhappy."

"I'm not unhappy. What do you mean, Porter?"

"You will be—if you go on as you are going. Mary—I took you to Colin's to-night on purpose, so that you could see the picture of the little saint in red, the Fra Angelico one."

"Yes."

"You know what you said about her—that she had such a trustful, childish face?"

"Yes."

"That was the picture of Roger Poole's wife, Mary."

She sat as still in her white dress as a marble statue.

At last she asked, "How do you know?"

"Quale told me. I fancy he hadn't heard that Poole had lived here, and that we knew him. So he let the name drop carelessly."

"Well?"

He turned on her flaming. "I know what you mean by that tone, Mary. But you're unjust. You think I've been meddling. But I haven't. It is only this. If Poole could break the heart of one woman, he can break the heart of another—and he sha'n't break yours."

"Who told you that he broke her heart?"

"You've seen the picture. Could a woman with a face like that do anything bad enough to wreck a man's life? I can't believe it, Mary. There are always two sides of a question."

She did not answer at once. Then she said, "How did you know about—Roger?"

"Delilah told me—he couldn't expect to keep it secret."

"He did not expect it; and he had much to bear."

"Then he has told you, and has pleaded with eloquence? But that child's face in the picture pleads with me."

It did plead. Remembering it, Mary was assailed by her first doubts. It was such a child's face, with saint's eyes.

Porter's voice was proceeding. "A man can always make out a case for himself. And you have only his word for what he did. Oh, I suppose you'll think I'm all sorts of a cad to talk this way. But I can't see you drifting, drifting toward a danger which may wreck your life."

"Why should it wreck my life?"

"Because Poole, whatever the merits of the case—doesn't seem to me strong enough to shape his destiny and yours. Was it strong for him to let go as he did, just because that woman failed him? Was it strong for him to hide himself here—like—like a criminal? A strong man would have faced the world. He would have tried to rise out of his wreck. His actions all through spell weakness. I could bear your not marrying me, Mary. But I can't bear to see you marry a man who isn't worthy of you. To see you unhappy would be torture for me."

In his earnestness he had struck a genuine note, and she recognized it.

"I know," she said, unsteadily. "I believe that you think you are fighting my battle, instead of your own. But I don't think Roger Poole would—lie."

"Not consciously. But he'd create the wrong impression—we can never see our own faults—and he would blame her, of course. But the man who has made one woman unhappy would make another unhappy, Mary."

Mary was shaken.

"Please don't put it so—inevitably. Roger hasn't any claim on me whatever."

"Hasn't he? Oh, Mary, hasn't he?"

There was hope in his voice, and she shrank from it.

"No," she said, gently, "he is just—my friend. As yet I can't believe evil of him. But I don't love him. I don't love any body—I don't want any man in my life."

She thought that she meant it. She thought it, even while her heart was crying out in defense of the man he had maligned.

"How can one know the truth of such a thing?" she went on,

unsteadily. "One can only believe in one's friends."

"Mary," eagerly, "you've known Poole only for a few months. You've known me always. I can give you a devotion equal to anybody's. Why not drop all this contrariness—and come to me?"

"Why not?" she asked herself. Roger Poole was obscure, and destined to be obscure. More than that, there would always be people like Porter who would question his past. "It is the whispers that kill," Roger had said. And people would always whisper.

She rose and walked to the end of the porch. Porter followed her, and they stood looking down into the garden. It was in a riot of summer bloom—and the fragrance rushed up to them.

The garden! And herself a flower! It was such things that Roger Poole could say, and which Porter could never say. And he could not say them because he could not think them. The things that Porter thought were commonplace, the things which Roger thought were wonderful. If she married Porter Bigelow, she would walk always with her feet firmly on the ground. If she married Roger Poole they would fly in the upper air together.

"Mary," Porter was insisting, "dear girl."

She held up her hand. "I won't listen," she said, almost passionately; "don't imagine things about me, Porter. I have my work—and my freedom—I won't give them up for anybody."

If she said the words with something less than her former confidence he was not aware of it. How could he know that she was making a last desperate stand?

When at last she sent him away, he went with an air of depression which touched her.

"I've risked being thought a cad," he said, "but I had to do it."

"I know. I don't blame you, dear boy."

She gave him her hand upon it, and he went away, and she was left alone in the moonlight.

And when the last echo of his purring car had died away into silence she went down and sat in the garden on the bench beside the hundred-leaved bush. Aunt Isabelle's light was still burning, and presently she would go up and say "Good-night," but for the moment she must be alone. Alone to face the doubts which were facing her. Suppose, oh, suppose, that the things which Roger had told her about his marriage had been distorted to make his story sound plausible? Suppose the little wife had suffered, had been driven from him by coldness, by cruelty? One never knew the real inner histories of such domestic tragedies. There was Leila, for example, who knew nothing of Barry's faults, and Barry had not told her. Might not other men have faults which they dared not tell? The world was full of just such tragedies.

When at last Mary reached the Tower Rooms, she undressed in the dark. She said her prayers in the dark, out loud, as had been her childish habit. And this was what she said: "Oh, Lord, I want to believe in Roger. Let me believe—don't let me doubt—let me believe."

When at last she slept, it was to dream and wake and to dream again. And waking or dreaming, out of the shadows came ghostly creatures, who whispered, "His little wife was a saint— how could she make him unhappy?" And again, "He may have been cruel, how do you know that he was not cruel?" And again, "If you were his wife, you would be thinking always of that other wife—thinking—thinking—thinking."

CHAPTER XX

In Which Mary Faces the Winter of Her Discontent; and in Which Delilah Sees Things in a Crystal Ball.

The summer slipped by, monotonously hot, languidly humid. And it was on these hot and humid days that Mary felt the grind of her new occupation. She grew to dread her entrance into the square close office room, with its gaunt desks and its unchanging occupants. She waxed restless through the hours of confinement, escaping thankfully at the end of a long day.

She longed for a whiff of the sea, for the deeps of some forest, for the fields of green which must be somewhere beyond the blue-gray haze which had settled over the shimmering city.

She began to show the effects of her unaccustomed drudgery. She grew pale and thin. Aunt Isabelle was worried. The two women sat much by the fountain. Mary had begged Aunt Isabelle to go away to some cooler spot. But the gentle lady had refused.

"This is home to me, my dear," she had said, "and I don't mind the heat. And there's no happiness for me in big hotels."

"There'd be happiness for me anywhere that I could get a breath of coolness," Mary said, restlessly. "I can hardly wait for the fall days."

Yet when the cooler days came, there was the dreariness of rain and of sighing winds. And now it was November, and Roger Poole had been away a year.

The garden was dead, and Mary was glad. Dead gardens seemed to fit into her mood better than those which bloomed. Resolutely she set herself to be cheerful; conscientiously, she told herself that she must live up to the theories which she had professed; sternly, she called herself to account that she did not exult in the freedom which she had craved. Constantly her mind warred with her heart, and her heart won; and she faced the truth that all seasons would be dreary without Roger Poole.

Her letters to him of late had lacked the spontaneity which had at first characterized them. She knew it, and tried to regain her old sense of ease and intimacy. But the doubts which Porter had planted had borne fruit. Always between her and Roger floated the vision of the little saint in red.

It was inevitable that Roger's letters should change. He ceased to show her the side which for a time he had so surprisingly revealed. Their correspondence became perfunctory—intermittent.

"It is my own fault," Mary told herself, yet the knowledge did not make things easier.

And now began the winter of her discontent. If any one had told her in her days of buoyant self-confidence that she would ever go to bed weary and wake up hopeless, she would have scorned the idea; yet the fact remained that the fruit of her independence was Dead Sea apples.

It was a letter from Barry which again brought her head up, and made her life march once more to a martial tune.

"I have found the work for which I am fitted," he wrote; "you don't know how good it seems. For so many years I went to my desk like a boy driven to school. But now—why, I work after hours for the sheer love of it—and because it seems to bring me nearer to Leila."

This from Barry, the dawdler! And she who had preached was whimpering about heat and cold, about long hours and hard work—as if these things matter!

Why, life was a Great Adventure, and she had forgotten!

And now she began to look about her—to find, if she could, some ray to illumine her workaday world.

She found it in the friendliness and companionship of her office comrades—good comrades they were—fighting the battle of drudgery shoulder to shoulder, sharing the fortunes of the road, needing, some of them, the uplift of her courage, giving some of them more than they asked.

As Mary grew into their lives, she grew away somewhat from her old crowd. And if, at times, her gallant fight seemed futile—if at times she could not still the cry of her heart, it was because she was a woman, made to be loved, fitted for finer things and truer things than writing cabalistic signs on a tablet and transcribing them, later, on the typewriter.

Leila had refused to be dropped from Mary's life. She came, whenever she could, to walk a part of the way home with her friend, and the two girls would board a car and ride to the edge of the town, preferring to tramp along the edges of the Soldiers' Home or through the Park to the more formal promenade through the city streets.

It was during these little adventures that Mary became conscious of certain reserves in the younger girl. She was closely confidential, yet the open frankness of the old days was gone.

Once Mary spoke of it. "You've grown up, all in a minute, Leila," she said. "You're such a quiet little mouse."

Leila sighed. "There's so much to think about."

Watching her, Mary decided. "It is harder for her than for Barry. He has his work. But she just waits and longs for him."

In waiting and longing, Little-Lovely Leila grew more mouse-like than ever. And at last Mary spoke to the General. "She needs a change."

He nodded. "I know it. I am thinking of taking her over in the spring."

"How lovely. Have you told her?"

"No—I thought it would be a grand surprise."

"Tell her now, dear General. She needs to look forward."

So the General, who had been kept in the house nearly all winter by his rheumatism, spoke of certain baths in Germany.

"I thought I'd go over and try them," he informed his small daughter, on the day after his talk with Mary, "and you could stop and call on Barry."

"Barry!" She made a little rush toward him. "Dad, *Dad*, do you mean it?"

"Yes."

She tucked her head into his shoulder and cried for happiness. "Dad, I've missed him so."

With this hope held out to her, Little-Lovely Leila grew radiant. Once more her feet danced along the halls, and the music of her voice trilled bird-like in the big rooms.

Delilah, discussing it with her artist, said: "Leila makes me believe in Romance with a big R. But I couldn't love like that."

Colin smiled. "You'd love like a lioness. I've subdued you outwardly, but within you are still primitive."

"I wonder—" Delilah mused.

"The man for you," Colin turned to her suddenly, "is Porter Bigelow. Of course I'm taking it from the artist's point of view. You're made for each other—a pair of young gods—his red head just topping your black one—It was that way at the garden party; any one could see it."

Delilah laughed. "His eyes aren't for me. With him it is Mary Ballard. If I were in love with him, I should hate Mary. But I don't; I love her. And she's in love with Roger Poole."

Colin looked up from the samples from which he and Delilah were choosing her spring wardrobe.

"Poole? I knew his wife," he said abruptly; "it was her picture that I showed you the other night—the little saint in the Fra Angelico pose—it didn't come to me until afterward that he might be the same Poole of whom I had heard you speak."

Delilah swept across the room, and turned the canvas outward. "Roger Poole's wife," she said, "of all things!" Then she stood staring silently.

"You didn't tell us who she was."

"No," he was weighing mentally Porter's attitude in the matter, "no one knew but Bigelow."

"And he showed this to Mary?" They looked at each other, and laughed. "Perhaps all's fair in love," Delilah murmured, at last, "but I wouldn't have believed it of him."

As she turned the picture toward the wall, Delilah decided, "Mary Ballard is worth a hundred of such women as this."

"A woman like you is worth a hundred of them," Colin stated deliberately.

Delilah flushed faintly. Colin Quale was giving to her something which no other man had given. And she liked it.

"Do you know what you are doing to me?" she said, as she sat down by the window. "You are making me think that I am like the pictures you paint of me."

"You are," was the quiet response; "it's just a matter of getting beneath the surface."

There was a pause during which his fingers and eyes were busy with the shining samples—then Delilah said: "If Leila and her father go to Germany in May, I'm going to get Dad to go too. I don't suppose you'd care to join us? You'll want to get back to that girl in Amesbury or Newburyport, or whatever it is."

"What girl?"

"The one you are going to marry."

"There is no girl," said Colin quietly, "in Amesbury or Newburyport; there never has been and there never will be." Coming close, he held against her cheek a sample of soft pale yellow. "Leila Dick wears that a lot, but it's not for you." He stood back and gazed at her meditatively.

"Colin," she protested, "when you look at me that way, I feel like a wooden model."

He smiled, "That's what you have come to mean to me," he said; "I don't want to think of you as a woman."

"Why not?" asked daring Delilah.

"Because it is, to say the least, disturbing."

He occupied himself with his samples, shaking his head over them.

"None of these will do for the Secretary's dinner. You must have lace with many flounces caught up in the new fashion. And I shall want your hair different. Take it down."

She was used to him now, and presently it fell about her in all its shining sable beauty; and as he separated the strands, it was like a thing alive under his hands.

He crowned her head with the braids in a sort of old-fashioned coronet. And so arranged, the old fashion became a new fashion, and Delilah was like a queen.

"You see—with the lace and your pearl ornaments. There is nothing startling; but no one will be like you."

And there was no one like her. And because of the dress, which Colin had planned, and because of the way which he had taught her to do her hair, Delilah annexed to her train of admirers on the night of the Secretary's dinner a distinguished titled gentleman, who was looking for a wife to grace his ancestral halls—and who was impressed mightily by the fact that Delilah looked the part to perfection.

He proposed to her in three weeks, and was so sure of his ability to get what he wanted that he was stunned by her answer:

"Perhaps I'll make up my mind to it. I'll give you your answer when I come over in the spring."

"But I want my answer now."

"I'm sorry. But I can't."

When she told Colin of her abrupt dismissal of the discomfited gentleman, she asked, almost plaintively, "Why couldn't I say 'yes' at once? It is the thing I've always wanted."

"Have you really wanted it?"

"Of course."

"Not of course. You want other things more."

"What for example?"

"I think you know."

She did know, and she drew a quick breath. Then laughed.

"You're trying to teach me to understand my—emotions, Colin, as you have taught me to understand my clothes."

"You're an apt pupil."

Tea came in, just then, and she poured for him, telling his fortune afterward in his teacup.

"Are you superstitious?" she asked him, having worked out a future of conventional happiness and success.

"Not enough to believe what you have told me." He was flickering his pale lashes and smiling. "Life shall bring me what I want because I shall make it come."

"Oh, you think that?"

"Yes. All things are possible to those of us who believe they are possible."

"Perhaps to a man. But—to a woman. There's Leila, for example. I'm afraid—"

"You mustn't be. Life will come right for her."

"How do you know?"

"It comes right for all of us, in one way or another. You'll find it works out. You're afraid for your little friend because of Ballard—he's pretty gay, eh?"

"Yes. More, I think, than she understands. But everybody else knows that they sent him away for that. And I can't see any way out. If he marries her he'll break her heart; if he doesn't marry her he'll break it—and there you have it."

"You must not put these 'ifs' in their way. There'll be some way out."

She rose and went to a table to a little cabinet which she unlocked.

"You wouldn't let me have my crystal ball in evidence," she said, "because it doesn't fit in with the rest of my new furnishings—but it tells things."

"What things?"

"I'll show you." She set it on the table between them. "Put your hand on each side of it."

He grasped it with his flexible fingers. "Don't invent—" he warned.

She began to speak slowly, and she was still at it when Porter's big car drove up to the door, and he came in with Mary and Leila.

"I picked up these two on their way home," Porter explained; "it is raining pitchforks, and I'm in my open car. And so, kind lady, dear lady, will you give us tea?"

Colin and Delilah, each a little pale, breathing quickly, rose to greet their guests.

"She's been telling my fortune," Colin informed them, while Delilah gave orders for more hot water and cups. "It's a queer business."

Porter scoffed. "A fake, if there ever was one."

Colin mused. "Perhaps. But she has the air of a seeress when she says it all—and she has me slated for a—masterpiece—and marriage."

Leila, standing by the table, touched the crystal globe with doubtful fingers. "Do you really see things, Delilah?"

"Sit down, and I'll prove it."

Leila shrank. "Oh, no."

But Porter insisted. "Be a sport, Leila."

So she settled herself in the chair which Colin had occupied, her curly locks half hiding her expectant eyes.

And now Delilah looked, bending over the ball.

There was a long silence. Then Delilah seemed to shake herself, as one shakes off a trance. She pushed the ball away from her with a sudden gesture. "There's nothing," she said, in a stifled voice; "there's really nothing to tell, Leila."

"I knew that you'd back out with all of us here to listen," Porter triumphed.

But Colin saw more than that.

"I think we want our tea," he said, "while it is hot," and he handed Delilah the cups, and busied himself to help her with the sugar and lemon, and to pass the little cakes, and all the time he talked in his pleasant half-cynical, half-earnest fashion, until their minds were carried on to other things.

When at last they had gone, he came back to her quickly.

"What was it?" he asked. "What did you see in the ball?"

She shivered. "It was Barry. Oh, Colin, I don't really believe in it—perhaps it was just my imagination because I am worried about Leila, but I saw Barry looking at me with such a white strange face out of the dark."

CHAPTER XXI

In Which a Little Lady in Black Comes to Washington to Witness the Swearing-in of a Gentleman and a Scholar.

It was in February that Roger wrote somewhat formally to ask if his Cousin Patty might have a room in Mary's big house during the coming inauguration.

"She is supremely happy over the Democratic victory, but in spite of her advanced ideas, she is a timid little thing, and she has no knowledge of big cities. I feel that many difficulties would be avoided if you could take her in. I want her, too, to know you. I had thought at first that I might come with her. But I think not. I am needed here."

He did not say why he was needed. He said little of himself and of his work. And Mary wondered. Had his enthusiasm waned? Was he, after all, swayed by impulse, easily discouraged? Was Porter right, and was Roger's failure in life due not to outside forces, but to weakness within himself?

She wrote him that she should be glad to have Cousin Patty, and it was on the first of March that Cousin Patty came.

Once in four years the capital city takes on a supreme holiday aspect. In other years there may be parades, in other years there may be pageants—it is an every-day affair, indeed, to hear up and down the Avenue the beat of music, and the tramp of many feet. There are funerals of great men, with gun carriages draped with the flag, and with the Marine Band playing the "Dead March." There are gay cavalcades rushing in from Fort Myer, to escort some celebrity; there are pathetic files of black folk, gorgeous in the insignia of some society which gives to its dead members the tribute of a conspicuousness which they have never known in life. There are circus parades, and suffrage parades, minstrel parades and parades of the boys from the high schools—all the display of military and motley by which men advertise their importance and their wares.

But the Inauguration is the one great and grand effort. All work stops for it; all traffic stops for it; all of the policemen in the town patrol it; half the detectives in the country are imported to protect it. All of fashion views it from the stands up-town; all of the underworld gazes at it from the south side of the street down-town. Packed trains bring the people. And the people are crowded into hotels and boarding-houses, and into houses where thresholds are never crossed at any other time by paying guests.

To the inauguration of 1913 was added another element of interest—the parade of the women, on the day preceding the changing of presidents. Hence the red and white and blue of former decorations were enlivened by the yellow and white and purple of the Suffrage colors.

Cousin Patty wore a little knot of yellow ribbon when Porter met her at the station.

Porter was not inclined to welcome any cousin of Roger Poole's with open arms. But he knew his duty to Mary's guests. He had offered his car, and had insisted that Mary should make use of it.

"For Heaven's sake, don't make me utterly miserable by refusing to let me do anything for you, Mary," he had said, when she had protested. "It is the only pleasure I have."

Cousin Patty, in spite of Porter's preconceived prejudices,

made at once a place for herself. She gave him her little bag, and with a sigh of such infinite relief, her eyes like a confiding child's, that he laughed and bent down to her.

"Mary Ballard is in my car outside. I didn't want her to get into this crowd."

Cousin Patty shuddered. "Crowd! I've never seen anything like—the people. I didn't know there were so many in the world. You see, I've never been far away from home. And they kept pouring in from all the stations, and when I reached here and stood on the steps of the Pullman, and saw the masses streaming in ail directions, I felt faint—but the conductor pointed out the way to go, and then I saw your—lovely head."

She said it so sincerely that Porter laughed.

"Miss Carew," he said, "I believe you mean it."

"Mean what?"

"That it's a lovely head."

"It is." The dark eyes were shining. "You were so tall that I could see you above the people, and Roger had described how you would look. Mary Ballard had said you would surely be here to meet me, and now—oh, I'm really in Washington!"

If she had said, "I'm really in Paradise," it could not have expressed more supreme bliss.

"I never expected to be here," Cousin Patty went on to explain, as they crossed the concourse, and Porter guided her through the crowd. "I never expected it. And now Roger's beautiful Mary Ballard has promised to show me everything."

Roger's beautiful Mary Ballard, indeed!

"Miss Ballard," he said, stiffly, "is taking a week off from her work. And she is going to devote it to sightseeing with you."

"Yes, Roger told me. Is that Mary smiling from that big car? Oh, Mary Ballard, I knew you'd be just—like this."

Well, nobody could resist Cousin Patty. There was that in her charming voice, in her vivid personality which set her apart from other middle-aged and well-bred women of her type.

Porter made a wide sweep to take in the Capitol and the Library; then he flew up the Avenue, disfigured now by the stands from which people were to view the parade.

But Cousin Patty's eyes went beyond the stand to the tall straight shaft of the Monument in the distance, and when they passed the White House, she simply settled back in her seat and sighed.

"To think that, after all these years, there'll be a gentleman and a scholar to live there."

"There have been other scholars—and gentlemen," Mary reminded her.

"Of course, my dear. But this is different. You see, in our section of the country a Republican is just a—Republican. And a Democrat is a—gentleman."

Mary's eyes were dancing. "Cousin Patty," she said, "may I call you Cousin Patty? What will you do when women vote? Will the women who are Republicans be ladies?"

"Oh, now you are laughing at me," Cousin Patty said, helplessly.

Mary gave Cousin Patty the suite next to Aunt Isabelle's, and the two gentle ladies smiled and kissed in the fashion of their time, and became friends at once.

When Cousin Patty had unpacked her bag, and had put all of her nice little belongings away, she tripped across the threshold of the door between the two rooms, to talk to Aunt Isabelle.

"Mary said that we should be going to the theater to-night with Mr. Bigelow. You must tell me what to wear, please. You see I've been out of the world so long."

"But you are more of it than I," Aunt Isabelle reminded her.

Cousin Patty, in her pretty wrapper, sat down in a rocking-chair comfortably to discuss it. "What do you mean?"

"Mary has been telling me how far ahead of me your thoughts have flown. You're taking up all the new questions, and you're a successful woman of business. I have envied you ever since I heard about the wedding cake."

"It's a good business," said Cousin Patty, "and I can do it at home. I couldn't have gone out in the world to make my fight for a living. I can defy men in theory; but I'm really Southern and feminine—if you know what that means," she laughed happily. "Of course I never let them know it, not even Roger."

And now Mary came in, lovely in her white dinner gown.

"Oh," she accused them, "you aren't ready."

Cousin Patty rose. "I wanted to know what to wear, and we've talked an hour, and haven't said a word about it."

"Don't bother," Mary said; "there'll be just four of us."

"But I want to bother. Roger helped me to plan my things. He remembered every single dress you wore while he was here."

"Really?" The look which Roger had loved was creeping into Mary's clear eyes. "Really, Cousin Patty?"

"Yes. He drew a sketch of your velvet wrap with the fur, and I made mine like it, only I put a frill in place of the fur." She trotted into her room and brought it back for Mary's inspection. "Is it all right?" she asked, anxiously, as she slipped it on, and craned her neck in front of Aunt Isabelle's long mirror to see the sweep of the folds.

"It is perfect; and to think he should remember."

Cousin Patty gave her a swift glance. "That isn't all he has remembered," she said, succinctly.

It developed when they went down for dinner that Roger had ordered a box of flowers for them—purple violets for Aunt Isabelle and Cousin Patty, white violets for Mary.

"How lovely," Mary said, bending over the box of sweetness. "I am perfectly sure no one ever sent me white violets before."

There were other flowers—orchids from Porter.

"And now—which will you wear?" demanded sprightly Cousin Patty, an undercurrent of anxiety in her tone.

Mary wore the violets, and Porter gloomed all through the play.

"So my orchids weren't good enough," he said, as she sat beside him on their way to the hotel where they were to have supper.

"They were lovely, Porter."

"But you liked the violets better? Who sent them, Mary?"

"Don't ask in that tone."

"You don't want to tell me."

"It isn't that—it's your manner." She broke off to say pleadingly, "Don't let us quarrel over it. Let me forget for to-night that there's any discord in the world—any work—any worry. Let me be Contrary Mary—happy, care-free, until it all begins over again in the morning."

Very softly she said it, and there were tears in her voice. He glanced down at her in surprise. "Is that the way life looks to you—you poor little thing?"

"Yes, and when you are cross, you make it harder."

Thus, woman-like, she put him in the wrong, and the question of violets vs. orchids was shelved.

Presently, in the great red dining-room, Porter was ordering things for Cousin Patty's delectation of which she had never heard. Her enjoyment of the novelty of it all was refreshing. She tasted and ate and looked about her as frankly as a happy child, yet never, with it all, lost her little air of serene dignity, which set her apart from the flaming, flaring type of femininity which abounds in such places.

The great spectacle of the crowded rooms made a deep impression on Cousin Patty. To her this was no gathering of people who were eating too much and drinking too much, and who were taking from the night the hours which should have been given to sleep. To her it was—fairy-land; all of the women were lovely, all of the men celebrities—and the gold of the lights, the pink of the azaleas which were everywhere in pots, the murmur of voices, the sweet insistence of the music in the balcony, the trail of laughter over it all—these were magical things, which might disappear at any moment, and leave her among her boxes of wedding cake, after the clock struck twelve.

But it did not disappear, and she went home happy and too tired to talk.

At breakfast the next morning, Mary announced their programme for the day.

"Delilah has telephoned that she wants us to have lunch with her at the Capitol. Her father is in Congress, Cousin Patty, and they will show us everything worth seeing. Then we'll go for a ride and have tea somewhere, and the General and Leila have asked us for dinner. Shall you be too tired?"

"Tired?" Cousin Patty's laugh trilled like the song of a bird. "I feel as if I were on wings."

Cousin Patty trod the steps of the historic Capitol with awe. To her these halls of legislation were sacred to the memory of Henry Clay and of Daniel Webster. Every congressman was a Personage—and many a simple man, torn between his desire to serve his constituents, and his need to placate the big interests of his state, would have been touched by the faith of this little Southern lady in his integrity.

"A man couldn't walk through here, with the statues of great men confronting him, and the pictures of other great men looking down on him, and the shades of those who have gone before him haunting the shadows and whispering from the galleries, without feeling that he was uplifted by their influence," she whispered to Mary, as from the Member's Gallery she gazed down at the languid gentlemen who lounged in their seats and listened with blank faces to one of their number who was speaking against time.

Colin Quale, who lunched with them, was delighted with her.

"She is an example of what I've been trying to show you," he said to Delilah. "She is so well bred that she absolutely lacks self-consciousness, and she is so clear-minded that you can't muddy her thoughts with scandals of this naughty world. She is a type worthy of your study."

"Colin," Delilah questioned, with a funny little smile, "is this a 'back to grandma' movement that you are planning for me?"

The pale little man flickered his blond lashes, but his face was grave.

"No," he said, "but I want you to be abreast of the times. There's going to be a reaction from this reign of the bizarre. We've gone long enough to harems and odalisques for our styles and our manners and presently we are going to see the blossoming of old-fashioned beauty."

"And do you think the old manners and morals will come?"

He shrugged. "Who knows? We can only hope."

It was to Colin that Cousin Patty spoke confidingly of her admiration of Delilah. "She's beautiful," she said. "Mary says that you plan her dresses. I never thought that a man could do such things until Roger took such an interest."

"Men of to-day take an interest," Colin said. "Woman's dress is one branch of art. It is worthy of a man's best powers because it adds to the beauty of the world."

"That's the funny part of it," Cousin Patty ventured; "women are taking up men's work, and men are taking up women's—it is all topsy turvy."

The little artist pondered. "Perhaps in the end they'll understand each other better."

"Do you think they will?"

"Yes. The woman who does a man's work learns to know what fighting means. The man who makes a study of feminine things begins to see back of what has seemed mere frivolity and love of admiration a desire for harmony and beauty, and self-expression. Some day women will come back to simplicity and to the home, because they will have learned things from men and will have taught things to men, and by mutual understanding each will choose the best."

Cousin Patty was inspired by the thought. "I never heard any one put it that way before."

"Perhaps not—but I have seen much of the world—and of men—and of women."

"Yet all women are not alike."

"No." His eyes swept the table. "You three—Miss Ballard, Miss Jeliffe—how far apart—yet you're all women—all, I may say, awakened women—refusing to follow the straight and narrow path of the old ideal. Isn't it so?"

"Yes. I'm in business—none of our women has ever been in business. Mary won't marry for a home—yet all of her women have, consciously or unconsciously, married for a home. And Miss Jeliffe I don't know well enough to judge. But I fancy she'll blaze a way for herself."

His eyes rested on Delilah. "She has blazed a way," he said, slowly; "she's a most remarkable woman."

Delilah, looking up, caught his glance and smiled.

"Are they in love with each other?" Cousin Patty asked Mary that night.

Mary laughed. "Delilah's a will-o'-the-wisp; who knows?"

With their days filled, there was little time for intimacy or confidential talks between Mary and Cousin Patty. And since Mary would not ask questions about Roger, and since Cousin Patty seemed to have certain reserves in his direction, it was only meager information which trickled out; and with this Mary was forced to be content.

Grace marched in the Suffrage Parade, and they applauded her from their seats on the Treasury stand. Aunt Frances, who sat with them, was filled with indignation.

"To think that *my* daughter—"

Cousin Patty threw down the gauntlet: "Why not your daughter, Mrs. Clendenning?"

"Because the women of our family have always been—different."

"So have the women of my family," calmly, "but that's no reason why we should expect to stand still. None of the women of my family ever made wedding cake for a living. But that isn't any reason why I should starve, is it?"

Aunt Frances shifted the argument. "But to march—on the street."

"That's their way of expressing themselves. Men march—and have marched since the beginning. Sometimes their marching doesn't mean anything, and sometimes it does. And I'm inclined," said Cousin Patty with an emphatic nod of her head, "to think that this marching means a great deal."

On and on they came, these women who marched for a Cause, heads up, eyes shining. There had been something to bear at the other end of the line where the crowd had pressed in upon them, and there had been no adequate police protection, but they were ready for martyrdom, if need be, perhaps, some of them would even welcome it.

But Grace was no fanatic. She met them afterward, and told of her experience gleefully.

"You should have been with me, Mary," she said.

Porter rose in his wrath. "What has bewitched you women?"

he demanded. "Do you all believe in it?"

And now Leila piped, "I don't want to march. I don't want to do the things that men do. I want to have a nice little house, and cook and sew, and take care of somebody."

They all laughed. But Porter surveyed Leila with satisfaction.

"Barry's a lucky fellow," he said.

"Oh, Porter," Mary reproached him, as he helped her down from her high seat on the stand.

"Well, he is. Leila couldn't keep her nice little house any better than you, Mary. But the thing is that she *wants* to keep it for Barry. And you—you want to march on the street—and laugh—at love."

She surveyed him coldly. "That shows just how much you understand me," she said, and turned her back on him and accepted an invitation to ride home in the Jeliffes' car.

On the day of the Inauguration, the same party had seats on the stand opposite the one in front of the White House from which the President reviewed the troops.

And it was upon the President that Cousin Patty riveted her attention. To be sure her little feet beat time to the music, and she flushed and glowed as the soldiers swept by, and the horses danced, and the people cheered. But above and beyond all these things was the sight of the man, who in her eyes represented the resurrection of the South—the man who should sway it back to its old level in the affairs of the nation.

"I couldn't have dreamed," she emphasized, as she talked it over that night with Mary, "of anything so satisfying as his smile. I shall always think of him as smiling out in that quiet way of his at the people."

Mary had a vision of another Inauguration and of another President who had smiled—a President who had captured the hearts of his countrymen as perhaps this scholar never would. It was at the shrine of that strenuous and smiling President that Mary still worshiped. But they were both great men—it was for the future to tell which would live longest in the hearts of the people.

The two women were in Cousin Patty's room. They were too excited to sleep, for the events of the day had been stimulating. Cousin Patty had suggested that Mary should get into something comfortable, and come back and talk. And Mary had come, in a flowing blue gown with her fair hair in shining braids. They were alone together for the first time since Cousin Patty's arrival. It was a moment for which Mary had waited eagerly, yet now that it had come to her, she hardly knew how to begin.

But when she spoke, it was with an impulsive reaching out of her hands to the older woman.

"Cousin Patty, tell me about Roger Poole."

Cousin Patty hesitated, then asked a question, almost sharply, "My dear, why did you fail him?"

The color flooded Mary's face. "Fail him?" she faltered.

"Yes. When he first came to me, there were your letters. He used to read bits of them aloud, and I could see inspiration in them for him. Then he stopped reading them to me, and they seemed to bring heaviness with them—I can't tell you how unhappy he was until he began to make his work fill his life. Do you mind telling me what made the change in you, my dear?"

Mary gazed into the fire, the blood still in her face.

"Cousin Patty, did you know his wife?"

"Yes. Is it because of her, Mary?"

"Yes. After Roger went away, I saw her picture. Colin had painted it. And, Cousin Patty, it seemed the face of such a little—saint."

"Yet Roger told you his story?"

"Yes."

"And you didn't believe him?"

"Oh, I don't know what to believe."

"I see," but Cousin Patty's manner was remote.

Mary slipped down to the stool at Cousin Patty's feet, and brought her clear eyes to the level of the little lady's. "Dear Cousin Patty," she implored, "if you only know how I *want* to believe in Roger Poole."

Cousin Patty melted. "My dear," she said with decision, "I'm going to tell you everything."

And now woman's heart spoke to woman's heart. "I visited them in the first year of their marriage. I wanted to love his wife, and at first she seemed charming. But I hadn't been there a week before I was puzzling over her. She was made of different clay from Roger. In the intimacy of that home I discovered that she wasn't—a lady—not in our nice old-fashioned sense of good manners, and good morals. She said things that you and I couldn't say, and she did things. I felt the catastrophe in the air long before it came. But I couldn't warn Roger. I just had to let him find out. I wasn't there when the blow fell; but I'll tell you this, that Roger may have been a quixotic idiot in the eyes of the world, but if he failed it was because he was a dreamer, and an idealist, not a coward and a shirk." Her eyes were blazing. "Oh, if you could hear what some people said of him, Mary."

Mary could fancy what they had said.

"Oh, Cousin Patty, Cousin Patty," she cried, "Do you think he will ever forgive me? I have let such people talk to me, and I have listened!"

CHAPTER XXII

In Which the Garden Begins to Bloom;
and in Which Roger Dreams.

March, which brings to the North sharp winds and gray days, brings to the sand-hill country its season of greatest beauty.

Straight up from the unpromising soil springs the green—the pines bud and blossom, everywhere there is the delicate tracery of pale leafage, there is the white of dogwood, the pink of peach trees and of apple bloom, and again the white of cherry trees and of bridal bush. There are amethystine vistas, and emerald vistas, and vistas of rose and saffron—the cardinals burn with a red flame in the magnolias, the mocking-birds sing in the moonlight.

It was through the awakened world that Roger drove one Sunday to preach to his people.

He did not call it preaching. As yet his humility gave it no such important name. He simply went into the sand-hills and talked to those who were eager to hear. Beginning with the boy, he had found that these thirsty souls drank at any spring. The boys listened breathless to his tales of chivalry, the men to his tales of what other men had achieved, the women were reached by stories of what their children might be, and the children rose to his bait of fairy books and of colored pictures.

Gradually he had gone beyond the tales of chivalry and the

achievements of men. Gradually he had brought them up and up. Other men had preached to them, but their preaching had not been linked with lessons of living. Others had cried, "Repent," but not one of them had laid emphasis on the fact that repentance was evidenced by the life which followed.

But Roger stood among them, his young face grave, his wonderful voice persuasive, and told them what it meant to be—saved. Planting hope first in their hearts, he led them toward the Christ-ideal. Manhood, he said, at its best was godlike; one must have purity, energy, education, growth.

And they, who listened, began to see that it was a spiritual as well as practical thing to set their houses in order, to plant and to till and to make the soil produce. They saw in the future a community which was orderly and law-abiding, they saw their children brought out of the bondage of ignorance and into the freedom of knowledge. And they saw more than that—they saw the Vision, faintly at first, but with ever-increasing clearness.

It was a wonderful task which Roger had set for himself, and he threw himself into his work with flaming energy. He hired a buggy and a little fat horse, and spent some of his nights *en route* in the houses of his friends along the way; other nights— and these were the ones he liked best—he slept under the pines. With John Ballard's old Bible under his arm, and his prayer-book in his pocket, he went forth each week, and always he found a congregation ready and waiting.

Over the stretches of that barren country they came to hear him, sailing in their schooner-wagons toward the harbor of the hope which he brought to them.

When he had preached from his pulpit, he had talked to men and women of culture and he had spent much of his time in polishing a phrase, or in rounding out a sentence. But now he spent his time in search of the clear words which would carry his—message.

For Mary had said that every man who preached must have a message.

Mary!

How far she had receded from him. When he thought of her now it was with a sense of overwhelming loss. She had chosen to withdraw herself from him. In every letter he had seen signs of it—and he could not protest. No man in his position could say to a woman, "I will not let you go." He had nothing to offer her but his life in the pines, a life that could not mean much to such a woman.

But it meant much to himself. Gradually he had come to see that love alone could never have brought to him what his work was bringing. He had a sense of freedom such as one must have whose shackles have been struck off. He began to know now what Mary had meant when she had said, "I feel as if I were flying through the world on strong wings." He, too, felt as if he were flying, and as it his wings were carrying him up and up beyond any heights to which he had hitherto soared.

He slept that night in one of the rare groves of old pines. He made a couch of the brown needles and threw a rug over them. The air was soft and heavy with resinous perfume. As he lay there in the stillness, the pines stretched above him like the arches of some great cathedral. His text came to him, "Come thou south wind and blow upon my garden." It was a simple people to whom he would talk on the morrow, but these things they could understand—the winds of heaven, and the stars, and the little foxes that could spoil the grapes.

When he woke there was a mocking-bird singing. He had gone to sleep obsessed by his sermon, uplifted. He woke with a sense of loneliness—a great longing for human help and under-standing—a longing to look once more into Mary Ballard's clear eyes and to draw strength from the source which had once inspired him.

John Ballard's Bible lay on the rug beside him. He opened it, and the leaves fell apart at a page where a rose had once been pressed. The rose was dead now, and had been laid away carefully, lest it should be lost. But the impress was still there, as the memory of Mary's frank friendliness was still in his mind.

It was a long time before he closed the book. But at last he sighed and rose from his couch. It was inevitable, this drifting apart. Fate would hold for Mary some brilliant future. As for him, he must go on with his work alone.

Yet he realized, even in that moment of renunciation, that it was a wonderful thing that he could at last go on alone. A year ago he had needed all of Mary's strength to spur him to the effort, all of her belief in him. Now with his heart still crying out for her, needing her, he could still go on alone!

He drew a long breath, and looked up through the singing tree-tops to the bit of sky above. He stood there for a long time, silent, looking up into the shining sky.

At ten o'clock when he entered the circle of young pines, his congregation was ready for him, sitting on the rough seats which the men had fashioned, their eager faces welcoming him, their eyes lighted.

The children whom he had taught led in the singing of the simple old hymns, and Roger read a prayer.

Then he talked. He withheld nothing of the poetry of his subject; and they rose to his eloquence. And when light began to fill a man's eyes or tears to fill a woman's—Roger knew that the work of the soul was well begun.

Afterward he went among them, becoming one of them in friendliness and sympathy, but set apart and consecrated by the wisdom which made him their leader.

Among a group of men he spoke of politics. "There's the new President," he said; "it has been a great week in Washington. His administration ought to mean great things for you people down here."

Thus he roused their interest; thus he led them to ask questions; thus he drew them into eager controversy; thus he waked their minds into activity; thus he roused their sluggish souls.

But he found his keenest delight in the children's gardens.

They were such lovely little gardens now—with violets blooming in their borders, with daffodils and jonquils and hyacinths. Every bit of bloom spoke to him of Mary. Not for one moment had she lost her interest in the children's gardens, although she had ceased, it seemed, to have interest in any other of his affairs.

Before he went, the children had to have their fairy tale. But to-night he would not tell them Cinderella or Red Riding Hood. The day seemed to demand something more than that, so he told them the story of the ninety and nine, and of the sheep that was lost.

He made much of the story of the sheep, showing to these children, who knew little of shepherds and little of mountains, a picture which held them breathless. For far back, perhaps, the ancestors of these sand-hill folk had herded sheep on the hills of Scotland.

Then he sang the song, and so well did he tell the story and so well did he sing the song that they rejoiced with him over the sheep that was found—for he had made it a little lamb— helpless and bleating, and wanting very much its mother.

The song, borne on the wings of the wind, reached the ears of a man with a worn face, who slouched in the shadow of the pines.

Later he spoke to Roger Poole. "I reckon I'm that lost sheep," he said, soberly, "an' nobody ain't gone out to find me—yit."

"Find yourself," said Roger.

The man stared.

"Find yourself," Roger said; "look at those little gardens over there that the children have made. Can you match them?"

"I reckon I've got somethin' else to do beside make gardens," drawled the man.

"What have you got to do that's better?" Roger demanded.

The man hesitated and Roger pressed his point. "Flowers for the children—crops for men—I'll wager you've a lot of land and don't know what to do with it. Let's try to make things grow."

"Us? You mean you and me, parson?"

"Yes. And while we plant and sow, we'll talk about the state of your soul." Roger reached out his hand to the lean and lank sinner.

And the lean and lank sinner took it, with something beginning to glow in the back of his eyes.

"I reckon I ain't got on to your scheme of salvation," he remarked shrewdly, "but somehow I have a feelin' that I ain't goin' to git through those days of plantin' crops with you without your plantin' somethin' in me that's bound to grow."

In such ways did Roger meet men, women and children, reaching out from his loneliness to their need, giving much and receiving more.

It was on Tuesday morning that he came back finally to the

house which seemed empty because of Cousin Patty's absence. The little lady was still in Washington, whence she had written hurried notes, promising more when the rush was over.

At the gate he met the rural carrier, who gave him the letters. There was one on top from Mary Ballard.

Roger tore it open and read it, as he walked toward the house. It contained only a scribbled line—but it set his pulses bounding.

"DEAR ROGER POOLE:

"I want to be friends again. Such friends as we were in the Tower Rooms. I know I don't deserve it—but—please.

"MARY BALLARD."

It seemed to him, as he finished it that all the world was singing, not merely the mocking-birds in the magnolias, but the whole incomparable chorus of the universe. It seemed an astounding thing that she should have written thus to him. He had so adjusted himself to the fact of repeated disappointment, repeated failure, that he found it hard to believe that such happiness could be his. Yet she had written it; that she wanted to be—his friend.

At first his thoughts did not fly beyond friendship. But as he sat down on the porch steps to think it over he began, for the first time since he had known her, to dream of a life in which she should be more to him than friend.

And why not? Why shouldn't he dream? Mary was not like other women. She looked above and beyond the little things. Might not a man offer her that which was finer than gold, greater than material success? Might not a man offer her a life which had to do with life and love—might he not share with her this opportunity to make this garden in the sand-hills bloom?

And now, while the mocking-birds sang madly, Roger Poole saw Mary—here beside him on the porch on a morning like this, with the lilacs waving perfumed plumes of mauve and white, with the birds flashing in blue and scarlet and gold from pine to magnolia, and from magnolia back to pine—with the sky unclouded, the air fresh and sweet.

He saw her as she might travel with him comfortably toward the sand-hills, in a schooner-wagon made for her use, fitted with certain luxuries of cushions and rugs. He saw her with him in deep still groves, coming at last to that circle of young pines where he preached, meeting his people, supplementing his labor with her loveliness. He saw—oh, dream of dreams—he saw a little white church among the sand-hills, a little church with a bell, such a bell as the boy had not heard before Whittington rang them all for him. Later, perhaps, there might be a rectory near the church, a rectory with a garden—and Mary in the garden.

So, tired after his journey, he sat with unseeing eyes, needing rest, needing food, yet feeling no fatigue as his soul leaped over time and space toward the goal of happiness.

He was aroused by the appearance of Aunt Chloe, the cook.

"I'se jus' been lookin' fo' you, Mr. Roger," she said. "A telegraf done come, yestiddy, and I ain't knowed what to do wid it."

She handed it to him, and watched him anxiously as he opened it.

It was from Cousin Patty.

"Mary has had sad news of Barry. We need you. Can you come?"

CHAPTER XXIII

In Which Little-Lovely Leila Looks Forward to the
Month of May; and in Which Barry Rides Into a
Town With Narrow Streets.

It was when Little-Lovely Leila was choosing certain gowns for her trip abroad that she had almost given away her secret to Delilah.

"I want a yellow one," she had remarked, "with a primrose hat, like I wore when Barry and I—" She stopped, blushing furiously.

"When you and Barry what?" demanded Delilah.

Leila having started to say, "When Barry and I ran away to be married," stumbled over a substitute, "Well, I wore a yellow gown—when—when—"

"Not when he proposed, duckie. That was the day at Fort Myer. I knew it the minute I came out and saw your face; and then that telephone message about the picture. Were you really jealous when you found it on my table?"

"Dreadfully." Leila breathed freely once more. The subject of the primrose gown was shelved safely.

"You needn't have been. All the world knew that Barry was yours."

"And he's mine now," Leila laughed; "and I am to see him in—May."

In the days which followed she was a very busy little Leila. On every pretty garment that she made or bought, she embroidered in fine silk a wreath of primroses. It was her own delicious secret, this adopting of her bridal color. Other brides might be married in white, but she had been different—her gown had been the color of the great gold moon that had lighted their way. What a wedding journey it had been—and how she and Barry would laugh over it in the years to come!

For the tragedy which had weighed so heavily began now to seem like a happy comedy. In a few weeks she would see Barry, in a few weeks all the world would know that she was his wife!

So she packed her fragrant boxes—so she embroidered, and sang, and dreamed.

Barry had written that he was "making good"; and that when she came he would tell Gordon. And the General should go on to Germany, and he and Leila would have their honeymoon trip.

"You must decide where we shall go," he had said, and Leila had planned joyously.

"Dad and I motored once into Scotland, and we stopped at a little town for tea. Such a queer little story-book town, Barry, with funny houses and with the streets so narrow that the people leaned out of their windows and gossiped over our heads, and I am sure they could have shaken hands across. There wasn't even room for our car to turn around, and we had to go on and on until we came to the edge of the town, and there was the dearest inn. We stopped and stayed that night—and the linen all smelled of lavender, and there was a sweet dumpling of a landlady, and old-fashioned flowers in a trim little garden—and all the hills beyond and a lake. Let's go there, Barry; it will be beautiful."

They planned, too, to go into lodgings afterward in London.

The thought of lodgings gave Leila a thrill. She hunted out her fat little volume of Martin Chuzzlewit and gloated over Ruth Pinch and her beef-steak pie. She added two or three captivating aprons to the contents of the fragrant boxes. She even bought a cook-book, and it was with a sigh that she laid the cook-book away when Barry wrote that in such lodgings as he would choose the landlady would serve their meals in the sitting-room. And this plan would give Leila more time to see the sights of London!

But what cared Little-Lovely Leila for seeing sights? Anybody could see sights—any dreary and dried-up fossil, any crabbed and cranky old maid—the Tower and Westminster Abbey were for those who had nothing better to do. As for herself, her horizon just now was bounded by primrose wreaths and fragrant boxes, and the promise of seeing Barry in May!

But fate, which has strange things in store for all of us, had this in store for little Leila, that she was not to see Barry in May, and the reason that she was not to see him was Jerry Tuckerman.

Meeting Mary in the street one day early in February, Jerry had said, "I am going to run over to London this week. Shall I take your best to Barry?"

Mary's eyes had met his squarely. "Be sure you take *your* best, Jerry," she had said.

He had laughed his defiance. "Barry's all right—but you've got to give him a little rope, Mary."

When he had left her, Mary had walked on slowly, her heart filled with foreboding. Barry was not like Jerry. Jerry, coarse of fiber, lacking temperament, would probably come to middle age safely—he would never be called upon to pay the piper as Barry would for dancing to the tune of the follies of youth.

She wrote to Gordon, warning him. "Keep Barry busy," she said. "Jerry told me that he intended to have 'the time of his young life'—and he will want Barry to share it."

Gordon smiled over the letter. "Poor Mary," he told Constance; "she has carried Barry for so long on her shoulders, and she can't realize that he is at last learning to stand alone."

But Constance did not smile. "We never could bear Jerry Tuckerman; he always made Barry do things."

"Nobody can make me do things when I don't want to do them," said Gordon comfortably and priggishly, "and Barry must learn that he can't put the blame on anybody's shoulders but his own."

Constance sighed. She did not quite share Gordon's sense of security. Barry was different. He was a dear, and trying so hard; but Jerry had always had some power to sway him from his best, a sinister inexplicable influence.

Jerry, arriving, hung around Barry for several days, tempting him, like the villain in the play.

But Barry refused to be tempted. He was busy—and he had just had a letter from Leila.

"I simply can't run around town with you, Tuckerman," he explained. "Holding down a job in an office like this isn't like holding down a government job."

"So they've put your nose to the grindstone?" Jerry grinned as he said it, and Barry flushed. "I like it, Tuckerman; there's something ahead, and Gordon has me slated for a promotion."

But what did a promotion mean to Jerry's millions? And Barry was good company, and anyhow—oh, he couldn't see Ballard doing a steady stunt like this.

"Motor into Scotland with me next week," he insisted; "get a week off, and I'll pick up a gay party. It's a bit early, but we'll stop in the big towns."

Barry shook his head.

"Leila and the General are coming over in May—she wants to take that trip—and, anyhow, I can't get away."

"Oh, well, wait and take your nice little ride with Leila," Jerry said, good-naturedly enough, "but don't tie yourself too soon to a woman's apron string, Ballard—wait till you've had your fling."

But Barry didn't want a fling. He, too, was dreaming. On half-holidays and Sundays he haunted neighborhoods where there were rooms to let. And when one day he chanced on a sunshiny suite where a pot of primroses bloomed in the window, he lingered and looked.

"If they're empty a month from now I'll take them," he said.

"A guinea down and I'll keep them for you," was the smiling response of the pleasant landlady.

So Barry blushingly paid the guinea, and began to buy little things to make the rooms beautiful—a bamboo basket for flowers—a Sheffield tray—a quaint tea-caddy—an antique footstool for Leila's little feet.

Yet there were moments in the midst of his elation when some chill breath of fear touched him, and it was in one of these moods that he wrote out of his heart to his little bride.

"Sometimes, when I think of you, sweetheart, I realize how little there is in me which is deserving of that which you are giving me. When your letters come, I read them and think and think about them. And the thing I think is this: Am I going to be able all my life to live up to your expectations? Don't expect too much, dear heart. I wonder if I am more cowardly about facing life than other men. Now and then things seem to loom up in front of me—great shadows which block my way—and I grow afraid that I can't push them out of your path and mine. And if I should not push them, what then? Would they engulf you, and should I be to blame?"

Mary found Leila puzzling over this letter. "It doesn't sound like Barry," she said, in a little frightened voice. "May I read it to you, Mary?"

Mary had stopped in for tea on her way home from the office. But the tea waited.

"Barry is usually so—hopeful," Leila said, when she had finished; "somehow I can't help—worrying."

Mary was worried. She knew these moods. Barry had them when he was fighting "blue devils." She was afraid—haunted by the thought of Jerry. She tried to speak cheerfully.

"You'll be going over soon," she said, "and then all the world will be bright to him."

Leila hesitated. "I wish," she faltered, "that I could be with him now to help him—fight."

Mary gave her a startled glance. Their eyes met.

"Leila," Mary said, with a little gasp, "who told you?"

"Barry"—the tea was forgotten—"before—before he went away." The vision was upon her of that moment when he had knelt at her feet on their bridal night.

Haltingly, she spoke of her lover's weakness. "I've wanted to ask you, Mary, and when this letter came, I just had to ask. If you think it would be better—if we were married, if I could make a home for him."

"It wouldn't be better for you."

"I don't want to think about myself," Leila said, passionately; "everybody thinks about me. It is Barry I want to think of, Mary."

Mary patted the flushed cheek. "Barry is a fortunate boy," she said. Then, with hesitation, "Leila, when you knew, did it make a difference?"

"Difference?"

"In your feeling for Barry?"

And now the child eyes were woman eyes. "Yes," she said, "it made a difference. But the difference was this—that I loved him more. I don't know whether I can explain it so that you will understand, Mary. But then you aren't like me. You've always been so wonderful, like Barry. But you see I've never been wonderful. I've always been just a little silly thing, pretty enough for people to like, and childish enough for everybody to pet, and because I was pretty and little and childish, nobody seemed to think that I could be anything else. And for a long time I didn't dream that Barry was in love with me. I just knew that I—cared. But it was the kind of caring that didn't expect much in return. And when Barry said that I was the only woman in the world for him—I had the feeling that it was a pleasant dream, and that—that some day I'd wake up and find that he had made a mistake and that he should have chosen a princess instead of just a little goosie-girl. But when I knew that Barry had to fight, everything changed. I knew that I could really help. More than the princess, perhaps, because you see she might not have cared to bother—and she might not have loved him enough to—overlook."

"You blessed child," Mary said with a catch in her voice, "you mustn't be so humble—it's enough to spoil any man."

"Not Barry," Leila said; "he loves me because I am so loving."

Oh, wisdom of the little heart. There might be men who could love for the sake of conquest; there might be men who could meet coldness with ardor, and affection with indifference. Barry was not one of these. The sacred fire which burned in the heart of his sweet mistress had lighted the flame in his own. It was Leila's love as well as Leila that he wanted. And she knew and treasured the knowledge.

It was when Mary left that she said, with forced lightness, "You'll be going soon, and what a summer you will have together."

It was on Leila's lips to cry, "But I want our life together to begin now. What's one summer in a whole life of love?"

But she did not voice her cry. She kissed Mary and smiled wistfully, and went back into the dusky room to dream of Barry—Barry her young husband, with whom she had walked in her little yellow gown over the hills and far away.

And while she dreamed, Barry, in Jerry Tuckerman's big blue car, was flying over other hills, and farther away from Leila than he had ever been in his life.

It was as Mary had feared. Barry's strength in his first resistance of Jerry's importunities had made him over-confident, so that when, at the end of the month, Jerry had returned and had pressed his claim, Barry had consented to lunch with him.

At luncheon they met Jerry's crowd and Barry drank just one glass of golden sparkling stuff.

But the one glass was enough to fire his blood—enough to change the aspect of the world—enough to make him reckless, boisterous—enough to make him consent to join at once Jerry's party in a motor trip to Scotland.

In that moment the world of work receded, the world of which

Leila was the center receded—the life which had to do with lodgings and primroses and Sheffield trays was faint and blurred to his mental vision. But this life, which had to do with laughter and care-free joyousness and forgetfulness, this was the life for a man who was a man.

Jerry was saying, "There will be the three of us and the chauffeur—and we will take things in hampers and things in boxes, and things in bottles."

Barry laughed. It was not a loud laugh, just a light boyish chuckle, and as he rose and stood with his hand resting on the table, many eyes were turned upon him. He was a handsome young American, his beautiful blond head held high. "You mustn't expect," he said, still with that light laughter, "that I am going to bring any bottles. Only thing I've got is a tea-caddy. Honest—a tea-caddy, and a Sheffield tray."

Then some memory assailing him, he faltered, "And a little foolish footstool."

"Sit down," Jerry said. There was something strangely appealing in that gay young figure with the shining eyes. In spite of himself, Jerry felt uncomfortable. "Sit down," he said.

So Barry sat down, and laughed at nothing, and talked about nothing, and found it all very enchanting.

He packed his bag and left a note for Gordon and when he piled finally with the others into Jerry's car, he was ready to shout with them that it was a long lane which had no turning, and that work was a bore and would always be.

And so the ride which Leila had planned for herself and her young husband became a wild ride, in which these young knights of the road pursued fantastic adventures, with memories blank, and with consciences soothed.

For days they rode, stopping at various inns along the way,

startling the staid folk of the villages by their laughter late into the night; making boon companions in an hour, and leaving them with tears, to forget them at the first turn of the corner.

Written as old romance, such things seem of the golden age; looked upon in the light of Barry's future and of Leila's, they were tragedy unspeakable.

And now the car went up and up, to come down again to some stretch of sand, with the mountains looming black against one horizon, the sea a band of sapphire against another.

And so, fate drawing them nearer and nearer, they came at last to the little town which Leila had described in her letter.

Going in, some one spoke the name, and Barry had a stab of memory. Who had talked of narrow streets, across which people gossiped—and shook hands?—who had spoken of having tea in that little shop?

He asked the question of his companions, "Who called this a story-book town?"

They laughed at him. "You dreamed it."

Steadily his mind began to work. He fumbled in his pocket, and found Leila's letter.

Searching through it, he discovered the name of the little place. "I didn't dream it," he announced triumphantly; "my wife told me."

"Wake up," Jerry said, "and thank the gods that you are single."

But Barry stood swaying. "My little wife told me—*Leila*!"

With a sudden cry, he lurched forward. His arm struck the arm of the driver beside him. The car gave a sudden turn. The streets were narrow—so narrow that one might almost shake hands across them!

And there was a crash!

Jerry was not hurt, nor the other adventurers. The chauffeur was stunned. But Barry was crumpled up against the stone steps of one of the funny little houses, and lay there with Leila's letter all red under him.

It was Porter and Mary who told Leila. The General had begged them to do it. "I can't," he had said, pitifully. "I've faced guns, but I can't face the hurt in my darling's eyes."

So Mary's arms were around her when she whispered to the child-wife that Barry was—dead.

Porter had faltered first something about an accident—that the doctors were—afraid.

Leila, shaking, had looked from one to the other. "I must go to him," she had cried. "You see, I am his wife. I have a right to go."

"*His wife?*" Of all things they had not expected this.

"Yes, we have been married a year—we ran away."

"When, dear?"

"Last March—to Rockville—and—and we were going to tell everybody the next day—and then Barry lost his place—and we couldn't."

Oh, poor little widow, poor little child! Mary drew her close. "Leila, Leila," she whispered, "dear little sister, dear little girl, we must love and comfort each other."

And then Leila knew.

But they did not tell her how it had happened. The details of that last ride the woman who loved him need never know. Barry was to be her hero always.

CHAPTER XXIV

In Which Roger Comes Once More to the Tower Rooms; and in Which a Duel is Fought in Modern Fashion.

It was Cousin Patty who had suggested sending for Roger. "He can look after me, Mary. If you won't let me go home, I don't want you to have the thought of me to burden you."

"You couldn't be a burden. And I don't know what Aunt Isabelle and I should have done without you."

She began to cry weakly, and Cousin Patty, comforting her, said in her heart, "There is no one but Roger who can say the right things to her."

As yet no one had said the right things. It seemed to Mary that she carried a wound too deep for healing. Gordon had softened the truth as much as possible, but he could not hide it from her. She knew that Barry, her boy Barry, had gone out of the world defeated.

It was Roger who helped her.

He came first upon her as she sat alone in the garden by the fountain. It was a sultry spring day, and heavy clouds hung low on the horizon. Thin and frail in her black frock, she rose to meet him, the ghost of the girl who had once bloomed like a flower in her scarlet wrap.

Roger took her hands in his.

"You poor little child," he said; "you poor little child."

She did not cry. She simply looked up at him, frozen-white. "Oh, it wasn't fair for him to go—that way. He tried so hard. He tried so hard."

"I know. And it was a great fight he put up, you must remember that."

"But to fail—at the last."

"You mustn't think of that. Somehow I can see Barry still fighting, and winning. One of a glorious company."

"A glorious company—Barry?"

"Yes. Why not? We are judged by the fight we make, not by our victory."

She drew a long breath. "Everybody else has been sorry. Nobody else could seem to understand."

"Perhaps I understand," he said, "because I know what it is to fight—and fail."

"But you are winning now." The color swept into her pale cheeks. "Cousin Patty told me."

"Yes. You showed me the way—I have tried to follow it."

"Oh, how ignorant I was," she cried, tempestuously, "when I talked to you of life. I thought I knew everything."

"You knew enough to help me. If I can help you a little now it will be only a fair exchange."

It helped her merely to have him there. "You spoke of Barry's still fighting and winning. Do you think that one goes on fighting?"

"Why not? It would seem only just that he should conquer. There are men who are not tempted, whose goodness is negative. Character is made by resistance against evil, not by lack of knowledge of it. And the judgments of men are not those which count in the final verdict."

He said more than this, breaking the bonds of her despair. Others had pitied Barry. Roger defended him. She began to think of her brother, not as her imagination had pictured him, flung into utter darkness, but with his head up—his beautiful fair head, a shining sword in his hand, fighting against the powers of evil—stumbling, falling, rising again.

He saw her relax as she listened, and his love for her taught him what to say.

And as he talked, her eyes noted the change in him.

This was not the Roger Poole of the Tower Rooms. This was a Roger Poole who had found himself. She could see it in his manner—she could hear it in his voice, it shone from his eyes. Here was a man who feared nothing, not even the whispers that had once had power to hurt.

The clouds were sweeping toward them, hiding the blue; the wind whirled the dead leaves from the paths, and stirred the budding branches of the hundred-leaved bush—touched with its first hint of tender green. The mist from the fountain was like a veil which hid the mocking face of the bronze boy.

But Mary and Roger had no eyes for these warnings; each was famished for the other, and this meeting gave to Mary, at least, a sense of renewed life.

She spoke of her future. "Constance and Gordon want me to come to them. But I hate to give up my work. I don't want to be discontented. Yet I dread the loneliness here. Did you ever think I should be such a coward?"

"You are not a coward—you are a woman—wanting the things that belong to you."

She sat very still. "I wonder—what are the things which belong to a woman?"

"Love—a home—happiness."

"And you think I want these things?"

"I know it."

"How do you know?"

"Because you have tried work—and it has failed. You have tried independence—and it has failed. You have tried freedom, and have found it bondage."

He was once more in the grip of the dream which he had dreamed as he had sat with Mary's letter in his hand on Cousin Patty's porch. If she would come to him there would be no more loneliness. His love should fill her life, and there would be, too, the love of his people. She should win hearts while he won souls. If only she would care enough to come.

It was the fear that she might not care which suddenly gripped him. Surely this was not the moment to press his demands upon her—when sorrow lay so heavily on her heart.

So blind, and cruel in his blindness, he held back the words which rose to his lips.

"Some day life will bring the things which belong to you," he said at last. "I pray God that it may bring them to you some day."

A line of Browning's came into her mind, and rang like a knell—"Some day, meaning no day."

She shivered and rose. "We must go in; there's rain in those clouds, and wind."

He rose also and stood looking down at her. Her eyes came up to his, her clear eyes, shadowed now by pain. What he might have said to her in another moment would have saved both of them much weariness and heartache. But he was not to say it, for the storm was upon them driving them before it, slamming doors, banging shutters in the big house as they came to it—a miniature cyclone, in its swift descent.

And as if he had ridden in on the wings of the storm came Porter Bigelow, his red mane blown like a flame back from his face, his long coat flapping.

He stopped short at the sight of Roger.

"Hello, Poole," he said; "when did you arrive?"

"This morning."

They shook hands, but there was no sign of a welcome in Porter's face.

"Pretty stiff storm," he remarked, as the three of them stood by the drawing-room window, looking out.

The rain came in shining sheets—the lightning blazed—the thunder boomed.

"It is the first thunder-storm of the season," Mary said. "It will wake up the world."

"In the South," Roger said, "the world is awake. You should see our gardens."

"I wish I could; Cousin Patty asked me to come."

"Will you?" eagerly.

"There's my work."

"Take a holiday, and let me show you the pines."

Porter broke in impatiently, almost insolently.

"Mary needs companionship, not pines. I think she should go to Constance. Leila and the General will go over as they planned in May, and the Jeliffes—"

"There's more than a month before May—which she could spend with us."

Porter stared. This was a new Roger, an insistent, demanding Roger. He spoke coldly. "Constance wants Mary at once. I don't think we should say anything to dissuade her. Aunt Isabelle and I can take her over."

And now Mary's head went up.

"I haven't decided, Porter." She was fighting for freedom.

"But Constance needs you, Mary—and you need her."

"Oh, no," Mary said, brokenly, "Constance doesn't need me. She has Gordon and the baby. Nobody needs me—now."

Roger saw the quick blood flame in Porter's face. He felt it flame in his own. And just for one fleeting moment, over the bowed head of the girl, the challenging eyes of the two men met.

Aunt Frances, who came over with Grace in the afternoon, went home in a high state of indignation.

"Why Patty Carew and Roger Poole should take possession of Mary in that fashion," she said to her daughter at dinner, "is beyond me. They don't belong there, and it would have been in better taste to leave at such a time."

"Mary begged Cousin Patty to stay," Grace said, "and as for Roger Poole, he has simply made Mary over. She has been like a stone image until to-day."

"I don't see any difference," Aunt Frances said. "What do you mean, Grace?"

"Oh, her eyes and the color in her cheeks, and the way she does her hair."

"The way she does her hair?" Aunt Frances laid down her fork and stared.

"Yes. Since the awful news came, Mary has seemed to lose interest in everything. She adored Barry, and she's never going to get over it—not entirely. I miss the old Mary." Grace stopped to steady her voice. "But when I went up with her to her room to talk to her while she dressed for dinner, she put up her hair in that pretty boyish way that she used to wear it, and it was all for Roger Poole."

"Why not for Porter?"

"Because she hasn't cared how she looked, and Porter has been there every day. He has been there too often."

"Do you think Roger will try to get her to marry him?"

"Who knows? He's dead in love with her. But he looks upon her as too rare for the life he leads. That's the trouble with men. They are afraid they can't make the right woman happy, so they ask the wrong one. Now if we women could do the proposing—"

"Grace!"

"Don't look at me in that shocked way, mother. I am just voicing what every woman knows—that the men who ask her aren't the ones she would have picked out if she had had the choice. And Mary will wait and weary, and Roger will worship and hang back, and in the meantime Porter will demand and demand and demand—and in the end he'll probably get what he wants."

Aunt Frances beamed. "I hope so."

"But Mary will be miserable."

"Then she'll be very silly."

Grace sighed. "No woman is silly who asks for the best. Mother, I'd love to marry a man with a mission—I'd like to go to the South Sea Islands and teach the natives, or to Darkest Africa—or to China, or India, anywhere away from a life in which there's nothing but bridge, and shopping, and deadly dullness."

She was in earnest now, and her mother saw it.

"I don't see how you can say such things," she quavered. "I don't see how you can talk of going to such impossible places —away from me."

Grace cut short the plaintive wail.

"Of course I have no idea of going," she said, "but such a life would furnish its own adventures; I wouldn't have to manufacture them."

It was with the wish to make life something more than it was that Grace asked Roger the next day, "Is there any work here in town like yours for the boy—you see Mary has told me about him."

He smiled. "Everywhere there are boys and girls, unawakened —if only people would look for them; and with your knowledge of languages you could do great things with the little foreigners—turn a bunch of them into good citizens, for example."

"How?"

"Reach them first through pictures and music—then through their patriotism. Don't let them learn politics and plunder on the streets; let them find their place in this land from you, and let them hear from you of the God of our fathers."

Grace felt his magnetism. "I wish you could go through the streets of New York saying such things."

He shook his head. "I shall not come to the city. My place is found, and I shall stay there; but I have faith to believe that there will yet be a Voice to speak, to which the world shall listen."

"Soon?"

"Everything points to an awakening. People are beginning to say, 'Tell us,' where a few years ago they said, 'There is nothing to tell.'"

"I see—it will be wonderful when it comes—I'm going to try to do my little bit, and be ready, and when Mary comes back, she shall help me."

His eyes went to where Mary sat between Porter and Aunt Frances.

"She may never come back."

"She must be made to come."

"Who could make her?"

"The man she loves."

She flashed a sparkling glance at him, and rose.

"Come, mother," she said, "it is time to go." Then, as she gave Roger her hand, she smiled. "Faint heart," she murmured, "don't you know that a man like you, if he tries, can conquer the—world?"

She left Roger with his pulses beating madly. What did she mean? Did she think that—Mary—? He went up to the Tower Rooms to dress for dinner, with his mind in a whirl. The windows were open and the warm air blew in. Looking out, he could see in the distance the shining river—like a silver ribbon, and the white shaft of the Monument, which seemed to touch the sky. But he saw more than that; he saw his future and Mary's; again he dreamed his dreams.

If he had hoped for a moment alone that night with the lady of his heart, he was doomed to disappointment, for Leila and her father came to dinner. Leila was very still and sweet in her widow's black, the General brooding over her. And again Roger had the sense that in this house of sorrow there was no place for love-making. For the joy that might be his—he must wait; even though he wearied in the waiting.

And it was while he waited that he lunched one day with Porter Bigelow. The invitation had surprised him, and he had felt vaguely troubled and oppressed by the thought that back of it might be some motive as yet unrevealed. But there had been nothing to do but accept, and at one o'clock he was at the University Club.

For a time they spoke of indifferent things, then Porter said, bluntly, "I am not going to beat about the bush, Poole. I've asked you here to talk about Mary Ballard."

"Yes?"

"You're in love with her?"

"Yes—but I question your right to play inquisitor."

"I haven't any right, except my interest in Mary. But I claim that my interest justifies the inquisition."

"Perhaps."

"You want to marry her?"

Roger shifted his position, and leaned forward, meeting Porter's stormy eyes squarely. "Again I question your right, Bigelow."

"It isn't a question of right now, Poole, and you know it. You're in love with her, I'm in love with her. We both want her. In days past men settled such things with swords or pistols. You and I are civilized and modern; but it's got to be settled just the same."

"Miss Ballard will have to settle it—not you or I."

"She can't settle it. Mary is a dreamer. You capture her with your imagination—with your talk of your work—and your people and the little gardens, and all that. And she sees it as you want her to see it, not as it really is. But I know the deadly dullness, the awfulness. Why, man, I spent a winter down there, at one of the resorts and now and then we rode through the country. It was a desert, I tell you, Poole, a desert; it is no place for a woman."

"You saw nothing but the charred pines and the sand. I could show you other things."

"What, for example?"

"I could show you an awakened people. I could show you a community throwing off the shackles of idleness and ignorance. I could show you men once tied to old traditions, meeting with eagerness the new ideals. There is nothing in the world more wonderful than such an awakening, Bigelow. But one must have the Vision to grasp it. And faith to believe it. It is the dreamers, thank God, who see beyond to-day into to-morrow. I haven't wealth or position to offer Mary, but I can offer her a world which needs her. And if I know her, as I think I do, she will care more for my world than for yours."

He did not raise his voice, but Porter felt the force of his restrained eloquence, as he knew Mary would feel it if it were applied to her.

And now he shot his poisoned dart.

"At first, perhaps. But when it came to building a home, there'd be always the stigma of your past, and she's a proud little thing, Poole."

Roger winced. "My past is buried. It is my future of which we must speak."

"You can't bury a past. You haven't even a pulpit to preach from."

Roger pushed back his chair. "I am tempted to wish," his voice was grim, "that we were not quite so civilized, not quite so modern. Pistols or swords would seem an easier way than this."

"I'm fighting for Mary. You've got to let go. None of her friends want it—Gordon would never consent."

It seemed to Roger that all the whispers which had assailed him in the days of long ago were rushing back upon him in a roaring wave of sound.

He rose, white and shaken. "Do you call it victory when one man stabs another through the heart? Well, if this is your victory, Bigelow—you are welcome to it."

CHAPTER XXV

In Which Mary Bids Farewell to the Old Life; and in Which She Finds Happiness on the High Seas.

Contrary Mary was Contrary Mary no longer. Since Roger had gone, taking Cousin Patty with him—gone without the word to her for which she had waited, she had submitted to Gordon's plans for her, and to Aunt Frances' and Porter's execution of them.

Only to Grace did she show any signs of her old rebellion.

"Did you ever think that I should be beaten, Grace?" she said, pitifully. "Is that the way with all women? Do we reach out for so much, and then take what we can get?"

Grace pondered. "Things tie us down, but we don't have to stay tied—and I am beginning to see a way out for myself, Mary."

She told of her talk with Roger and of her own strenuous desire to help; but she did not tell what she had said to him at the last. There was something here which she could not understand. Mary persistently refused to talk about him. Even now she shifted the topic.

"I don't want to strive," she said, "not even for the sake of others. I want to rest for a thousand years—and sleep for the next thousand."

And this from Mary, buoyant, vivid Mary, with her almost boyish strength and energy.

The big house was to be closed. Aunt Isabelle would go with Mary. Susan Jenks and Pittiwitz would be domiciled in the kitchen wing, with a friend of Susan's to keep them company.

Mary, wandering on the last day through the Tower Rooms, thought of the night when Roger Poole had first come to them. And now he would never come again.

She had not been able to understand his abrupt departure. Yet there had been nothing to resent—he had been infinitely kind, sympathetic, strong, helpful. If she missed something from his manner which had been there on the day of his arrival, she told herself that perhaps it had not been there, that her own joy in seeing him had made her imagine a like joy in his attitude toward her.

Cousin Patty had cried over her, kissed her, and protested that she could not bear to go.

"But Roger thinks it is best, my dear. He is needed at home."

It seemed plausible that he might be needed, yet in the back of Mary's mind was a doubt. What had sent him away? She was haunted by the feeling that some sinister influence had separated them.

A pitiful little figure in black, she made the tour of the empty rooms with Pittiwitz mewing plaintively at her heels. The little cat, with the instinct of her kind, felt the atmosphere of change. Old rugs on which she had sprawled were rolled up and reeking with moth balls. The little white bed, on which she had napped unlawfully, was stripped to the mattress. The cushions on which she had curled were packed away—the fire was out—the hearth desolate.

Susan Jenks, coming up, found Mary with the little cat in

her lap.

"Oh, honey child, don't cry like that."

"Oh, Susan, Susan, it will never be the same again, never the same."

And now once more in the garden, the roses bloomed on the hundred-leaved bush, once more the fountain sang, and the little bronze boy laughed through a veil of mist—but there were no gay voices in the garden, no lovers on the stone seat. Susan Jenks kept the paths trim and watered the flowers, and Pittiwitz chased butterflies or stretched herself in the sun, lazily content, forgetting, gradually, those who had for a time made up her world.

But Mary, on the high seas, could not forget what she had left behind. It was not Susan Jenks, it was not Pittiwitz, it was not the garden which called her back, although these had their part in her regrets—it was the old life, the life which had belonged to her childhood and her girlhood the life which had been lived with her mother and father and Constance—and Barry.

As she lay listless in her deck chair, she could see nothing in her future which would match the happiness of the past. The days lived in the old house had never been days of great prosperity; her father had, indeed, often been weighed down with care—there had been times of heavy anxieties—but, there had been between them all the bond of deep affection, of mutual dependence.

In Gordon's home there would be splendors far beyond any she had known, there would be ease and luxury, and these would be shared with her freely and ungrudgingly, yet to a nature like Mary Ballard's such things meant little. The real things in life to her were love and achievement; all else seemed stale and unprofitable.

Of course there would be Constance and the baby. On the

hope of seeing them she lived. Yet in a sense Gordon and the baby stood between herself and Constance—they absorbed her sister, satisfied her, so that Mary's love was only one drop added to a full cup.

It was while she pondered over her future that Mary was moved to write to Roger Poole. The mere putting of her thoughts on paper would ease her loneliness. She would say what she felt, frankly, freely, and when the little letters were finished, if her mood changed she need not send them.

So she began to scribble, setting down each day the thoughts which clamored for expression.

Porter complained that now she was always writing.

"I'd rather write than talk," Mary said, wearily; and at last he let the matter drop.

In Mid-Sea.

DEAR FRIEND O' MINE:

You asked me to write, and you will think that I have more than kept my promise when you get this journal of our days at sea. But it has seemed to me that you might enjoy it all, just as if you were with us, instead of down among your sand-hills, with your sad children (are they really sad now?) and Cousin Patty's wedding cakes.

There's quite a party of us. Leila and her father and the Jeliffes and Colin kept to their original plan of coming in May, and we decided it would be best to cross at the same time, so there's Aunt Frances and Grace and Aunt Isabelle, and Porter—and me—ten of us. If you and Cousin Patty were here, you'd round out a dozen. I wish you were here. How Cousin Patty would enjoy it—with her lovely enthusiasms, and her interest in everything. Do give her much love. I shall write to her when I reach London, for I know she will be traveling with us in spirit; she said she was going to live in England by proxy this summer, and I shall help her all I can by sending pictures, and you must tell her the books to read.

To think that I am on my way to the London of your Dick Whittington! I call him yours because you made me really see him for the first time.

"*There was he an orphan, O, a little lad alone.*"

And I am to hear all the bells, and to see the things I have always longed to see! Yet—and I haven't told this to any one but you, Roger Poole, the thought doesn't bring one little bit of gladness—it isn't London that I want, or England. I want my garden and my old big house, and things as they used to be.

But I am sailing fast away from it—the old life into the new!

So far we have had fair weather. It is always best to speak of the weather first, isn't it?—so that we can have our minds free for other things. It hasn't been at all rough; even Leila, who isn't a good sailor, has been able to stay on deck and people are so much interested in her. She seems such a child for her widow's black. Oh, what children they were, my boy Barry and his little wife, and yet they were man and woman, too. Leila has been letting me see some of his letters; he showed her a side which he never revealed to me, but I am not jealous. I am only glad that, for her, my boy Barry became a man.

But I am going to try to keep the sadness out of my scribbles to you, only now and then it will creep in, and you must forgive it, because you see it isn't easy to think that we are all here who loved him, and he, who loved so much to be with us, is somewhere—oh, where is he, Roger Poole, in that vast infinity which stretches out and out, beyond the sea, beyond the sky, into eternity?

All day I have been lying in my deck chair, and have let the world go by. It is clear and cool, and the sea rises up like a wall of sapphire. Last night we seemed to plough through a field of gold. The world is really a lovely place, the big outside world, but it isn't the outside world which makes our happiness, it is the world within us, and when the heart is tired—

But now I must talk of some one else besides my self.

Shall I tell you of Delilah? She attracts much attention, with her gracious manner and her wonderful clothes. All the people are crazy about her. They think she is English, and a duchess at least. Colin is as pleased as Punch at the success he has made of her, and he just stands aside and watches her, and flickers his pale lashes and smiles. Last night she danced some of the new dances, and her tango is as stately as a minuet. She and Porter danced together—and everybody stopped to look at them. The gossip is going the rounds that they are engaged. Oh, I wish they were—I wish they were! It would be good for him to meet his match. Delilah could hold her own; she wouldn't let him insist and manage until she was positively mesmerized, as I am. Delilah has such a queenly way of ruling her world. All the men on board trail after her. But she makes most of them worship from afar. As for the women, she picks the best, instinctively, and the ice which seems congealed around the heart of the average Britisher melts before her charm, so that already she is playing bridge with the proper people, and having tea with the inner circle. Even with these she seems to assume an air of remoteness, which seems to set her apart— and it is this air, Grace says, which conquers.

When people aren't coupling Porter's name with Delilah's, they are coupling it with Grace's. You should see our "red-headed woodpeckers," as poor Barry used to call them. When they promenade, Grace wears a bit of a black hat that shows all of her glorious hair, and Porter's cap can't hide his crown of glory. At first people thought they were brother and sister, but since it is known that they aren't I can see that everybody is puzzled.

It is all like a play passing in front of me. There are charming English people—charming Americans and some uncharming ones. Oh, why don't we, who began in such simplicity, try to remain a simple people? It just seems to me sometimes as if everybody on board is trying to show off. The rich ones are trying to display their money, and the intellectual ones their brains. Is there any real difference between the new-rich and the new-cultured, Roger Poole? One tells about her three motor cars, and the other tells about her three degrees. It is all tiresome. The world is a place to have things and to know things, but if the having them and knowing them makes them so important that you have to talk about them all the time there's something wrong.

That's the charm of Grace. She has money and position—and I've told you how she simply carried off all the honors at college; she paints wonderfully, and her opinions are all worth listening to. But she doesn't throw her knowledge at you. She is interested in people, and puts books where they belong. She is really the only one whom I welcome without any misgivings, except darling Aunt Isabelle. The others when they come to talk to me, are either too sad or too energetic.

Doesn't all that sound as if I were a selfish little pig? Well, some day I shall enjoy them all—but now—my heart is crying—and Leila, with her little white face, hurts. Mrs. Barry Ballard! Shall I ever get used to hearing her called that? It seems to set her apart from little Leila Dick, so that when I hear people speak to her, I am always startled and surprised.

And now—what are you doing? Are you still planting little gardens, and talking to your boy—talking to your sad people? Cousin Patty has told me of your letter to your bishop, who was so kind during your—trouble—and of his answer—and of your hope that some day you may have a little church in the sand-hills, and preach instead of teach.

Surely that would make all of your dreams come true, all of *our* dreams, for I have dreamed too—that this might come.

Sometimes as I lie here, I shut my eyes, and I seem to see you in that circle of young pines, and I pretend that I am listening; that you are saying things to me, as you say them to those poor people in the pines—and now and then I can make myself believe that you have really spoken, that your voice has reached across the miles. And so I have your little sermons all to myself—out here at sea, with all the blue distance between us—but I listen, listen—just the same.

In the Fog.

Out of the sunshine of yesterday came the heavy mists of to-day. The sea slips under us in silver swells. Everybody is wrapped to the chin, and Porter has just stopped to ask me if I want something hot sent up. I told him "no," and sent him on to Leila. I like this still world, and the gray ghosts about the deck. Delilah has just sailed by in a beautiful smoke-colored costume—with her inevitable knot of heliotrope—a phantom lady, like a lovely dream.

Did I tell you that a very distinguished and much titled gentleman wants to marry Delilah, and that he is waiting now for her answer? Porter thinks she will say "yes." But Leila and I don't. We are sure that she will find her fate in Colin. He dominates her; he dives beneath the surface and brings up the real Delilah, not the cool, calculating Delilah that we once knew, but the lovely, gracious lady that she now is. It is as if he had put a new soul inside of the worldly shell that was once Delilah. Yet there is never a sign between them of anything but good comradeship. Grace says that Colin is following the fashionable policy of watchful waiting—but I'm not sure. I fancy that they will both wake up suddenly to what they feel, and then it will be quite wonderful to see them.

Porter doesn't believe in the waking-up process. He says that love is a growth. That people must know each other for years and years, so that each can understand the faults and virtues of the other. But to me it seems that love is a flame, illumining everything in a moment.

Porter came while I was writing that—and made me walk with him up and down, up and down. He was afraid I might get chilled. Of course he means to be kind, but I don't like to have him tell me that I must "make an effort"—it gives me a sort of Mrs. Dombey feeling. I don't wonder that she just curled up and died to get rid of the trouble of living.

I knew while I walked with Porter that people were wondering who I was—in my long black coat, with my hair all blown about. I fancy that they won't link my name, sentimentally, with the Knight of the Auburn Crest. Beside Grace and Delilah I look like a little country girl. But I don't care—my thick coat is comfortable, and my little soft hat stays on my head, which is all one needs, isn't it? But as I write this I wonder where the girl is who used to like pretty clothes. Do you remember the dress I wore at Constance's wedding? I was thinking to-day of it—and of Leila hippity-hopping up the stairs in her one pink slipper. Oh, how far away those days seem—and how strong I felt—and how ready I was to face the world, and now I just want to crawl into a corner and watch other people live.

Leila is much braver than I. She takes a little walk every morning with her father, and another walk every afternoon with Porter—and she is always talking to lonesome people and sick people; and all the while she wears a little faint shining smile, like an angel's. Yet I used to be quite scornful of Leila, even while I loved her. I thought she was so sweetly and weakly feminine; yet she is steering her little ship through stormy waters, while I have lost my rudder and compass, and all the other things that a mariner needs in a time of storm.

Before the storm.

The fog still hangs over us, and we seem to ride on the surface of a dead sea. Last night there was no moon and to-day Aunt

Frances has not appeared. Even Delilah seems to feel depressed by the silence and the stillness—not a sound but the beat of the engines and the hoarse hoot of the horns. This paper is damp as I write upon it, and blots the ink, but—I sha'n't rewrite it, because the blots will make you see me sitting here, with drops of moisture clinging to my coat and to my little hat, and making my hair curl up in a way that it never does in dry weather.

I wonder, if you were here, if you would seem a ghost like all the others. Nothing is real but my thoughts of the things that used to be. I can't believe that I am on my way to London, and that I am going to live with Constance, and go sightseeing with Aunt Frances and Grace, and give up my plans for the—Great Adventure. Aunt Isabelle sat beside me this morning, and we talked about it. She will stay with Aunt Frances and Grace, and we shall see each other every day. I couldn't quite get along at all if it were not for Aunt Isabelle—she is such a mother-person, and she doesn't make me feel, as the rest of them do, that I must be brave and courageous. She just pats my hand and says, "It's going to be all right, Mary dear—it is going to be all right," and presently I begin to feel that it is; she has such a fashion of ignoring the troublesome things of this world, and simply looking ahead to the next. She told me once that heaven would mean to her, first of all, a place of beautiful sounds—and second it would mean freedom. You see she has always been dominated by Aunt Frances, poor thing.

Do you remember how I used to talk of freedom? But now I'm to be a bird in a cage. It will be a gilded cage, of course. Even Grace says that Constance's home is charming—great lovely rooms and massive furniture; and when we begin to go again into society, I am to be introduced to lots of grand folk, and perhaps presented.

And I am to forget that I ever worked in a grubby government office—indeed I am to forget that I ever worked at all.

And I am to forget all of my dreams. I am to change from the

Mary Ballard who wanted to do things to the Mary Ballard who wants them done for her. Perhaps when you see me again I shall be nice and clinging and as sweetly feminine as you used to want me to be—Roger Poole.

The mists have cleared, and there's a cloud on the horizon—I can hear people saying that it means a storm. Shall I be afraid? I wonder. Do you remember the storm that came that day in the garden and drove us in? I wonder if we shall ever be together again in the dear old garden?

After the storm.

Last night the storm waked us. It was a dreadful storm, with the wind booming, and the sea all whipped up into a whirlpool.

But I wasn't frightened, although everybody was awake, and there was a feeling that something might happen. I asked Porter to take me on deck, but he said that no one was allowed, and so we just curled up on chairs and sofas and waited either for the storm to end or for the ship to sink. If you've ever been in a storm at sea, you know the feeling—that the next minute may bring calm and safety, or terror and death.

Porter had tucked a rug around me, and I lay there, looking at the others, wondering whether if an accident happened Delilah would face death as gracefully as she faces everything else. Leila was very white and shivery and clung to her father; it is at such times that she seems such a child.

Aunt Frances was fussy and blamed everybody from the captain down to Aunt Isabelle—as if they could control the warring elements. Surely it is a case of the "ruling passion."

But while I am writing these things, I am putting off, and putting off and putting off the story of what happened after the storm—not because I dread to tell it, but because I don't know quite how to tell it. It involves such intimate things—yet it makes all things clear, it makes everything so beautifully clear, Roger Poole.

It was after the wind died down a bit that I made Porter take me up on deck. The moon was flying through the ragged clouds, and the water was a wild sweep of black and white. It was all quite spectral and terrifying and I shivered. And then Porter said; "Mary, we'd better go down."

And I said, "It wasn't fear that made me shiver, Porter. It was just the thought that living is worse than dying."

He dropped my arm and looked down at me.

"Mary," he said, "what's the matter with you?"

"I don't know," I said. "It is just that my courage is all gone—I can't face things."

"Why not?"

"I don't know—I've lost my grip, Porter."

And then he asked a question. "Is it because of Barry, Mary?"

"Some of it."

"And the rest?"

"I can't tell you."

We walked for a long time after that, and I was holding all the time tight to his arm—for it wasn't easy to walk with that sea on—when suddenly he laid his hand over mine.

"Mary," he said, "I've got to tell you. I can't keep it back and feel—honest. I don't know whether you want Roger Poole in your life—I don't know whether you care. But I want you to be happy. And it was I who sent him away from you."

And now, Roger Poole, what can I say? What can *any* woman say? I only know this, that as I write this the sun shines over a blue sea, and that the world is—different. There are still things in my heart which hurt—but there are things, too, which make it sing!

MARY.

When Mary Ballard came on deck on the morning after the storm, everybody stared. Where was the girl of yesterday—the frail white girl who had moped so listlessly in her chair, scribbling on little bits of paper? Here was a fair young beauty, with her head up, a clear light shining in her gray eyes—a faint flush on her cheeks.

Colin Quale, meeting her, flickered his lashes and smiled: "Is this what the storm did to you?"

"What?"

"This and this." He touched his cheeks and his eyes. "To-day, if I painted you, I should have to put pink on my palette— yesterday I should have needed only black and white."

Mary smiled back at him. "Do you interpret things always through the medium of your brush?"

"Why not? Life is just that—a little color more or less, and it all depends on the hand of the artist."

"What a wonderful palette He has!" Her eyes swept the sea and the sky. "This morning the world is all gold and blue."

"And yesterday it was gray."

Mary flashed a glance at him. His voice had changed. Delilah was coming toward them. "There's material I like to work with," he said, "there's something more than paint or canvas—living, breathing beauty."

"He's saying things about you," Mary said, as Delilah joined them.

Delilah, coloring faintly, cast down her eyes. "I'm afraid of him, Mary," she said.

Colin laughed. "You're not afraid of any one."

"Yes, I am. You analyze my mental processes in such a weird fashion. You are always reading me like a book."

"A most interesting book," Colin's lashes quivered, "with lovely illustrations."

They laughed, and swept away into a brisk walk, followed by curious eyes.

If to others Mary's radiance seemed a miracle of returning health, to Porter Bigelow it was no miracle. Nothing could have more completely rung the knell of his hopes than this radiance.

Her attitude toward him was irreproachable. She was kinder, indeed, than she had been in the days when he had tried to force his claims upon her. She seemed to be trying by her friendliness to make up for something which she had withdrawn from him, and he knew that nothing could ever make up.

So it came about that he spent less and less of his time with her, and more and more with Leila—Leila who needed comforting, and who welcomed him with such sweet and clinging dependence—Leila who hung upon his advice, Leila who, divining his hurt, strove by her sweet sympathy to help him.

Thus they came in due time to London. And when Leila and her father left for the German baths, Porter went with them.

It was when he said "Good-bye" to Mary that his voice broke.

"Dear Contrary Mary," he said, "the old name still fits you. You never could, and you never would, and now you never will."

Followed for Mary quiet days with Constance and the beautiful baby, days in which the sisters were knit together by the bonds of mutual grief. The little Mary-Constance was a wonderful comfort to both of them; unconscious of sadness, she gurgled and crowed and beamed, winning them from sorrowful thoughts by her blandishments, making herself the center of things, so that, at last, all their little world seemed to revolve about her.

And always in these quiet days, Mary looked for a letter from across the high seas, and at last it came in a blue envelope.

It arrived one morning when she was at breakfast with Constance and Gordon. Handed to her with other letters, she left it unopened and laid it beside her plate.

Gordon finished his breakfast, kissed his wife, and went away. Constance, looking over her mail, read bits of news to Mary. Mary, in return, read bits of news to Constance. But the blue envelope by her plate lay untouched, until, catching her sister's eye, she flushed.

"Constance," she said, "it is from Roger Poole."

"Oh, Mary, and was that why Porter went away?"

"Yes." It came almost defiantly.

For a moment the young matron hesitated, then she held out her arms. "Dearest girl," she said, "we want you to be happy."

Mary, with eyes shining, came straight to that loving embrace.

"I am going to be happy," she said, almost breathlessly, "and perhaps my way of being happy won't be yours, Con, darling. But what difference does it make, so long as we are both—happy?"

The letter, read at last in the shelter of her own room, was not long.

Among the Pines.

Even now I can't quite believe that your letter is true—I have read it and reread it—again and again, reading into it each time new meanings, new hope. And to-night it lies on my desk, a precious document, tempting me to say things which perhaps I should not say—tempting me to plead for that which perhaps I should not ask.

Dear woman—what have I to offer you? Just a home down here among the sand-hills—a little church that will soon stand in a circle of young pines, a life of work in a little rectory near the little church—for your dreams and mine are to come true, and the little church will be built within a year.

Yet, I have a garden. A garden of souls. Will you come into it? And make it bloom, as you have made my life bloom? All that I am you have made me. When I sat in the Tower Rooms hopeless, you gave me hope. When I lost faith in myself, it shone in your eyes. When I saw your brave young courage, my courage came back to me. It was you who told me that I had a message to deliver.

And I am delivering the message—and somehow I cannot feel that it is a little thing to offer, when I ask you to share in this, my work.

Other men can offer you a castle—other men can give to you a life of ease. I can bring to you a life in which we shall give ourselves to each other and to the world. I can give you love that is equal to any man's. I can give you a future which will make you forget the past.

Not to every woman would I dare offer what I have to give— but you are different from other women. From the night when you first met me frankly with your brave young head up and your eyes shining, I have known that you were different from the rest—a woman braver and stronger, a woman asking more of life than softness.

And now, will you fight with me, shoulder to shoulder? And win?

Somehow I feel that you will say "Yes." Is that the right attitude for a lover? But surely I can see a little way into your heart. Your letter let me see.

If I seem over-confident, forgive me. But I know what I want for myself. I know what I want for you. I am not the Roger Poole of the Tower Rooms, beaten and broken. I am Roger Poole of the Garden, marching triumphantly in tune with the universe.

As I write, I have a vision upon me of a little white house not far from the little white church in the circle of young pines—a house with orchards sweeping up all pink behind it in April, and with violets in the borders of the walk in January, and with roses from May until December.

And I can see you in that little house. I shall see you in it until you say something which will destroy that vision. But you won't destroy it. Surely some day you will hear the mocking-birds sing in the moonlight—as I am hearing them, alone, to-night.

I need you, I want you, and I hope that it is not a selfish cry. For your letter has told me that you, too, are wanting—what?

Is it Love, Mary dear, and Life?

ROGER.

CHAPTER XXVI

In Which a Strange Craft Anchors in a Sea of Emerald Light;
and in Which Mocking-Birds Sing in the Moonlight.

Sweeping through a country of white sand and of charred trees run hard clay highways. When motor cars from the cities and health resorts began to invade the pines, it was found that the old wagon trails were inadequate; hence there followed experiments which resulted in intersecting orange-colored roads, throughout the desert-like expanse.

It was on a day in April that over the road which led up toward the hills there sailed the snowy-white canopy of one of the strange land-craft of that region—a schooner-wagon drawn by two fat mules who walked at a leisurely but steady pace, seemingly without guidance from any hand.

Yet that, beneath the hooded cover, there was a directing power, was demonstrated, as the mules turned suddenly from the hot road to a wagon path beneath the shelter of the pines.

It was strewn thick with brown needles, and the sharp hoofs of the little animals made no sound. Deeper and deeper they went into the wood, until the swinging craft and its clumsy steeds seemed to swim in a sea of emerald light.

On and on breasting waves of golden gloom, where the sunlight sifted in, to anchor at last in a still space where the great trees sang overhead.

Then from beneath the canopy emerged a man in khaki.

He took off his hat, and stood for a moment looking up at the great trees, then he called softly, "Mary."

She came to the back of the wagon and he lifted her down.

"This is my cathedral," he said; "it is the place of the biggest pines."

She leaned against him and looked up. His arm was about her. She wore a thin silk blouse and a white skirt. Her soft fair hair was blown against his cheek.

"Roger," she said, "was there ever such a honeymoon?"

"Was there ever such a woman—such a wife?"

After that they were silent. There was no need for words. But presently he spread a rug for her, and built their fire, and they had their lunch. The mules ate comfortably in the shade, and rested throughout the long hot hours of the afternoon.

Then once more the strange craft sailed on. On and on over miles of orange roadway, passing now and then an orchard, flaunting the rose-color of its peach trees against the dun background of sand; passing again between drifts of dogwood, which shone like snow beneath the slanting rays of the sun—sailing on and on until the sun went down. Then came the shadowy twilight, with the stars coming out in the warm dusk—then the moonlight—and the mocking-birds singing.

ABOUT THE AUTHOR

Irene Temple Bailey (c.1885 - July 6, 1953) was an American novelist and short story writer.

Beginning around 1902, Temple Bailey was contributing stories to national magazines such as The Saturday Evening Post, Cavalier Magazine, Cosmopolitan, American Magazine, McClure's, Woman's Home Companion, Good House-keeping, McCall's and others.

In 1914, Bailey wrote the screenplay for the Vitagraph Studios film "Auntie" and two of her books were filmed. She also had three of her books on the list of bestselling novels in the United States in 1918, 1922, and 1926 as determined by the New York Times.

Choose from Thousands of 1stWorldLibrary Classics By

A. M. Barnard
Ada Leverson
Adolphus William Ward
Aesop
Agatha Christie
Alexander Aaronsohn
Alexander Kielland
Alexandre Dumas
Alfred Gatty
Alfred Ollivant
Alice Duer Miller
Alice Turner Curtis
Alice Dunbar
Allen Chapman
Alleyne Ireland
Ambrose Bierce
Amelia E. Barr
Amory H. Bradford
Andrew Lang
Andrew McFarland Davis
Andy Adams
Angela Brazil
Anna Alice Chapin
Anna Sewell
Annie Besant
Annie Hamilton Donnell
Annie Payson Call
Annie Roe Carr
Annonaymous
Anton Chekhov
Archibald Lee Fletcher
Arnold Bennett
Arthur C. Benson
Arthur Conan Doyle
Arthur M. Winfield
Arthur Ransome
Arthur Schnitzler
Arthur Train
Atticus
B.H. Baden-Powell
B. M. Bower
B. C. Chatterjee
Baroness Emmuska Orczy
Baroness Orczy
Basil King
Bayard Taylor
Ben Macomber
Bertha Muzzy Bower
Bjornstjerne Bjornson

Booth Tarkington
Boyd Cable
Bram Stoker
C. Collodi
C. E. Orr
C. M. Ingleby
Carolyn Wells
Catherine Parr Traill
Charles A. Eastman
Charles Amory Beach
Charles Dickens
Charles Dudley Warner
Charles Farrar Browne
Charles Ives
Charles Kingsley
Charles Klein
Charles Hanson Towne
Charles Lathrop Pack
Charles Romyn Dake
Charles Whibley
Charles Willing Beale
Charlotte M. Braeme
Charlotte M. Yonge
Charlotte Perkins Stetson
Clair W. Hayes
Clarence Day Jr.
Clarence E. Mulford
Clemence Housman
Confucius
Coningsby Dawson
Cornelis DeWitt Wilcox
Cyril Burleigh
D. H. Lawrence
Daniel Defoe
David Garnett
Dinah Craik
Don Carlos Janes
Donald Keyhoe
Dorothy Kilner
Dougan Clark
Douglas Fairbanks
E. Nesbit
E. P. Roe
E. Phillips Oppenheim
E. S. Brooks
Earl Barnes
Edgar Rice Burroughs
Edith Van Dyne
Edith Wharton

Edward Everett Hale
Edward J. O'Biren
Edward S. Ellis
Edwin L. Arnold
Eleanor Atkins
Eleanor Hallowell Abbott
Eliot Gregory
Elizabeth Gaskell
Elizabeth McCracken
Elizabeth Von Arnim
Ellem Key
Emerson Hough
Emilie F. Carlen
Emily Bronte
Emily Dickinson
Enid Bagnold
Enilor Macartney Lane
Erasmus W. Jones
Ernie Howard Pie
Ethel May Dell
Ethel Turner
Ethel Watts Mumford
Eugene Sue
Eugenie Foa
Eugene Wood
Eustace Hale Ball
Evelyn Everett-green
Everard Cotes
F. H. Cheley
F. J. Cross
F. Marion Crawford
Fannie E. Newberry
Federick Austin Ogg
Ferdinand Ossendowski
Fergus Hume
Florence A. Kilpatrick
Fremont B. Deering
Francis Bacon
Francis Darwin
Frances Hodgson Burnett
Frances Parkinson Keyes
Frank Gee Patchin
Frank Harris
Frank Jewett Mather
Frank L. Packard
Frank V. Webster
Frederic Stewart Isham
Frederick Trevor Hill
Frederick Winslow Taylor

Friedrich Kerst
Friedrich Nietzsche
Fyodor Dostoyevsky
G.A. Henty
G.K. Chesterton
Gabrielle E. Jackson
Garrett P. Serviss
Gaston Leroux
George A. Warren
George Ade
Geroge Bernard Shaw
George Cary Eggleston
George Durston
George Ebers
George Eliot
George Gissing
George MacDonald
George Meredith
George Orwell
George Sylvester Viereck
George Tucker
George W. Cable
George Wharton James
Gertrude Atherton
Gordon Casserly
Grace E. King
Grace Gallatin
Grace Greenwood
Grant Allen
Guillermo A. Sherwell
Gulielma Zollinger
Gustav Flaubert
H. A. Cody
H. B. Irving
H.C. Bailey
H. G. Wells
H. H. Munro
H. Irving Hancock
H. R. Naylor
H. Rider Haggard
H. W. C. Davis
Haldeman Julius
Hall Caine
Hamilton Wright Mabie
Hans Christian Andersen
Harold Avery
Harold McGrath
Harriet Beecher Stowe
Harry Castlemon
Harry Coghill
Harry Houidini

Hayden Carruth
Helent Hunt Jackson
Helen Nicolay
Hendrik Conscience
Hendy David Thoreau
Henri Barbusse
Henrik Ibsen
Henry Adams
Henry Ford
Henry Frost
Henry James
Henry Jones Ford
Henry Seton Merriman
Henry W Longfellow
Herbert A. Giles
Herbert Carter
Herbert N. Casson
Herman Hesse
Hildegard G. Frey
Homer
Honore De Balzac
Horace B. Day
Horace Walpole
Horatio Alger Jr.
Howard Pyle
Howard R. Garis
Hugh Lofting
Hugh Walpole
Humphry Ward
Ian Maclaren
Inez Haynes Gillmore
Irving Bacheller
Isabel Cecilia Williams
Isabel Hornibrook
Israel Abrahams
Ivan Turgenev
J.G.Austin
J. Henri Fabre
J. M. Barrie
J. M. Walsh
J. Macdonald Oxley
J. R. Miller
J. S. Fletcher
J. S. Knowles
J. Storer Clouston
J. W. Duffield
Jack London
Jacob Abbott
James Allen
James Andrews
James Baldwin

James Branch Cabell
James DeMille
James Joyce
James Lane Allen
James Lane Allen
James Oliver Curwood
James Oppenheim
James Otis
James R. Driscoll
Jane Abbott
Jane Austen
Jane L. Stewart
Janet Aldridge
Jens Peter Jacobsen
Jerome K. Jerome
Jessie Graham Flower
John Buchan
John Burroughs
John Cournos
John F. Kennedy
John Gay
John Glasworthy
John Habberton
John Joy Bell
John Kendrick Bangs
John Milton
John Philip Sousa
John Taintor Foote
Jonas Lauritz Idemil Lie
Jonathan Swift
Joseph A. Altsheler
Joseph Carey
Joseph Conrad
Joseph E. Badger Jr
Joseph Hergesheimer
Joseph Jacobs
Jules Vernes
Julian Hawthrone
Julie A Lippmann
Justin Huntly McCarthy
Kakuzo Okakura
Karle Wilson Baker
Kate Chopin
Kenneth Grahame
Kenneth McGaffey
Kate Langley Bosher
Kate Langley Bosher
Katherine Cecil Thurston
Katherine Stokes
L. A. Abbot
L. T. Meade

L. Frank Baum
Latta Griswold
Laura Dent Crane
Laura Lee Hope
Laurence Housman
Lawrence Beasley
Leo Tolstoy
Leonid Andreyev
Lewis Carroll
Lewis Sperry Chafer
Lilian Bell
Lloyd Osbourne
Louis Hughes
Louis Joseph Vance
Louis Tracy
Louisa May Alcott
Lucy Fitch Perkins
Lucy Maud Montgomery
Luther Benson
Lydia Miller Middleton
Lyndon Orr
M. Corvus
M. H. Adams
Margaret E. Sangster
Margret Howth
Margaret Vandercook
Margaret W. Hungerford
Margret Penrose
Maria Edgeworth
Maria Thompson Daviess
Mariano Azuela
Marion Polk Angellotti
Mark Overton
Mark Twain
Mary Austin
Mary Catherine Crowley
Mary Cole
Mary Hastings Bradley
Mary Roberts Rinehart
Mary Rowlandson
M. Wollstonecraft Shelley
Maud Lindsay
Max Beerbohm
Myra Kelly
Nathaniel Hawthrone
Nicolo Machiavelli
O. F. Walton
Oscar Wilde
Owen Johnson
P.G. Wodehouse
Paul and Mabel Thorne

Paul G. Tomlinson
Paul Severing
Percy Brebner
Percy Keese Fitzhugh
Peter B. Kyne
Plato
Quincy Allen
R. Derby Holmes
R. L. Stevenson
R. S. Ball
Rabindranath Tagore
Rahul Alvares
Ralph Bonehill
Ralph Henry Barbour
Ralph Victor
Ralph Waldo Emmerson
Rene Descartes
Ray Cummings
Rex Beach
Rex E. Beach
Richard Harding Davis
Richard Jefferies
Richard Le Gallienne
Robert Barr
Robert Frost
Robert Gordon Anderson
Robert L. Drake
Robert Lansing
Robert Lynd
Robert Michael Ballantyne
Robert W. Chambers
Rosa Nouchette Carey
Rudyard Kipling
Saint Augustine
Samuel B. Allison
Samuel Hopkins Adams
Sarah Bernhardt
Sarah C. Hallowell
Selma Lagerlof
Sherwood Anderson
Sigmund Freud
Standish O'Grady
Stanley Weyman
Stella Benson
Stella M. Francis
Stephen Crane
Stewart Edward White
Stijn Streuvels
Swami Abhedananda
Swami Parmananda
T. S. Ackland

T. S. Arthur
The Princess Der Ling
Thomas A. Janvier
Thomas A Kempis
Thomas Anderton
Thomas Bailey Aldrich
Thomas Bulfinch
Thomas De Quincey
Thomas Dixon
Thomas H. Huxley
Thomas Hardy
Thomas More
Thornton W. Burgess
U. S. Grant
Upton Sinclair
Valentine Williams
Various Authors
Vaughan Kester
Victor Appleton
Victor G. Durham
Victoria Cross
Virginia Woolf
Wadsworth Camp
Walter Camp
Walter Scott
Washington Irving
Wilbur Lawton
Wilkie Collins
Willa Cather
Willard F. Baker
William Dean Howells
William le Queux
W. Makepeace Thackeray
William W. Walter
William Shakespeare
Winston Churchill
Yei Theodora Ozaki
Yogi Ramacharaka
Young E. Allison
Zane Grey